*Me on the Floor, Bleeding*

# ME ON THE FLOOR, BLEEDING

## JENNY JÄGERFELDT

Translated by Susan Beard

STOCKHOLM TEXT

**Stockholm Text**
stockholm@stockholmtext.com
www.stockholmtext.com

© 2010, 2014 Jenny Jägerfeld, by agreement with Grand Agency
Stockholm Text, Stockholm 2014
Translation: Susan Beard
Cover: Ermir Peci
ISBN 978-91-7547-011-5

This book was partly founded by a grant given by The Swedish Arts Council

To my sweet siblings Patric, John and Caroline.
(I think Maja would have wished that she had some.)

## THURSDAY, 12 APRIL

*Spurting Blood*

It was a quarter to one on Thursday the twelfth of April, one day before the so-called unlucky thirteenth and I had just sawn off the tip of my left thumb with an electric saw.

I stared at my thumb – what was left of it, I mean – with its pale midwinter skin and the pinky-red stuff inside. The flesh. In a detached kind of way I thought I'd sawn it off quite neatly, that the edges of the cut were straight, which was good. Wasn't it? I searched my mind for relevant experiences but it was blank. Empty. My knowledge of sawn-off body parts was clearly limited. Anyway, the cut was pretty difficult to make out because a massive stream of blood suddenly spurted right up into the air. Like a little geyser.

The saw fell to the floor with a violent crash. Perhaps I dropped it, perhaps I threw it away from me, I don't remember. I grabbed my thumb with my right hand and held it tight, so tight my knuckles turned white. One second passed, then another. I watched as the saw jerked across the floor, its blade wildly vibrating.

Everything in front of me swam about like bad television reception and a stream of blood forced its way out between the thumb and index finger of my right hand. As if on cue blood began pouring out between every finger and my right hand gradually turned bright red. I tried to squeeze even tighter but the blood kept gushing through. It dropped onto the white worktop with such relentless speed you'd think someone was spraying it with red paint.

Suddenly it felt as if my stomach was emptying itself of its contents, as if I was in a lift and the cable had just snapped, and instead of slowly travelling upwards I found myself freefalling down the shaft. I was forced to let go of my thumb and grab the back of the chair to keep my balance. That was the starting signal for the blood: it spiralled and poured and pumped out from what had once been one of my most important digits. The starched front of my dress shirt was sprayed red.

*Shit. Dad's going to be angry.*

*This ought to be hurting,* I thought objectively. *Why isn't it hurting?*

At that very moment a bomb detonated right in the middle of my hand.

And then another.

And then another.

The pain was red hot and hard. The pain was absolutely, *inconceivably* agonising. I tried to breathe but I couldn't. My throat had closed up. The oxygen had run out.

I looked around in mute panic. All work had stopped. No one was at the potter's wheel. No-one was moulding plaster, bending metal or messing about with papier-mâché. They were just staring silently in my direction, in the direction of the pool of fresh blood on the floor. At my bloodstained hands and the blood-red hand print on the back of the wooden chair.

They were silent.

They had never been so silent. The only thing you

8

could hear was the saw aggressively attacking the floor. The sound of metal teeth against stone.

It was like I was forty metres under the sea. The pressure of thousands of square metres of water prevented any quick movements and made my body slow and sluggish. My vision became indistinct and cloudy and the sound of the saw was elongated and distorted. I looked at my classmates. They were gently undulating at their workbenches. *Like seaweed,* I thought in the split second before I finally managed to gasp in some air and scream at the top of my lungs. It was a raw and rasping sound, as if I hadn't opened my mouth all day.

I screamed, wide-eyed, as one explosion after another went off in my thumb. I screamed like I had never, and I mean *ever*, screamed before and it was impossible, totally out of the question, to stop. I tried to meet Enzo's eyes but his expression was difficult to read behind his protective goggles. The elastic around his head was so tight that it dug into his skin and pushed his chubby cheeks upwards, squashing them together underneath the scratched lenses. He broke away from the frozen crowd, moving jerkily like a robot. Without taking his eyes off me he bent down and picked up something small from the floor, something a pinky-red colour, and he stretched out his arm to give it to me. When I didn't make any attempt to take it he placed it in the palm of my right hand. Then he sank silently to the blood-covered floor, less than one metre away from the saw.


Valter ran. He ran so fast his soft curls flapped about. Normally his movements were slow and dignified. Not now. Never before had I seen him move so fast from his desk to the work benches at the back. I didn't hear the characteristic clicking of his heels against the stone floor and that surprised me until I realised it was my own voice, my own continuous bellowing, that prevented every other sound from reaching my ears.

I looked down at my unmangled right hand and studied the object in my palm. I knew what was lying there but still I couldn't understand it. I just couldn't, somehow. It was too . . . absurd. Plain disgusting too, for that matter.

There in the palm of my hand lay a part of my body. A part of *me*.

The tip of my thumb.

It was so light, no heavier than a pea, or maybe two. I could hardly feel it.

I didn't want to look at it but it was impossible not to.

The upper rounded surface of the nail was intact. A little sliver of wood shaving had fastened in the bloody, fleshy side. I glimpsed something white behind the blood and realised it was my bone. My own skeleton.

I was wrong. The edges of the cut were not straight. They were shredded, like minced meat. For a second everything went black. Unfortunately I did not faint. Not then. Instead, a violent nausea bubbled up into my throat and with the self-control worthy of a Russian gymnast I succeeded in holding back the vomit.

Abruptly the aggressive hacking of the saw stopped. Valter had wrenched the plug from the wall. And at that exact moment I stopped too, as if the saw and I had been connected to the same socket.

There was silence. An echoing silence.

Valter took a step towards me. He stood too close, like he had poor social skills, and his breath hit my face in small minty puffs. He gulped and in his grey-blue eyes I could see alarm. Maybe even panic. It was something about the speed of his irises racing from side to side in tiny, hardly perceptible movements. A few seconds passed as we stood like that, our eyes locked together.

Then there was a noise, a drawn-out whimper. Simultaneously Valter and I looked down at the floor. There was Enzo. It was like someone had paused a frame in a horror movie. The saw was less than ten centimetres from his right ear. He had blood on his cheek and in his hair, and splashes of blood on his goggles. My blood. His brown eyes were staring and his mouth was gaping as if he was about to scream but had been distracted. I noticed the zip of his flies wasn't done up properly.

Suddenly there was the sound of tentative footsteps and electronic clicking. I looked quickly over my shoulder and a blinding bluish-white flash went off right in my face.

*Click.*

It was Simon. Naturally it was Simon. He moved his mobile closer to my hand.

*Click.*

Then he pointed it at the floor and Enzo.

*Click.*

The blood, the goggles, his flies. Everything was illuminated by that deadly flash.

*Click. Click. Click.*

Self-consciously Enzo shut his mouth. He cleared his throat. From his humiliating position on the floor he said:

'Stick your thumb in … in your mouth. The tip of your thumb, I mean. That'll make it easier to sew it back on, that's … that's what I've heard.'

Everything started spinning. I heard the click and his voice like an echo, but weirdly distorted:

*Click. Stick your thumb in … in your mouth.*
I fell backwards and my head hit something hard.
*Click.*
It was a merciful release when everything went black.

*Status: Sawn-off Thumb*

'Right,' said Dr Levin, leaning over her desk and fixing me with her eyes. They were blood-shot and framed in layer upon layer of black mascara, which glued her eye-lashes together in clumps of spiky spiders' legs. She had a small graze on her nose and I thought that she must have fallen over, that perhaps she was an alcoholic.

'Well, we've almost finished. Now ...' The beautiful, dark-haired nurse, who was called Maryam according to her name badge, unintentionally interrupted Dr Levin by asking me to keep my hand still. She raised my arm and instinctively I pulled back, only to relax when I realised there was no pain. Gratefully I remembered the local anaesthetic. Maryam gave a smile revealing a fascinating amount of even teeth and gently placed a sort of thin net over the stitches and a compress on top of that. Then she wrapped a layer of wadding around my thumb.

'To stop it getting bumped,' she said.

I nodded. I was finding it hard to stop staring at Maryam. Expertly she wound a narrow bandage around my wrist and thumb. Her hands were warm and dry. Dr Levin looked bored, her lower lip jutting out irritably and her eyes half closed, as if trying but failing to imagine she was somewhere else. She took a breath and was about to continue talking but looked first at me, then at Maryam, then back at me, to make sure she would not be interrupted again.

'Any more questions?'

I thought frantically. She made me nervous.

'Nope,' I said. 'Or, well …yes. What are you going to do with the thumb?'

'What do you mean?'

'Well, um, what are you going to do with the actual … tip?'

'Oh, that. Throw it away, of course,' she said bluntly, looking down at her papers.

'Throw it away?' My voice rose to a falsetto.

'Yes. You can't do anything with it. You do understand that, I hope? It's incredibly difficult to re-attach the tip of a thumb once it's been sawn off and the edges are shredded. It would be a hell of a job stitching back nerves and blood vessels and all that sort of thing. We don't go to that much trouble, quite frankly. Not for a tiny thumb tip you can manage without.'

*Shredded?* Wasn't there some nice medical term that wouldn't make you want to projectile vomit?

'It would have been much better if you had cut it off cleanly, with some pliars, say. A much cleaner wound. *Much* easier to stitch together.'

I stared at her. She was unbelievable.

'I'll bear that in mind next time,' I said.

'What?' She drummed her fingernails impatiently on her desk but didn't bother waiting for my answer.

'And the tip of your thumb was so full of splinters, dust, and God knows what else. I doubt you'd have been able to use it anyway, but that didn't make the job any easier. Any more questions?'

14

I shook my head.

'Right then,' said Dr Levin.

She spun her chair round so that her back was partially towards me and she started speaking into a microphone that looked like a pen.

'This is Dr Marie-Louise Levin dictating an emergency visit by Maja Müller. Reason for visit, colon, sawn-off thumb tip.'

She fell silent, cleared her throat, and looked over her shoulder at me. Maryam patted my arm and told me to come back on Monday for a check-up and to have the dressing changed. After ten days I could go to my local surgery and have the stitches removed. I nodded, my eyes still fixed on Dr Levin, who at that very moment began dictating again:

'Background, colon, seventeen-year-old girl, comma, lives with her father in Örnsberg, comma, parents separated, full stop. Occupation, colon, student, full stop. First year of creative arts course, comma, art and design, comma, St Erik's Sixth Form Collage, comma, Stockholm, full stop. Non-smoker, full stop. Basically non-drinker, full stop.'

*On the other hand I've dealt a lot of heroin,* I thought, and couldn't hold back a smile.

She continued:

'Current status, colon, the patient was sawing a shelf during a woodwork lesson, with an electric…'

'It wasn't woodwork.'

'Pardon?'

Her voice was sharp. Her eyes narrowed. I imagined those spidery eyelashes breaking off in thick lumps and slowly crawling down over her cheeks.

'It wasn't woodwork. It was sculpture. A sculpture lesson.'

'Why were you making a shelf, then?'

'I … I was exempt, you could say. I'm not that keen on sculpture.'

Dr Levin demonstratively picked up the microphone again:

'The patient was making a shelf using an electric jig-saw during a *sculpture lesson, full stop.*'

She stared at me. Those tired eyes seemed to look right through me and out the other side.

'The saw slipped causing her to saw off the tip of her left thumb, full stop. Sawn-off left thumb, comma, approximately twenty-three, twenty-four millimetres from the IP joint, comma, approximately five millimetres missing, comma, a small piece of bone protruding, full stop. Visible nail damage, comma, joint not engaged by injury, full stop. No further damage, full stop. General condition, colon, patient appears to be in shock from pain and somewhat … detached.'

She stopped abruptly.

'I was going to cut out a flamingo,' I said. 'That was when the saw … slipped. I was going to cut the outline of a flamingo on the side piece.'

She looked at me blankly.

'You can go now,' she said, and I nodded and stood up quickly, as if I had received an electric shock. I looked around. Maryam had left the room without me noticing.

'Thank you,' I said, backing out through the door.

She didn't even look up. Was she going to have a drink after I left? Would she get out some tax-free vodka from her desk drawer and take a few swigs straight from the bottle? I shut the door. I would never know.

I sat down in the waiting room, which was empty apart from a young black woman wearing big gold earrings. She stared at me, at my shirt and the dried blood that drop by drop had stained the front of my shirt and most of the sleeves.

Outside it started to rain; thin small drops that fell sporadically against the glass. *Detached*, I thought. *Is that what I am? Slightly detached?*

Valter walked past the waiting room three times before he discovered me.

'So this is where you are!' he said, breathlessly. He smelled of smoke. Not a normal cigarette but something spicier, more like incense.

I didn't say anything. It was kind of like obvious.

He had put his T-shirt back on, the one he had wrapped around my thumb in the taxi a few hours earlier, and the blood stain on the front was an almost perfect circle. It looked as if he had been shot at close range. He sat down on the chair next to mine and I thought that was too close. There were thirty chairs in this waiting room and he had to sit ten centimetres away from me.

The young woman with the earrings stared first at Valter and then at me. It must have looked totally bizarre, all that blood.

'Bloody hell, what a day,' he said, taking a small box of throat sweets out of his jacket pocket.

I couldn't disagree with him there.

'I've phoned your dad, at least.'

He shoved a throat sweet into his mouth and held out the packet. I shook my head.

'I couldn't get hold of your mum but I left a message.

'Oh. What did you say?'

My voice revealed a kind of eager desperation and I didn't like it.

'Um, what did I say? I said there had been an accident but everything was under control.'

*"Under control?" Was everything really "under control"?*

'I left my number so she could ring before she came here, in case you had already left. But she'll probably phone you. Have you got your mobile switched on?'

'Yeah.'

I couldn't be bothered explaining that she wouldn't be coming anyway. I wasn't prepared to answer the probing questions that would no doubt follow.

'Is Dad coming here?'

'Yes, I guess he'll be here in twenty.'

'Minutes?' I had no idea what I was doing. Of course he meant minutes. Every other unit of time would have been absurd. Valter gave a lopsided smile.

'Yes,' he said. 'Minutes.'

We sat there for a while, next to each other. It was a relief he had his T-shirt on. It had been hard not to stare at his chest when that carpet of light-brown curly hair was exposed. Judging from the looks of the A&E nurses, they felt the same. Dr Levin was the only person who had managed to look him in the eyes.

I looked out of the window. Murky grey clouds were gathering on the horizon. It made the sky dark, like it was evening.

'Well,' said Valter. 'What did the doctor say?'

I shrugged. Valter had rushed out of the room when Dr Levin had started to examine my sawn-off thumb. He excused himself by saying he had to phone my parents. It was pretty transparent but I understood him: I would have liked to leave too. The image of Dr Levin clipping off my thumb bone and then filing it down a bit so she could stitch the skin together would be forever burned into my memory. I thought about her choice of vocabulary before the procedure: how she was just going to "trim the bone slightly." "Trim?" "Yes, she would just "file it down a bit" because it was so "shredded".

I squeezed my eyes shut. It was as if I could feel the vibration from the file against the bone all over again. Instinctively I lifted my bandaged hand towards my heart.

'What did she say about, you know, putting it in your mouth?'

'What?'

For a split second I thought Valter has said something really perverted.

'You know, what Enzo said. That you should put the sawn-off bit into your mouth.'

'Oh, that.'

I breathed out.

'She said that if I'd stuck it into my mouth I might just as well have stuck it up my arse.'

'What? She said that?'

Valter sucked energetically on his throat sweet and looked at me sceptically.

'Yeah. Sort of. There are just as many bacteria there. So she said.'

He shook his head and sighed heavily.

'I should never have agreed to lend you that saw from the machine workshop. I should have put a stop to it right from the beginning and said: "I can't take responsibility for this! Saws are outside my field of competence. You'll have to do a sculpture like everyone else, Maja!" Then none of this would have happened. I'm too soft. I'm far too soft. Always have been. Oh hell, what's the principal going to say?'

19

We sat in silence for a while. I felt ever so slightly guilty. But hang on a minute. A sculpture? What was the point?

'A shelf is also a kind of sculpture.'

'No, Maja. A shelf is *not* a sculpture.'

◆

The first thing Dad said when he came tearing into the waiting room half an hour later was:

'Good Lord! *What have you got on!*'

Not: 'Good Lord! *What's happened?*' Not: 'Good Lord, you poor thing!' Nothing sympathetic or even suitably shocked either.

A few weeks earlier I had been rooting through Dad's wardrobe and had found these fantastic midnight-blue uniform trousers with red and gold trim. There were three shiny gold buttons at each ankle and a velvet stripe down each leg in brothel red.

I had no idea Dad had played in an orchestra and I had assumed the trousers belonged to someone else because they were so small at the waist. The uniform trousers, along with the starched white dress shirt and a pair of red, white and blue braces, had made me feel like the Queen of Fucking Everything when I left home that morning.

'And the shirt ...' he said slowly, staring at the once blindingly-white shirt front that was now totally drenched in darkening blood. I could feel the material sticking to my skin.

Dad lifted his eyes and caught sight of Valter.

'Hi,' said Valter, stretching out his hand.

'Jonas,' said Dad, and squeezed Valter's hand so tight his knuckles turned white. A little habit he had.

'Valter,' said Valter, not letting on that his hand was

being crushed. 'I teach Maja art and design and, er, sculpture. I was the one who was with her when she …'

He paused.

'…sawed off her thumb.'

Dad's eyes travelled between Valter's face and the football-sized blood stain on his T-shirt. Then he turned to me. He took hold of my hand and studied the bandage suspiciously.

'Oh Maja,' he said, his voice indicating disappointment rather than concern. Then he scratched his head, stood up and took Valter to one side. With his back to me he muttered in a worried voice:

'You, um … you don't think she did this deliberately, do you Valter?'

*Verbalise Your Anxiety*

'Honestly! Are you completely mental? Obviously I didn't do it deliberately!'

I tried to block the way but Dad pushed past me and ran into the bathroom. I slammed the front door and the pain as I knocked my thumb against the door frame made everything go black. Clearly the local anaesthetic had worn off. Silently I grimaced. In the hall mirror I caught sight of my contorted face below the long black bangs and noted that the hair on each side had grown horribly long. It needed to be shaved again instantly.

'How do I know?' he shouted from the bathroom.

'Shut the door when you're having a pee!'

I hardly had time to say the words before I heard my heart beat loudly in my ears, as if the volume had been turned up. A regular, almost metallic, pulse.

*The saw. The grating, piercing sound.*
*The metal teeth, hacking into me.*
*The flesh. Exposed.*
*The blood. Spiralling, pulsating, spurting.*
*The explosions. The pain.*

Small, sharp flashes immediately began to dart across my field of vision. Each time I blinked another one appeared. I stumbled and crouched down, my pulse beating loudly in my ears, and tried to grab hold of the doorway but missed and half fell, half sat, on the hall floor. I shut my eyes tightly but the lightning continued to flash behind my closed eyelids. I sat like that for what seemed like minutes, but it couldn't have been. Slowly, very slowly, my senses returned to normal. The flashes grew faint and disappeared and the sound of my heartbeats faded away, as if someone was gradually turning down the volume before completely switching it off. The only thing that remained was the dizziness. What was happening to me?

I began to untie my boot laces. With only one hand it was tortuously slow. I heard Dad flush the toilet and then turn the tap on and off in the space of two seconds. He walked out of the bathroom drying his hands on his jeans. I pictured them being impregnated with a mixture of water and urine. He eased off his trainers with his feet and threw his leather jacket onto the stool.

'No one sodding well saws off their thumb deliberately,' I said crossly.

'I was thinking you might not be feeling very well.'

Who did he think he was, actually? Did we know each other?

'I might not be completely euphoric every day, but I don't go around mutilating myself because of it.'

I glared at him.

'No, Maja, I know. But I thought ... perhaps you were unable to verbalise your anxiety.'

Oh Lord. "Verbalise your anxiety." What course had he been on, what book had he read, what idiot had he been listening to? Our eyes met and he ran his hand through his hair, trying without success to push back a few curly strands.

'Do you know you've got pee in your hair now?'

'What?'

True to habit he pretended not to hear when he didn't like what I was saying.

'Pee in your hair! Oh, forget it. But believe me, I can verbalise my anxiety. If there is one thing I can do with my anxiety it is to verbalise it.'

*Was that right?* I sounded confident but of course that didn't mean I *was* confident. Dad said nothing. He stuffed his hands into his back trouser pockets and looked at me as I sat there. I tugged at a shoe lace and continued:

'If you're worried that I'm not very well perhaps you ought to ask *me* about it? Not my art and design teacher. And not the first time you meet him!'

Dad exhaled through his nose. Was he snorting or was he simply amused? Neither reaction was suitable.

'I promised we would wash his T-shirt. Or replace it. It looks expensive.'

I finally managed to get my boots off and stood up carefully, afraid that the lightning would return. I walked into the sitting room and sat down heavily on the sofa. Dad followed me in.

'Maja,' he said gently. 'How's your thumb now?'

'Not so good,' I said, and the burning hot tears invaded my eyes, threatening to spill over.

'So what actually happened?' he asked.

'I was sawing …'

I hesitated before continuing and he interrupted.

'Yes, well, I understood *that* much at least.'

The tears quickly retreated at the sound of his pompous voice. It was hardly loud enough to hear, but it was there. I so *hated* that arrogance! He always maintained it was an occupational hazard. What he meant was that he had interviewed so many self-obsessed people in his life that it had become a form of defence that kicked in automatically.

'I was sawing a shelf,' I went on.

'But why were you sawing a shelf in a sculpture lesson? Aren't you supposed to be doing things with clay or something?'

I tried again. 'A shelf is also a form of sculpture.'

'No, Maja, a shelf is not a sculpture. A shelf is a shelf and a sculpture is …'

My voice was hard as I interrupted him:

'Anyway, it's for Jana.'

'For Jana?' he repeated stupidly, and I saw the astonishment in his eyes. It was not often we spoke about her.

'It's her birthday next week. She's forty-five.'

'I know that,' he said slowly, but I knew he was lying. He even had trouble remembering my birthday and he had a reminder of that in his mobile.

He sat down beside me and put his arm around my shoulders. It was warm and heavy. He smelled of that aftershave I hate, and possibly a bit sweaty too. I presumed he had been in a hurry to get to A&E. The leather creaked as he sank down into the shallow dip in the cushion where the stuffing had given way.

That sofa was actually quite disgusting. Tacky. But once I had got used to sitting on the skin of a dead cow or whatever it was I had to admit it was amazingly comfortable. Still, you couldn't get away from the fact that it looked ugly and cheap. As far as Dad was concerned it was love at first sight in the furniture shop. After trying it out for less than a minute he informed me that he simply *had* to have it. The sofa had been incredibly expensive. I thought of what Dolly Parton had once said: "You'd be surprised how much it costs to look this cheap."

The leather sofa could not have said it better itself.

Dad removed his arm and leaned back. It turned a bit colder. He sighed and said:

'I suppose I'd better ring her.'

'Who?'

'Well, Jana of course.'

'Why.'

'What do you mean, why? You've shown extremely poor judgment and sawn off your thumb, that's why.'

He laughed but immediately became serious again.

'She should be informed. She is your mother, after all.'

'I can tell her at the weekend instead,' I said quickly, looking at the clock. It was eight-fifteen, almost half an hour until I could take the next painkiller. The feeling in my thumb was returning at full speed and what had been a dull continuous ache was fast becoming a series of aggressive hammer blows. What the eff. I took the blister pack out of my jacket pocket and pressed out a round white tablet. I flicked it up into the air with the help of my right thumb and caught it in my mouth like a peanut. Dad did not appear impressed.

'Do you really think you can go to Norrköping tomorrow?' he said, wrinkling his forehead.

'Well of course I can.'

'Are you sure?'

'Well, it isn't my feet I've sawn off.'

He opened his mouth to say something but kept quiet. I smiled at him in a way I hoped would signal "rest assured". At least, that was what I thought when I had practised the expression in the mirror. I said:

'It's cool. I promise.'

Dad did not return my smile. The crease in his forehead seemed to have become a permanent fixture and he peered at me doubtfully. When he looked like that he really did look forty-two, despite his hip T-shirt and ripped jeans. I realised I was happy about that.

After a while he stood up and said indecisively:

'You know, I think it's just as well I phone her anyway.'

'Watch out you don't fall over with enthusiasm.'

He pretended not to hear what I had said.

I switched on the TV and lay down gingerly on the sofa, but as soon as the back of my head came into contact with the cushion I felt as if I had been whacked right on the bump. A wave of nausea washed over me and my mouth suddenly produced a mass of iron-tasting saliva. I had to lie on my side instead. Marginally better.

I hopped randomly between the channels. Images flashed past: grey-suited men smiling stiffly and shaking hands, young women dancing and slapping each other provocatively on the butt to the beat of a monotonous rhythm, and a lion moving lethargically through long grass. I looked down at my hand. My left thumb, which Maryam had so carefully wrapped in a cream-coloured bandage, was rigid with pain. I tried to position it to ease the pain but it didn't matter how I held my hand, it hurt just as much anyway, as if someone had hammered a rusty nail right through it.

As I remembered the vibrations of the file against the bone I felt a gagging sensation dangerously high up in my throat and regretted that I hadn't suggested a general anaesthetic, that I hadn't actually demanded one. Regretted that as usual I had pretended to deal with it all so well. The absolute worst thing was not the agonising pain but the fact that a bit of me was missing. That a part of my body was gone forever, nonchalantly discarded in some rubbish bin at St. Göran's Hospital. I felt like, incomplete, somehow. I felt dismembered.

Mechanically I reached for my mobile and went online and logged onto Dad's email. It was excruciatingly slow, but what did I have if not plenty of time? I entered the password, the predictable "maja", lazily spelled without a capital letter, and checked his inbox. Mostly work-related. Some editor who had emailed suggestions for changes to some article. Dad's replies. I looked at his Facebook page. The only interesting thing there was a message from Dad's mate Ola who mentioned some woman Dad had evidently met the weekend before last. Denise, she was called and she was, according to Ola, "completely crazy".

*Completely crazy.*

Something told me that was spot on.

It was so revolting it made me shudder, and I shut my eyes.

◆

When Dad came back I realised I had been out of it for some time. Perhaps I'd fainted? Or, to be less dramatic, slept for a while.

He cleared his throat and scratched the stubble on his chin.

'She didn't answer.'

I longed to be able shut my eyes again.

'She's probably busy,' I mumbled.

'Jana? Busy? That's not very likely, is it? I left a message, told her you'd sawn off your thumb. It's odd,' he said, scraping his nails hard against his stubbly beard. 'I called her when I was on my way to the hospital too. She didn't answer that time, either. And she usually answers when I phone.'

I thought: what do you mean, "usually"? They didn't speak more than once every six months. Or did they?

He put the phone down on the table and exclaimed:

'It's itching like mad! I've *got* to have a shower. I've *got* to have a shave!'

As if he was afraid someone was going to stop him.

Then he disappeared into the bathroom. I reached for the phone and tapped the buttons. The coagulated blood on my shirt front chafed. If anyone should be having a shower it was me, but how was I going to summon up the energy? How would I find the strength? I heard the water splash against the tiles and after a while Dad's low humming. He never closed the door when he showered, either, even though I had nagged him for the past five years. He was so chilled he was on the verge of being comatose.

I hesitated for a moment and then keyed in Mum's number. I heard the ringing tones one after the other and eventually got the answerphone message. Phoned again and then once more after that.

But still no one answered.

*Reclaim the Whore*

'I won't ask. If it hurts, I mean. Cos I know it does …
it has to, I mean, what with that saw. Blimey … all that
blood! I heard it took the caretaker an hour to clean it up
and he could hardly get it off your desk and that … that
it's kind of like of rust-coloured now. There was blood all
the way to the door. It must have made you go mental,
the agony … and I … I can understand that, obviously,
so … so that's why I won't ask.'

Enzo was digging a hole for himself with his own
words, as usual. The thought of yesterday instinctively
made me lift my hand to my chest as if to protect it.

*The saw. The grating, piercing sound.*
*The metal teeth, hacking into me.*

I shuddered but tried to shake off the uncomfortable
feeling, tried to suppress the flashbacks. It was difficult.

*The flesh. Exposed.*
*The blood. Spiralling, pulsating, spurting.*

It was impossible.

*The explosions.*
*The pain.*

I set my face in a smile that was so stiff it made the corners of my mouth hurt. We walked along the narrow corridor that was quickly filling with students. Shrieking and laughing like monkeys, they poured out of the classrooms. It was nine forty and first break.

'So I mean, I really, really understand, absolutely! So I won't ask. Whether it hurt.'

'You *can* ask if you want.'

'Okay. Well, er, okay then.'

He smiled and turned to face me. His cheeks looked so soft, like vanilla fudge, and they had that same light brown colour. I had an impulse to stroke those round cheeks, but I resisted. Our relationship does not permit that level of physical contact.

'Ask, then!'

'Does it hurt?'

'Well of course it frigging well hurts, you cretin! Surely even you can understand that!'

I struggled to look pissed off, glaring at him and letting my mouth drop open. But I couldn't keep it up and after a few seconds burst out laughing, and I laughed so hard I was forced to grab my stomach.

'Oh, sorry, Enzo! But your expression, it was fantastic!'

Enzo aimed a slap at my head with his maths book but I ducked, feeling the gust of air rush over my hair.

'You little shit,' he said.

I carried on laughing like I couldn't stop, but Enzo kept quiet and it made me worry that I'd gone too far.

'Enzo-Benzo! Stand up straight!'

I sighed to myself. That voice was easily recognisable. It was clear and sharp, kind of like high-pitched. Vendela. And next to her was FAS-Lars with the obligatory can of Coke in his hand. FAS as in Foetal Alcohol Syndrome, which you can get if your mum drinks while she's pregnant. We had read about it in biology and Lars ticked all the criteria: small head, flat face, turned-up nose, hyperactive, low intelligence. Those last two were the total opposite of me: underactive, high intelligence. It was obvious we didn't get on. Obvious we didn't like each other.

Enzo jumped and automatically straightened up. It was true his posture was bad, as if he wanted to hide himself, hide his own body. But you noticed him even more when he walked about hunched over like that.

'Maja manky Müller. Sawn off any more fingers lately?' said Vendela, looking at me confrontationally. Rumours of the bloodbath had clearly spread. Probably Simon had posted pictures on every idiot site he could find. Hooray.

FAS-Lars laughed maniacally and slurped the last of his Coke loudly.

There was one unusual thing about Vendela: she was a bully even though she was studying science. Weren't bright, academic girls supposed to be kind? Wasn't that written in the small print in a clause somewhere on the confirmation letter? In which case she had definitely not read it.

I said nothing, only looked at her indifferently. Her short blond hair. Her large blue eyes. The little turned-up nose. She could be pretty. If she wasn't so flipping ugly, of course.

I tried to imagine I was looking at a dead object. A stone. She was a stone. That was another look I had practised in front of the mirror: trying to look unmoved and cold. Very handy. I had tested it on Dad and it had driven him mad. "Stop staring at me like that!" he had yelled, waving his hands. "You look like Jana. You've got the same … look"'

Even though I really didn't like him saying that, there was some truth in it. The look did remind me of Mum. When she sort of "drifted off", as she described it herself. When she became, like, distant and detached.

*Detached.*

Is that what we were like, me and her? Was I really like her?

'Answer then, bitch,' said Lars, who seemed to go in for the role of sidekick one hundred percent.

'I asked a polite question,' said Vendela. 'Have you sawn off any more fingers lately?'

'Not this one, anyway.' I gave her the finger. Almost stuck it right up her nose.

'My, you're in a bad mood,' said Vendela, managing to sound offended. 'I was only asking. Because I absolutely get it, you know. That you want to harm yourself, I mean. I imagine I would want to do that too, if I were you. But I thought you emo kids were more discreet about cutting yourselves.'

Oh my God. Was she just being a bitch or did people really think I had done it deliberately?

I lowered my finger.

And thought to myself: *She's a stone.*

FAS-Lars laughed out loud and grabbed one of my braces. It was narrow and black and attached to my mint-green jogging bottoms. I had bought a complete 1980s tracksuit in shiny polyester from the City Mission. Fifty kronor and never been worn! It was still in its original wrapping, a rustling transparent bag, when I bought it.

'And what is this? Everyone knows your emo stuff is ugly but this wins first prize! You look like you come from a fucking *mental institution*.'

He said those last words in English. Then he pulled out the strap as far as he could and let it go. It stung my nipple for an instant but I didn't show it. I only looked at him indifferently.

*He is a stone.*

'Yes, what is the matter with you?' asked Vendela, pretending to be sympathetic. 'Do you earn so little from sucking dicks that you have to steal clothes from poor retards?'

Over and over again I thought: *She is a stone. She is a stone.*

Eventually I said:

'I earn shitloads, Vendela, but your mother has a problem. She's undercutting everyone. Selling blow jobs for a few kronor. All the other whores are mad as hell.'

Only if you looked at her really closely could you detect a reaction. Perhaps she had also been practising how to shut off her facial expressions, how to look at people coldly. But I noticed. I saw the muscles round her neck tense up and her eyes narrow.

Out of the corner of my eye I also noticed Enzo slowly edging a few centimetres away and wondered if that was being disloyal, but decided it was mainly understandable. He hadn't chosen this strategy. I had.

I stared calmly first at Vendela and then at Lars for a long time, and then pushed my way past. Lars's body was compact and tense, like a fighting dog's. Even though I despised him with all my heart there was something inexplicably sexual about that hard, aggressive body. No doubt some sick learned behaviour.

As I passed he whacked my head with the palm of his hand. It wasn't an especially hard slap but it hit me right on the swelling. The unexpected pain made me sink to the floor with a loud groan. FAS-Lars looked astounded. He probably hadn't expected the slap to have such a powerful effect.

'You filthy little *slut!*' Vendela hissed down at me. Small, hardly noticeable drops of saliva sprayed from the corners of her mouth. She wiped them away with the back of her hand, turned round, and walked off. FAS-Lars and I looked at each other in confusion. I guess we were both thinking: 'Did I just win, or what?'

Some passing students I vaguely recognised were forced to step aside to avoid my body. I made no attempt to stand up but just lay there with the sound of the smack echoing in my ears. The pain was hard and hot.

FAS-Lars made a face that I think was supposed to be threatening and then hurried after Vendela like a randy but well-trained dog. Sadly I understood that the opportunity for making a caustic remark had passed.

Enzo cautiously approached, clearly ready to flee should they return. He leaned over me and reached out his hand and helped me up. His cheeks hung heavily. He started to speak, fast and disjointed.

'Whoa, I know you can't … you can't expect anything else from *them* but I get so … so mad … so *incredibly* angry at all that … talk about whores … that's no way to … to talk about girls … women …'

While he was searching for the right words I interrupted him.

'I don't. I don't understand what's so wrong about having sex and charging for it. Millions have sex without getting paid. Is that really any better? Isn't it better to get some remuneration than to work for nothing? I think we should reclaim the whole whore concept, bring back "whore" and sort of upgrade it. You know, like the neo-Nazis have done with the Swedish flag.'

Enzo squirmed. I was being disloyal, I knew. He only wanted to show that he was on my side. But it was a little late for that. He mumbled:

'Remuneration? Can't you speak in a language I can understand?'

I sighed. Sometimes it was remarkable how little it took to totally make you lose heart.

'Yes. *Money*. Perhaps you've heard of it? That you get paid?'

He shook his head. It was clear he didn't agree with me. I couldn't blame him. I didn't agree myself. I was only trying to rescue some of my dignity. I think he understood. In a show of solidarity he said nothing.

The corridors had emptied of students and Enzo and I walked quickly to the next lesson.

'Reclaim the whore!' I said, to cheer things up, and blew my nose on a tissue I found in my pocket. It's harder than you think to blow your nose with only one hand.

Two shy girls with messy hair and a thick layer of foundation walked past, late for class. They clung close together, whispering conspiratorially. They fell silent and looked at me in terror, their eyes wide. I stared back, but they carried on walking, throwing glances over their shoulders. It aggravated me. The silence of girls who were best friends did that to me. People always thought they were sweet and considerate, but how would you know that if they never said anything? They made me suspicious. They could just as easily be, well, neo-Nazis.

'Maja?' said Enzo, following the direction of my gaze.

'What?' I said, distractedly, feeling the thumping, blood-filled bump on my head. I couldn't help moaning.

'Excuse my asking,' he grinned. 'But did *that* hurt?'

'Yes, Enzo, it did. Happy now?'

'Yep, happy now!'

## A Stab in the Heart

A minute later we were sitting next to each other in our Swedish lesson. Hanne had just run through the various poetry metric variations and now it was our turn to write a haiku: a Japanese poetic form with five syllables in the first line, seven in the second, and five in the third, she explained.

'Give the third line a kind of twist,' said Hanne, turning her freckly face towards me.

'Something that … surprises!'

She smiled warmly and I gave her a tired smile in return. She liked me, I knew that. I suppose I liked her too; it was hard not to. She often came up to me after the lesson to discuss something I had said or written. Her written comments on my assignments were always profusely positive. "Brilliant!" was her constant opinion about almost everything I wrote. At our progress assessment before Christmas she had said that I have, and I quote: "an exceptionally good ability to express myself both verbally and in writing" and she also said that I was probably "the most gifted pupil in Swedish she had ever had." Of course, she's only been teaching for two years, but still.

An A-star was a given. I needed that grade. In every

other subject I was depressingly mediocre. Studying art and design called for a certain amount of artistic talent, at the very least. I had kind of used up all my talents taking the entrance exam. I never painted or drew as well before or since. I made a sculpture even though I hate sculptures. Venus de Milo. You know, that beautiful woman with bare breasts and sawn-off arms. I gave it the title "No arms, no cake," and who knows, perhaps it was a premonition of what was to come? "No thumb, no …", well, what? But after I had sent in those assignments for the entrance exam it was like there was nothing more to give. Once the inspiration was gone, my artistic ability burnt out like sulphur on a matchstick.

Hanne walked up and down in front the white board on which she had written the guide lines for composing a haiku in handwriting that was as immaculate as it was impersonal. Then all of a sudden she strode up to Simon's desk and took his mobile away from him. He looked up and managed an astonished:

'But …'

Hanne went back to her desk at the front, pulled out a drawer and dropped in the mobile without saying a word. Then she continued walking up and down.

My thumb was hurting like mad and a vague feeling of reluctance worked its way through my body.

*Why didn't she phone? I mean, I had sawn off my thumb and she knew it.*

Hanne came to a halt and leaned over her desk, supporting herself with her hands, her fingers outspread like a sprinter at the starting block. She looked down at her notes. Enzo passed me a slip of paper asking if we could hang out that evening. I shook my head and mouthed 'Norrköping', looking apologetic, and without taking my eyes off Hanne.

Her blouse was very low cut and you could see her pale breasts heaving up and down. Each time she breathed in it looked as if her breasts would pop over the top, so overloaded was the neckline. I hoped they would; I was longing for something to happen. I looked around the classroom, sighing silently. A beam of sunlight had found its way through the window and I could see millions of dust particles, all lit up. Infinitely slowly they whirled around as if they were weightless. They looked like flying glitter. Flying glitter over Hanne's lowered face, flowing glitter over her pale skin ...

Abruptly she straightened up, catching out all of us who were blatantly staring at her bosom. Embarrassed, Enzo immediately looked down and perhaps he was not the only one because she clicked her fingers to regain eye contact. But wasn't that a small self-satisfied smile I saw, flitting like a summer cloud across her freckly face?

'And,' she said, 'Here's a little suggestion. Write about something related to the environment, to nature or the seasons, such as spring ... and, well, why not the approaching summer? That will make it a little more ... Japanese!'

She nodded graciously. That was her way of saying we could start writing.

Counting the syllables on my fingers I quickly wrote:

*Enzo cannot write*
*A haiku. That's because he's*
*Way, way too stupid*

I shoved the poem across to Enzo who opened his eyes wide in an insulted expression. He grabbed the piece of paper, stood up, pointed at me and whispered:

'That's it. This is war.'

Then he went and sharpened his pencil. It was so obvious that he was doing it to gain time and I wondered if I should tease him about it. He moved slowly, waddling a bit. Enzo had been fat since he was a child. Yes, fat. Describing it any other way would be embellishing the truth, he said so himself. But something had happened during the past few months. Apart from growing a few centimetres he had also lost weight. His body had become more defined. I suspected he had started going to the gym, but it wasn't something we talked about. I think it would have embarrassed both of us. Now he was quite a bit above average height and only a touch overweight. But even though he had lost a few negligible kilos he still moved the same way as before. As if he was, well, fat.

Enzo returned to his seat with his sharpened pencil and I decided not to say anything about him giving himself time to think, for once letting go of the impulse to tease. After a while he retaliated happily with:

*Stupid? Pardon me!*
*So who was it then who sawed*
*Off their flipping thumb?*

I laughed out loud because it was so good, and Hanne looked at me, her eyes like slits. I knew that was a warning. Even a favourite was given warnings. So I swallowed my laughter and tried to look as if I was thinking intensely. And I was. I always did. With my bangs falling in my eyes I wrote:

*I saw thumbs, it's cool!*
*But who faints at the sight of*
*Others' blood? You nerd!*

41

My cheeks hurt from holding in the laughter. I bent over my writing pad and looked sideways at Enzo. He met my eyes, looking wronged, but I didn't know if it was real or pretend. Perhaps I'd been cruel. He was ashamed of his weak side. He tried to grab hold of my paper but I held on to it. Eventually he did manage to pull it away from me but it tore with a noisy ripping sound. Hanne was leaning over Simon, who as usual didn't have a clue what he was supposed to be doing. She lifted her head and looked around, but couldn't localise the sound. Enzo and I stared innocently straight ahead. Hanne gave us a suspicious look and returned to Simon. Enzo began writing frantically. He wrote, crossed out, made changes. Then he thought for a while with a faraway look, waggling his pencil between his fingers, before starting to write again. I waited impatiently. Several minutes passed. I looked out of the window. The caretaker went past on his ride-on mower. Was it just me or was there blood on his blue overalls?

Enzo was still writing. I whispered:

'Is it a flipping haiku suite in seven parts, or what?'

He didn't answer. I gave up waiting and tried to write a real haiku, one I could show to Hanne.

*Diamond-like frost*
*Enfolds black and naked trees*
*In glittering cold.*

It was hardly spring related, but I was happy with it anyway. I thought it was beautiful. I also wrote:

*Shimmering dust specks*
*Whirl around swelling bosom*
*The fabric splits! Help!*

I giggled silently. It was a perfect haiku, with a description of the environment and a twist at the end. Pity I would never be able to show it to her.

Smiling broadly, Enzo at last slid his haiku, which had become two, over to me. My smile faded.

The poem was like a stab in the heart. I'm sure he hadn't meant to hurt me. I'd asked for it. I always asked for it. So why did it hurt so badly?

*You think you're so smart*
*Sure. Smart, cool, tough. Makes me laugh!*
*Because the truth is:*

*You are so ugly,*
*So stupid that not even*
*Your own mum wants you!*

I forced out a laugh that did in fact sound natural and tried to pretend that I was thinking up a new haiku in response to his. But in reality I had already given up.

Discretely I took a painkiller out of my pocket, put it into my mouth and swallowed. But it didn't help.

It still hurt.

*Innocence and Idiocy*

I put my book on my lap and looked out through the window, watching the open fields with newly-sprouting crops, birches with chlorophyll-green leaves and stately pines flash by. The landscape was veiled in a fine mist, as if it was early morning when in fact it was late afternoon. The sun was struggling to break through the haze. It was beautiful. I usually liked to read on the train but this time I couldn't. I was unable to concentrate. The words evaded me, wouldn't stick. Perhaps it was the ache in my thumb? I wasn't sure.

I took out my mobile and scrolled through my contacts, but there was no one I wanted to call, no one I wanted to text. Not that I had that many to choose from. I went online and onto Dad's Facebook page. He had loads of friends. Four hundred and sixteen. That was madness. He had one friend request, an invitation to some event and a message from that Denise. So, nearly four hundred and seventeen then.

Playing hard to get was clearly not her thing. She might just as well create a fansite in his honour while she was at it. The completely crazy Denise. Totally effing man-mad. Reluctantly I clicked on the message. There was a dull feeling of uneasiness in my stomach.

Hi Jonas!

Really REALLY nice to meet last time! Hope you weren't too tired next morning. I had a headache for two days afterwards, but it was worth it ;)

I'm having a little party tomorrow. Nothing big, just a few friends coming over, some wine, nibbles. Ola's coming. Check out the event! I know it's short notice but I thought I'd send you an invite anyway – come if you can! Party starts at 8. And of course you know where I live… . . .

It is your free weekend, isn't it? (talking about that I just want to say how impressed I am with you. Being on your own with a teenage girl can't be easy! There are so many men who don't bother with their kids but you seem to take wholehearted responsibility, and that's commendable. I understand, just like you said, that it must be tough sometimes, but I think it's an inspiration to others. So, all praise to you!)

And: really hope to see you tomorrow …

Hug, Denise

I almost spontaneously threw up into my own mouth.

*Oh my God.*

I squeezed my eyes closed. I squeezed them so hard that small dots of light appeared and exploded over my retina.

*Oh. My. God.*

"Inspiration to others?" What a *joke!* What crap! Is it *commendable* behaviour to look after a child that you've brought into the world yourself by shagging? A child who,

45

please note, didn't ask to be brought anywhere. Giving Dad "praise" because he took "wholehearted responsibility" for me was like giving him praise because he went to the toilet and had a dump once a day. It's what you did. It's something every parent ought to be able to manage.

*For crying out loud!*

Not that the others Dad had dated were gifted with more than mediocre intelligence, but this one! Shit. She won first prize. I slapped the palm of my hand down on the seat and took a few deep breaths in an attempt to calm myself down. I'd read in a self-help column somewhere that you should do that when you were worked up about something. But naturally it didn't work. Has it ever worked for anyone?

And then that thought again, revolving round and round: *Why didn't she phone?*

I picked up a free newspaper that someone had left on the seat next to mine and flicked through it aimlessly without reading anything. Right at the back was the long personal column: short, poorly spelled text messages, one after the other. The irritation made my skin itch, as if I'd been attacked by a swarm of angry gnats. My eyes ran over the rows: needy declarations of love, embarrassing one-sided obsessions and pathetic statements of broken hearts.

Don't understand – is it friendship or something more? U wont let me kno. Can't u get in touch I've told u wet I feel bout u. E.

I'm an older guy. Plan to go Puttgarden Germany @ w/e. Seeking older woman for company. Have Mercedes 300 and trailer. Get in touch!

1 mnth till we move 2 our new abode

Lunacy. Nothing but downright lunacy. How could such gravely retarded behaviour be revealed in so few words? But then, suddenly:

The person who came home with me Friday took not only my virginity but also the key to the laundry room. Why? Unnecessary. This relationship lacks communication. R.

Carefully I tore it out and put it into my purse. I was breathing more calmly now. I smiled and looked out across the fields.

*Hit on the Head with a Hammer*

When I got off the train at Norrköping station Mum wasn't there to meet me like she usually was. I scrutinised the platform systematically from right to left, saw people getting off and on, and others waiting and looking, just like I was. But she really wasn't there.

It was odd: Mum wasn't normally late.

I walked with the stream of people towards the white station building and carried on out to the car park to see if her dark blue Saab was parked there, but it wasn't. A taxi driver chewing gum was leaning over his car door and he looked at me, raising his eyebrows, but I shook my head. Did I look like someone who went by taxi?

I walked back into the ticket hall. It was empty apart from a couple of lingering passengers. A grey-haired elderly woman was trundling her shiny red rollator across the polished floor, her head erect. Then it hit me like the blow of a silver hammer on my head.

Wrong weekend.

I had come on the wrong weekend.

I stopped, dropping my bag to the floor so I could think more clearly.

But no, it couldn't be. I wasn't here last weekend

and the tickets had today's date on them. I picked up my bag again, went out through the main entrance and leaned against the white wall, feeling its rough exterior against my shoulder blades through my jacket. I debated several alternatives in my head and rejected them immediately.

No, Mum couldn't have forgotten that I was coming. She didn't forget things like that.

No, she hadn't said anything about going away.

No, she hadn't told me to take the bus and make my own way to her house.

And no, she wasn't usually late. But perhaps she really was. Late.


The haze had dissipated and the sun was low, shining orangey-red against the pale blue sky. I slumped down onto my bag. I had to screw up my eyes to make out the faces of the people passing by, but Mum wasn't one of them. Finally I phoned her. I shut my eyes and wished she would answer, but I got the answering machine just like the day before.

'Hi Jana, it's Maja. I'm here at the station and ... well, it's nearly six and I wonder ... well, I haven't heard from you so I suppose I'll get the bus to your house. So, see you at home in Smedby. You may have heard ... I think Dad told you yesterday that I sawed off my thumb. Not deliberately, I mean. Um, well, bye. See you later.'

It ended up being a strange message. I hadn't managed to make my voice as nonchalant as I'd hoped.

Something was scraping my chest.

I stood up and looked around me. I picked up the bag, took a few hesitant steps forwards, leapt out of the way of a tram and crossed Norra Promenad. I wandered slowly through Carl Johan Park, which was very neat, and crossed Saltängs Bridge, looking down at the grey and glistening surface of the water. I held my mobile in my hand. I should have told her to ring me, of course. I hoped she would realise that, but you couldn't count on it. She didn't always understand things too well.

I carried on along Drottninggatan towards the shopping centre. The streets were deserted but that was nothing unusual. It's just that today it seemed like they were especially deserted.

At the town hall the number three tram pulled up alongside me and I took it to Söder where I had to stand for a while outside the futuristic glass and concrete library, waiting for the bus to Smedby. I looked across at the museum of art and that great rotating spiral which always made me think of a contraceptive.

I really tried not to think too much but it was incredibly hard not to. I always thought too much.

◆

I was rummaging about in my bag for the key when I realised her car wasn't in the drive. The key turned easily in the lock as if it was newly oiled. Not like at home in Örnsberg where you had to throw yourself against the door to unlock it. I opened the door and walked in.

'Hello? Jana?'

No answer. Only silence.

I heard the fridge rumble in the kitchen and then fall

silent. When I closed the front door it was like stepping into a vacuum.

I realised I'd known it all the time.

Mum wasn't there.

*How About Using the Crisis as an Opportunity to Grow?*

I tried to think coldly and act logically. There had to be a reasonable explanation for Mum not being there. I crept through the hall, past the sitting room and into the kitchen. It was quiet. Numbingly quiet.

I looked around the room, over at the table and its chairs that didn't match, the draining board, the rarely used cooker. The heap of newspapers by the larder was almost as tall as me. I didn't quite get it. Clearly something wasn't right. I couldn't put my finger on it at first. But then I noticed.

The sink. It was overflowing with dirty plates, sticky saucepans, and coffee-stained mugs.

That wasn't like Mum.

Not at all.

She always rinsed the tiniest little glass immediately after she had used it. I felt the pulse in my thumb start to thud.

*The saw. The grating, piercing sound.*
*The metal teeth, hacking into me.*
*The flesh. Exposed.*
*The blood. Spiralling, pulsating, spurting.*
*The explosions. The pain.*

I heard my breathing amplified in my ears.

I backed out of the kitchen and into the sitting room, and looked at all the familiar things: the misshapen seventies sofa in green and black, the dilapidated coffee table with its piles of journals, the overloaded book shelves with books crammed into every available space. I spun round and ran up to the first floor. The stairs creaked under my weight.

Her office looked like it always did with the chair neatly tucked under the desk, books stacked one on top of the other, piles of papers, masses of journals: *Psychology Today, The Psychologist, The American Journal of Psychology.*

I walked slowly towards my room, my heart thumping against my ribcage. Then I caught sight of something moving in there, something that sort of swept past. Something white. A dress, perhaps? I stood still.

'Jana,' I said.

My voice fragile. Scared?

No one answered. I pressed my hand hard against the door. It flew open the way they do in gangster films, banged violently against the end of the bed and swung back again.

But I had time to see.

There was no one there.

I pushed open the door, slower this time. Yes, the room was empty. The unmade bed was empty, the chair beside the desk was empty, and the armchair at the far end of the bed was also empty, all except for my forgotten pair of black jeans.

The window was open and in front of it, flapping in the draft, was my white curtain.

I went downstairs again and sat apathetically on the sofa. My thumb was aching so badly. I closed my eyes and leaned back against the lumpy cushions.

I realised what it was I had vainly hoped to find, what I had been looking for: a note. A note that would explain everything. A note that said she had tried to contact me but hadn't been able to get through. One that said she was sorry but she was forced to work late, that she would be home *soon, soon, soon*. And maybe the note would end with a "Hug, Mum."

I laughed at myself, drily. Who was I trying to kid? Mum would never write "Hug, Mum." She never wrote "Mum." She was "Jana", to me and to everyone else. That's the way it had always been. It was only in my own head that I called her Mum. And also if I had to mention her to someone I didn't know, just to avoid their astonished reaction to me calling my own mother by her first name.

As for "hug" – that was a completely foreign concept to her, both in words and action. Up until a few years ago she had hugged me only sporadically. When one Sunday morning I gave a cough and said I would really like to have a hug from time to time, she had looked up from her newspaper in surprise. She questioned me in detail about my request, as if she was taking an order for something. When did I want them and where, she wondered. And how many had I been thinking of? I mumbled awkwardly that it might be nice when I arrived and when I left, what did she think about that? At the train station, perhaps? Wasn't that fairly normal when you hadn't seen each other or weren't going to see each other for a while? Mum nodded thoughtfully, her grey-green eyes fixed on mine. Then she said that it sounded like a "reasonable request" and went back to her newspaper.

After that I received the hugs I had ordered. It never felt really comfortable. Her arms went wrong, somehow, and were too tense, and her face too close or too far away. Mostly too far away.

It was as if she didn't know how to end the hug, either. She would suddenly let go, without looking at me, making a half turn with her arms hanging limply and her gaze somewhere in the distance.

And exactly at that moment, exactly when she let go, when her arms loosened and she kind of like disappeared, that's when I always felt so chillingly alone. As if a wind was blowing right through me. It was so hard to get on the train then. My feet sort of stuck to the platform.

No, those hugs never came naturally to her and sometimes I regretted that I had ever asked. But she never forgot them.


I stood up, called Mum's mobile once more and heard the ringing tone as I wandered through the sitting room and out towards the hall. The wooden flooring creaked at the threshold between the rooms, as it had always done. I stopped in front of the dusty hall mirror and saw something like desperation in my expression and decided it suited me. Didn't it make my eyes so very glittery and mournful? Didn't it make my face fascinatingly pale but my cheeks attractively pink? Perhaps I should be desperate more often.

*What was I doing?*

I slapped myself. Two quick slaps, right in the middle of those pink cheeks. It stung and it was if I suddenly had a revelation. I looked around blearily. My thumb started to thud again.

*What was I doing?*

What if something had happened to Mum? If something had really happened to her. And here I was, acting flirtatiously with my own desperation.

I called her number again. I heard the ringing and watched in surprise as my finger drew a penis in the dust on the mirror.

Then I thought I heard a sound from the other side of the house, a kind of squeaking, getting louder. I stiffened, standing motionless. Perhaps she was in the house after all? Was she lying somewhere, paralysed from a fall, unable to get up?

I walked through the hall, past the sitting room, and then stopped. I looked towards the stairs, towards the bedroom door. Mum's bedroom. I hadn't looked in there. That's where the sound was coming from.

Obviously.

There.

Why hadn't I looked in there?

What if she …

The door stood ajar and I peered cautiously in, my heart in my throat.

… what if she … if she was …

But she wasn't there.

Her bed was unmade. If I hadn't known better I would have thought: Aha, she left in a hurry. But no. Mum's bed was always unmade, so that was not going to get me anywhere. There on her bedside table, beside a pile of seven or eight books, a mouth guard and a glass half full of water, lay Mum's mobile. The ringing tone sounded like the dramatic intro to a news bulletin. I picked up the phone and saw the missed call: Maja mobile.

◆

The phone gave a few more muffled, apocalyptic rings before it abruptly stopped. It felt as if someone had placed a soundproof hat over my head. The entire house was echoingly, worryingly silent.

It was *not* like Mum to go out without her mobile.

I lay down on the bed, pulling the lilac, patterned duvet over my head. I closed my eyes and breathed in the smell of the fabric. It smelled as if she hadn't changed her bedding for a while: it didn't smell bad, exactly, just a bit stale and something else, something sweet. Floral.

I didn't have the energy to think so I squeezed my thumb hard and very obligingly it began to thud with pain. I closed my eyes tight. It was hard to breathe, so I gave the duvet a right hook and freed my face from the heavy material.

'She'll be here soon,' I said out loud to myself.

My voice was calm; it actually reassured me. I allowed my face to form the rest-assured expression of confidence: smooth forehead, eyes wide open, mouth in a relaxed smile. A minute passed. Two. My face muscles were tense.

*Rest assured. Rest assured.*

I took a picture of myself with the camera on my mobile.

I didn't look as if I was in a state of confidence.

I looked as if I was in a state of total lobotomisation.

*Fuck it.*

I shook my head violently, shouted, and stuck out my tongue. I clasped my mobile and shut my eyes, letting the smooth, cool display caress my cheek, and wondered so intensely where she could be that it hurt.

As I lay there under the duvet I suddenly realised that I ought to call Dad. I considered it for a second or two, but what would he be able to do about the situation? I would have to go home again, of course, and I didn't feel like doing that. I didn't want to get on the train again and I didn't want him to have to cancel his unsound plans that reeked of alcohol, which he would do because he wouldn't want me to know about the unsuitable life he was leading. Which I already got. But most of all, I did not want him to be even more irritated with Mum than he was already.

I stared at the display on Mum's mobile. There were several missed calls that I assumed was a cause for concern. The first one dated back to Wednesday. I recognised my home number from yesterday and my mobile number from today. She had several voicemails too. Did this mean she hadn't checked her voicemail since last Wednesday? So didn't she know about my thumb?

I scrolled through her contacts. There were about fifteen numbers but I only recognised one or two names apart from mine, my dad's, and Gran and Granddad's in Germany. Mum didn't have many friends but she didn't seem worried about it. She didn't seem to care, not like I did. It was as if she didn't really need other people.

I had a prickling, unpleasant thought: *Not even me?*

I shivered and pulled the duvet tighter around my body.


The number for the university switchboard was listed in her mobile, so I phoned it. I talked myself into believing she was there, that she was working late and the note she had written had simply blown off the table in a gust of wind when she had shut the door that morning.

*Hug, Mum.*

I spoke to a woman whose Östergötland dialect was so strong it made me smile. She put me through and immediately the answer machine kicked in.

"You have reached Jana Müller at the Institute of Psychology. Leave a message with your name and telephone number. Speak slowly and clearly, and I'll phone you back as soon as possible."

I hung up. Ever so clearly and slowly I said to the empty room:

'This is Maja, your daughter. It is Friday and I am here in Norrköping. It is my weekend. Or your weekend, depending on how you look at it. Our weekend. Do you remember? Ring me, I have sawn off my thumb and I need a mother's tender, loving care.'

Right. What now? I lay on my side and read the book spines. *The Existential Conversation* by Emmy van Deurzen, *The Interpretation of Dreams* by Sigmund Freud, *Crisis and Development* by Johan Cullberg.

I suddenly remembered today's date. Friday the thirteenth. Maybe there was something in it after all? Maybe something had happened? Something unlucky.

*Perhaps she had ... she was ...*

If so, how ironic. Mum, who was so dismissive about superstitions that she demonstratively walked under ladders and left her keys on the table.

I opened the drawer of the bedside table with my toes – it took a while – and pushed the mouth guard into it with my foot. I didn't want to look at it any more. To tell the truth it disgusted me a bit. I stood up, saying loudly to myself:

'Well, how about using this crisis as an opportunity to develop a little?'

*A Diabolical Conspiracy*

I put on an old yellow down jacket that I found in the wardrobe and took a cushion outside to the sun lounger which was still on the terrace. Mum had left it there all winter and there was rust on the hinges.

It was here I used to spend most of my weekends during the summer months. Right here, in this chair, with Mum a few metres away in an identical sun lounger, reading. Always reading. Books about psychology. Always. Her head bowed, her neck bent over like a flamingo's. That was the reason for the shelf. A bookshelf.

We didn't say much but sometimes she asked me what I thought about something she had just read. It could be about associations, developmental psychology or different types of therapy. Things I knew absolutely nothing about, of course. She wanted to hear my opinion anyway, she said, and always listened closely with a worried wrinkle between her eyebrows. She took great care to understand exactly what I meant and asked me loads of follow-up questions. That kind of attention made me feel important, made me feel she really was taking me seriously. But at times it was hard to formulate the words exactly the way she wanted, and I could feel backed against a wall by her sharp, fixed stare and her constant "In what way? What do you mean?"

The chair creaked as I sat down and I was unexpectedly thrown backwards into the maximum horizontal position. I found I could look straight up into space from that angle. The air was clear and cold and the sky a deep blue, turning whiter towards the horizon. A car drove into a driveway somewhere close by: I heard the tyres crunch on the gravel and then the engine being switched off. And perhaps, only perhaps, I saw a shooting star, or was it an aircraft coming down to land at Kungsängen airport? *I ought to make a wish,* I thought.

When Mum was expecting me she saw a shooting star. She did the only superstitious thing she has ever done in her entire life and made a wish.

She wished for a little girl, she said.

She wished for me.

'It was probably only the hormones,' she later commented.

But even so. She wished for me.

And me? I wished for Mum.


My body was relaxed and heavy. A pleasant tiredness came over me and I let the thoughts come and go like the clouds that were leisurely gliding across the evening sky. I could smell the earth and the dampness and hear last year's leaves rustling in the wind. It was so lovely that I almost forgot my mum had been officially missing for a couple of hours.

I was woken by a cool breeze on my face and I had no idea how long I'd been asleep. I looked around me, thinking perhaps I ought to get a book and do a bit of reading. Because if I sat in the chair and read I could pretend everything was normal.

*And perhaps it would make her come home.*

I hauled myself up and went back into the house without putting on my shoes. I got my socks damp, naturally; it was only April after all. I took them off and hung them over a radiator. Then I grabbed one of the many books that were lying on the kitchen table and went outside again to my chair. I had just reached it when I felt a sudden burning under my foot, like a wasp sting.

I had to go back once more into the kitchen. I leaned against the kitchen table and lifted the sole of my foot to the light. Of course. Three really thick, dark splinters had burrowed their way under the skin on the ball of my foot, immediately below my toes. One was perhaps half a centimetre but the others were over a centimetre long. I shook my head and said out loud to myself:

'What the flipping hell is going on? What kind of diabolical conspiracy am I the victim of, exactly?'

I limped into the bathroom to get a pair of tweezers and searched through drawers, shelves, and small woven baskets, which without doubt my Mum had been given by someone else. I observed she had very few bathroom-related items in the bathroom, mainly things easily damaged by water: books, newspapers, receipts. Oh, and loo paper, of course. A whole pack of them, wrapped in plastic, in the bath.

Why would you save receipts from the supermarket in a little basket in the bathroom? Yet another question to ask her when she finally turned up. The weird thing was I had never thought about it before, even though now I could recall it being there for years. Mum's absence seemed to highlight the oddness of it all.

But no tweezers as far as the eye could see. This was almost worse than sawing off my thumb, I thought, and as soon as I thought "thumb" I felt the pain wake up and make itself known in pulsating, aggressive thuds. I sat down in the middle of the floor and tried to get the splinters out using my fingernails, but it was hard to turn the sole of my foot up towards the light when one hand was practically useless. I almost succeeded with one splinter and felt the beginnings of the sweet smell of victory until the splinter broke off and I had to admit defeat.

In the first round, at least.

*Crapping the Internet*

The house to the right, a bungalow built of greyish-white bricks, was in darkness. There was no car parked outside. The one to the left, on the other hand, was bathed in light and when I listened I could make out the rhythmic thud of a heavy-duty bass. Two cars were parked in the drive, one a yellow American sports car and the other a cherry-red rusty, old Volvo.

I rang the door of the grey brick house, hoping someone was hiding inside in the darkness, a nurse or someone similar, who did nothing but slice open feet and remove splinters quickly and pain free. After five minute's silence that was broken only by my insistent ringing on the doorbell, I had to admit there was no one home, which I could in fact have worked out with my arse.

Dispirited I limped across to the other house.

I stood looking in at the yellow light and at the people moving about inside. Their illuminated faces suggested belonging and company. I felt like the girl in that story by Hans Christian Andersen, the one with the matchsticks.

Except I had mine in my foot.

Shit.

I stood there weighing up whether to go back to Mum's

house again, but when I rested my weight on the foot with the splinters I was convinced I had to do something about it. And to be honest, I was feeling quite lonely.

I summoned up my courage, hobbled up to the front door and rang the bell. I waited. No one opened. Cautiously I tried the handle. The door was unlocked. I stopped, took a deep breath, and then opened the door.

A wave of sound met me: loud, thumping music and people shouting and laughing.

A party, in fact.

Parties are not really my thing. At least, not the kind I had so far had the honour of being invited to. They were so chaotic. I missed a concrete plan of action. What was the point, exactly? What were you supposed to *do?* Obviously I got that it was a social thing, I wasn't that much of a loser. But the social aspect was so loosely maintained, so frayed at the edges, that it sort of fell apart for me. Introduce an activity – bowling, ping-pong relay or whatever you flipping well like – and that was cool. But I couldn't just stand there and talk and drink alcohol for seven hours. Not without doing something else. Luckily I didn't have to put myself through it too often. Party invitations were hardly dropping out of the sky and into my lap.

I walked through the doorway, my heart beating so fast that you'd think I was on the way to my own execution. I inched my way through the hall, partly because I couldn't walk any other way with those splinters in my foot and partly because I was actually scared.

At first I didn't see anyone, and then I still didn't see anyone, and then I saw everyone all at the same time. They were in the kitchen. I backed away slightly, half hiding myself behind the door frame. the majority of them must have been about twenty to twenty-five years old. They were standing chatting and laughing in groups of three or four, so loudly that I felt like I would go deaf. The contrast to the silence in Mum's house was enormous.

'Hello?' I said.

But my voice couldn't break through. There was kind of like no room for it in between their thick dialect, beside the fat l's and exaggerated i's and er's. A guy with a hat that was far too small laughed so violently that he had to grab his stomach and bend over. His hat fell off but he didn't seem to care.

No one took any notice of me. Someone yelled:

'Don't make me laaarrrff. I'm allorrgeck!'

It took a while before I realised she meant "allergic". I cleared my throat and said, slightly louder this time:

'Excuse me …er…hello.'

A dark-haired guy with orangey-brown freckles turned around and looked at me in a bored way. In places the freckles were so close together that they formed little islands and made his cheeks look dirty. He studied me critically. I actually saw his eyes move from place to place over my body. My hair. My face. My breasts. The bandage.

I was suddenly conscious of the puffy yellow jacket, hoping it was so outrageously ugly that it was cool, but I was forced to painfully admit that it didn't quite make the grade. The freckly one was wearing a bizarre T-shirt showing a hot dog high-fiving a can of lemonade. He looked down at my naked feet and turned back to his mates.

I stood there for a long time, not quite knowing what to do with myself, wondering if it was possible to back out without attracting anyone's attention. I slid one foot back slightly, then the other. I was just about to disappear into the hall when an ultra-blonde girl with bangs that ended three or four centimetres above her eyebrows broke away from the crowd. Her hips swayed exaggeratedly with each step, as if she was on a catwalk and she was wearing black boots with stiletto heels as thin as pencils. She wasn't entirely unlike Debbie Harry, the one from Blondie. She must have been twenty-four, twenty-five, something like that.


'You moonwalking?' she asked, taking a deep gulp of her lime-green drink. She looked at me, narrowing her eyes above the rim of the glass.

I was so ashamed at being caught in the act of escape that I couldn't answer. I just looked at her, wide eyed. She looked worn out, as if she hadn't slept for several days. Her skin was milky white and her mouth was painted a bright cerise. She was wearing a yellow dress with a very low neckline and, as far as I could see, no bra.

'What a lovely colour your … hair is,' she went on in a drawl. She had a slight accent that may have been British and her voice was as rough as sandpaper. It sounded like she had smoked two packets of ciggs a day since her confirmation. She pushed my long, quite ordinary, black-dyed bangs out of my eyes and ran her hand down my temple, where the hair was shorter and the skin so fine that her touch seemed to leave an imprint. It made me remember I hadn't had time to shave it.

'You're not leaving already? The party's hardly got started. We've got to dance!'

I coughed but couldn't manage a reply this time either. She smiled warmly and pulled me playfully by the arm in the direction of the kitchen. Unwillingly I went back in with her. When we reached the doorway she left me without saying a word and walked right into the crowd of laughing people. Then she clapped her hands, a few short claps like a teacher who is impatiently waiting for the children to be quiet. She staggered momentarily on the high heels and put her hands on her hips as if to steady herself. It did not look entirely relaxed.

'Hello, hello!'

Faces turned towards her, most of them amused and clearly interested, one or two looking slightly irritated.

'I have a question!'

A guy who was unusually young to have an arm full of blue-black tattoos shouted:

'The answer's yes! No problem, my bed is wide enough and I always use a condom.'

'You wish,' said Debbie, rolling her eyes. 'As I said, I have a question!'

'You already said that,' said a girl with long curly hair. Dramatically she threw her head back and took a swallow of her beer. Her hair bounced on her shoulders like in a shampoo ad. Not in slow motion, obviously, but even so.

'Look I'm just wondering ...' Debbie tried to make herself heard.

'Ou' weth it then!' yelled the bloke with the little hat.

'You can shut your BIG MOUTH!' bellowed Debbie so loudly that it made me jump. She looked around the kitchen furiously, her eyes black with anger.

'*Fucking farmers!* What does it take to ask a question round here?'

'Well, ask it then for God's sake!' shouted the girl with the advertisement hair.

'That's exactly what I'm *trying* to do!' Look, is there

anyone here who can download music? I want to listen to Five Minutes by Justin Timberlake,' said Debbie.

The anger made her voice hoarse. She went on:

'But I can't get find it. Can anyone help me?'

Someone said:

'Hello? Spotify?'

'Yeah but it's not there! You've got to download it from somewhere else.'

'Perhaps that's because it's called Four Minutes,' said the guy with the sausage T-shirt.

Debbie hissed: 'You think I don't know what it's called? It's Five Minutes!'

She gave him such a look of hate it made me flinch. The sausage guy didn't seem to care.

'In that case he's done another one because the one he did with Madonna is called Four Minutes, I bet you a million.'

'Take your sodding million and stuff it up your arse! It's called Five *fucking* Minutes.'

Debbie was fuming.

'Isn't there anyone who can help me?'

Someone over at the kitchen table mumbled: 'After being called fucking farmers? Shouldn't think so.'

Debbie swore, tottered to one side and fell against a cupboard with large leaded glass doors. There was a massive clatter as cups and glasses crashed into each other and broke. After a last little clink from a broken shard as it hit the floor, I noticed the music in the other room had gone quiet.

Debbie struggled up onto her feet, straightened her dress and clicked her neck. Then she turned towards me. A thin index finger was pointed directly at my nose. The nail was short with peeling cerise nail varnish.

'You! You're young! Aren't you?'

I looked around in embarrassment. The eyes that had been directed towards her now turned their attention to me and stuck like glue. Instinctively I lifted my bandaged left hand to my chest, holding it carefully with my right hand. It felt like my whole skeleton ached, if that was possible.

Debbie came a few steps closer without lowering her finger.

'Um, yes.'

Yes, I was young. But she was hardly at death's door, was she?

'Young people know all about technology, right? They are *one* with technology. They were born with the internet. They eat, sleep and *crap* the internet. *You* can download, surely? You know what to do?'

I scraped my foot over the floor like some nervous old mare.

'Well … I don't know that I've done much internet crapping. I don't think I can help you. Unfortunately.'

In actual fact I would easily have been able to find that track for her, but because the atmosphere at that moment was so nasty I didn't dare say yes. But of course I crap the internet. I wasn't a hacker exactly but I crap the internet just as well as anyone else my age, although I think my use of the internet is different from most other people. I take pride in using that particular medium in a meaningful way: to search for information. Not to upload pictures of myself in a series of degrading poses. Not to write some onanistic, introverted blog about what I've just eaten or bought, to trick myself into believing that someone is actually *interested*. Not to collect pretend friends in some overrated community with enough pop-ups to trigger an epilepsy attack. And not to press the "like" button when one of these pretend friends updates their status bar with exclamations such as "film night with Katta and Jessi! Cosy!" If people really were having such a flipping cosy time why did they waste time shouting about it on Facebook? Why weren't they just *doing* it? Why does every other idiot have to know?

Debbie slunk past me, swearing.

'Who'd have thought it would be so hard to hear a bit of *Justin fucking Timberlake*?'

Silence fell like a blanket over the gathering.

It was unbearable.

I don't usually feel like that. I usually like silences. They are often more relevant than words, but this silence was in fact unbearable. So I broke it the only way I could think of:

'Er, has anyone got any tweezers?'

*Justin Case*

I sat on the toilet lid with my foot ten centimetres away from the concentrated face of a totally unknown young man. He was crouching in front of me and if I wasn't mistaken he had, only minutes earlier, presented himself as Justin Case. Maybe a stage name, maybe a joke. What did I know?

He must have been twenty-three or thereabouts and he was incredibly tall, you could see that even when he was sitting down. Almost two metres, easily. His eyes were the palest blue I have ever seen and his hair was reddish-blond and greasy and combed forward diagonally in a style that actually resembled Hitler's. No other similarities, I hoped.

He was wearing a pair of extremely tight trousers which had probably been red once upon a time but had faded so much in the wash they were now pink, and a white T-shirt with some image in black, a face maybe. I assumed he lived in the house because he had taken charge of the tweezers situation and moved about the bathroom with familiarity. I couldn't ever remember seeing him before, even though Mum had lived in the area for at least twelve years. But we didn't exactly socialise with the neighbours.

In the doorway three girls were standing watching,

apathetically. One of them, an elfin-like thing who was so tiny she looked as if she had been made to half-scale, turned to the others and whispered something. I looked at her. She had fair hair and her skin was so thin it looked transparent.

'How did this happen, then?' asked Justin severely, but his nose was so blocked it kind of took the edge off his words.

'I, er, I was walking on the terrace, my Mum's terrace, I mean. We're neighbours, yeah? She lives ... she lives in that red house.'

I pointed vaguely to the left.

'What's your name?'

'Maja. Maja Müller.'

'Maja. Hadn't you donned any socks?'

'No, no, I hadn't *donned* ... I wasn't wearing socks, no.'

He studied my foot closely and I hoped it smelled okay. I thought of Mum's hatred of socks, her sermons about how they trapped your feet, made them hot and sweaty. She always tore off her socks the minute she got home, in an irritated and almost aggressive way, as if the socks were offending her personally. She started wearing sandals as soon as she possibly could in the spring and as a rule continued wearing them right up until the first frost arrived. I always hoped it would come early because I was embarrassed about her naked feet in October. She walked about barefoot indoors all the time and was always trying to get me to do the same, even though I had told her a hundred times that I would much rather wear socks. That they didn't bother me the way they bothered her. All she did was shake her head. It was impossible for her to take it in, something she couldn't possibly understand.

'I need more than tweezers to do this,' said Justin abruptly, and went on:

'They are completely embedded in your skin.'

I swallowed. He put my foot down and ordered the elf in the doorway to lend him the safety pin that was holding her top together, a top that looked as if it was made out of one long piece of fabric.

'You are aware it's only April?' he asked, his gaze directed at my foot.

I looked at the girls but none of them answered.

'Are you talking to me?' I asked.

'Who else? Are you?'

'Yes. Yes, course I am. April,' I said quietly, nodding to myself.

I didn't dare look at him. Was he joking?

'Is it really suitable to go barefoot in April?' he said, scolding me.

I looked at him, puzzled.

'You're pulling my leg …'

He looked up briefly and gave me a teasing smile.

'Yes, I am.'

The tiny blonde crept up to him and handed over the safety pin, holding her top closed. I looked at her but she shyly lowered her gaze. You could make out the thin veins forming an irregular network over her eyelids. Her skin seemed to glow a light violet colour.

Justin didn't say thank you; instead he got out a cigarette lighter and held the flame against the point. After a while the metal glowed a shining orange. I gulped. He blew on the pin.

'What have you done to your thumb?' wondered the elfin's friend, a girl with enormous horn-rimmed spectacles. The hint of an Östgöta accent crept in even though she struggled to suppress it.

'I've sawn it off.'

'You've *what?*' she said in disbelief, and the Östgöta accent threatened to take over completely.

'Sawn it off. With an electric saw.'

'Why?'

She took a step forward to get a better look.

'I was tired of it.'

I smiled slyly, but after a moment – usually I can hold out longer, at least with Enzo I can hold out for at least a minute if I force myself – I said:

'No, only joking. It was an accident. I was sawing the side pieces of a shelf.'

'You doing some kind of craft course, then?'

'No, it was a sculpture lesson.'

'Why were you sawing a shelf in a sculpture lesson?'

She pushed her glasses higher up on her nose.

'A shelf can be a sculpture too, can't it?'

'No-o, I don't know if I can agree with you there ...'

To think people can be so flipping conservative!

Justin raised his voice:

'Sit still. Now then ...'

I could feel him digging. And digging. And digging. Every so often he went back to using the tweezers. I tried not to look but my eyes were irresistibly drawn to the silvery metal instrument.

'There. Got one.'

He lifted up the thick splinter triumphantly. I felt sick. The girls in the doorway applauded. The little elf smiled at me encouragingly.

A moment later he pulled out another one, but the third was hard to get at because it had snapped off in two places. 'Nearly there. I've just got to slit open this little bit of skin.'

Everything went black. Only for a nanosecond, but

because I was wearing polyester trousers and a shiny down jacket, and because the toilet seat was made of slippery porcelain, I slid down and banged the back of my head against the toilet. In exactly the same place as the day before. And in exactly the same place where FAS-Lars had hit it only hours earlier.

I actually saw stars. Blue-white flashes anyway, the kind you see if you rub your eyes really hard.

You would think the removal of a little patch of skin isn't so bad when you've lost part of a digit but I suppose it was all too much, what with Mum's disappearance and everything so to tell you the truth, a tear trickled from my eye. That *so* irritated me because they might think it was because I'd bashed myself. It *so* irritated me that they might think I was a wimp.

'Perhaps you would like some water?' asked Justin kindly.

The elfin-like girl raised her voice.

'No, I know. You've got to have some alcohol and then a towel to bite on when he takes out the last bit. It helps. I've seen it on a film.'

'She's underage,' snapped Justin to the elf, but she didn't reply and only slipped out quickly through the doorway.

I felt a bit disappointed, not because I might not be getting any alcohol, but because I realised it showed. I made my voice as chilled as I could as I said:

'I am *not* underage.'

Justin looked at me sceptically but when the elf came back with a glass of whisky he didn't protest. I took two over-confident gulps – I was excused the towel – and managed to keep the gagging under control. I mean, I don't *think* it showed on the outside that I wanted to throw up. But isn't it strange that something that looks like liquid gold can taste so disgusting?

The final splinter was quickly dealt with. I didn't even feel it and even managed to check my mobile at the same time, but it was worryingly silent and blank and pointless. When Justin handed me the splinter I saw that it was as thick as a toothpick and jagged, and full of small protruding wood fibres. *There is something about wood,* I thought. *It doesn't like me.*

Justin pulled out a metre of loo roll and blew his nose in such a way that everyone in his presence could see the contents of his nostrils. I turned away politely and drained my glass.

That whisky, those totally disgusting mouthfuls, made me open up. Yes, I know it was pathetic, but that's how it was. I just wasn't used to alcohol. When the blonde Debbie Harry look-alike walked haughtily past the bathroom it was probably the whisky that made me dare to call out:

'I can get Justin Timberlake. If you want.'

She came to an abrupt halt as if someone had put on the hand brake, then she turned and in an unhurried cat-like way walked towards me.

'Can you?'

'Yes.'

'We can all do that,' said Justin, tossing his bangs. 'You've just got to put in his name, I told you.'

She took no notice of him.

'Do you want me to do it?'

Her eyes glittered as she said:

'Abso*fucking*lutely. What are you waiting for?'

And I saw that her eyes were slanted, like a feline predator.

*Hang the DJ*

I think I sat for three hours on Justin's sofa, downloading tracks with his laptop resting on my knees and always with someone sitting beside me. They sat close, their thighs pressed against mine, their shoulders hard, their breath hot. Greasy fingers on the screen: "That one. Get that one!"

Of course I played tracks from Spotify too, but anyone could use Spotify. Downloading – that was something else. People seem to have forgotten how to do it, seem to have forgotten that you can still hear those obscure B-sides, unobtainable albums, artists who didn't want anything to do with it. Frank Zappa. Sonic. Girl Talk.

I loved it. *Loved.* There is no other word for it. It was as if every spotlight was directed at me. My body became warm and my skin tingled. The pain in my thumb eased and faded away, and the anxiety about Mum sort of got lost and disappeared somewhere into the background.

*Is this what it feels like,* I wondered. *Is this what it feels like to be popular?*

Mum asked me once in her rather weirdly direct way if I was popular at school. I didn't know what to say, so I said nothing. I wasn't popular but I wasn't unpopular either; I wasn't someone people avoided or bullied. Or was I? Vendela and FAS-Lars bullied me at regular intervals, but I was pretty good at bullying back. But in my class? I don't think my classmates found me especially interesting. Like, weird and uninteresting at the same time.

But there! There in the warmth of that crowded sofa, something happened. Someone else could have done it. Obviously. But they wanted me to do it, and I did it well. I varied the music: mellow sounds, dance numbers, pop, alternative, and when there were adverts I played a downloaded track instead. I was as fair as a mum with five kids, all the time giving equal turns: "Yes, we'll play your track next, after this one."

Maybe I was being naïve, maybe it was only the music they wanted, but even if that was the case I didn't give a toss because it felt as if they wanted me.

*Just for once. Me.*

I started with Justin, obviously. Justin *fucking* Timberlake. Anything else would have been unthinkable. Four Minutes. Debbie's eyes almost filled with tears. I don't know whether she didn't hear or whether she totally didn't care that he was actually singing *four* and not *five* minutes, but she yelled a happy:

'We only got FIVE minutes to save the world!'

Then in quick succession: Cry Me a River, Like I Love You, SexyBack, Rock your Body.

After that a random mix of other artists. Some of them good, most of them total rubbish. But always back to Justin.

Justin Timberlake had never impressed me before – music after 1987 seldom did – but there was something about Debbie's aggressive enthusiasm that was infectious. She danced wildly a few metres in front of me, her arms above her head, and every time I looked up I met those

79

predatory eyes. It was as if they were constantly fixed on me. Her heels stamped hard against the floor and made tiny, tiny circular marks in the wooden boards. Every so often she squeezed herself onto the sofa beside me to demand a new track, totally ignoring the fact that someone else was sitting there. She took a firm grip on my bandaged hand and whispered in my ear so it tickled:

'Honey! You are such a fucking techgirl! I love you!'

Then she kissed me hard on the cheek, leaving a trail of wet saliva on my skin and a half-empty glass of some lime drink in my hand. And I took the credit for something that mostly an online music service had done.

Only occasionally did the anxiety bubble up to the surface. Like a little whirlwind appearing on the edge of a thunderstorm, the anxiety began to rotate, lifting those little nagging thoughts, that chilling fear, the way a whirlwind lifts leaves and paper from the street and makes them fly violently around.

*What had happened?*

Then I stood up and looked through the window towards Mum's house. It looked just as dark and empty as when I had left it. I told myself that I really should call the police, because wasn't that what you did when someone disappeared? But I couldn't make up my mind whether to phone the emergency number or the one for less urgent cases. I couldn't even get my phone out of my pocket. I was too afraid it would be silent. Too afraid the display would be blank.

◆

Justin Case kept away; I was conscious of that the whole time. I didn't get a glimpse of him for over two hours, but in the silence between two tracks I heard his voice from the kitchen. Then all of a sudden he appeared, walking towards me with his hands in his back pockets, so tall that he had to duck to avoid a ceiling lamp. I noticed what he had on his feet: white basketball boots with long laces tied around his trouser legs like ballet shoe ribbons.

He did a circuit of the sofa and came and stood nonchalantly behind me. I could feel his hot breath on my neck. Then he leaned over and just happened to throw an arm around my shoulders. He stood with his cheek so close to mine that I could almost feel the heat coming off his face. He smelt vaguely of cologne and sweat. My heart did a double somersault.

'Have you got Panic?'

'No, it's cool. Or – what did you mean?'

'The Smiths. Panic.'

And then he sang:

'Burn down the disco, hang the blessed DJ, because the music that they constantly play IT SAYS NOTH-ING TO ME ABOUT MY LIFE!'

He shouted that last line.

'Ha-a-ang the blessed DJ. Hang the DJ, hang the DJ, hang the DJ. If I hear one more Timberlake song I will hang first the DJ and then myself. In a double loop.'

'I'm not DJ-ing! I'm only doing what the others want me to do.'

'Are you? Do you always do that? That doesn't seem very *sound*.'

He shook his head exaggeratedly and knocked back a mouthful of my drink.

I smiled and looked down at the screen. He was a bit

plastered, at least. I stared at the letters and tried to re-member which ones I had been going to click, trying to understand what was written there, but the letters ran together and blurred.

'So what would it be if the DJ herself chose?' he said, teasing me.

'Well, not this, that's for sure.'

Through the speakers you could hear some latest dance stuff by Madonna. Clearly I must have clicked on it a minute earlier even if I didn't remember doing so.

'What, then?'

'I – I only listen to 80s music, that and some 70s stuff, late 70s. Not disco or crap like that. A lot of … new ro-mantic stuff, if you know what that is. And new wave.'

'What?' he asked in amusement, tossing back his bangs. He went on:

'But were you even born then?'

I looked up at him, backwards. Met those pale, pale eyes.

'And?'

The irritation rose up in me.

'I know what you're thinking,' I said.

'Do you? How handy,' he said, and his face was so close to mine that I could have licked the tip of his nose if I had turned sideways and made an effort.

'You think it's pathetic to like the same music as your parents. And sure, maybe it is. But I can tell you after I listened to my dad's music collection it seemed like the crap my classmates listen to is completely pathetic.'

I sounded more irritated than I intended, and aware of this I pinched my lips together tightly, to hold back the words. It didn't work too well. They just poured out. I expect I had heard those amused comments one time too many.

'And what current band can compare with … with Human League, Spandau Ballet and Duran Duran? Both musically and … and stylistically. Not to mention Joy Division and … and New Order? Yeah? None. None at all? None *at all*.'

He held up his hands as if to fend me off, and backed away.

'No, of course not,' he said gently.

Then he walked off.

Away. Away from me. His arms dangling at his sides.

And I regretted immediately that I had sounded off like that.

*Regretted.*

Regretted that I'd mentioned *Dad*, that I'd mentioned *classmates. That* was pathetic if anything was. Childish. The shame washed over me, warm and damp as if someone had placed a sauna heater in the middle of the table in front of me and thrown a cup of ice-cold water onto it. I was expiring from the steam. From the regret.

And I regretted snubbing him like that.

Because otherwise I would still be feeling his breath on my neck, his arm round my shoulder.

I felt the pain from my thumb radiate into my hand and up towards my wrist. I chose a track for myself for once. Don't You Want Me? by the Human League. I sung a quiet duet with Philip Oakey.

*Don't, don't you want me?*
*You know I can't believe it when I hear that you won't see me*
*Don't, don't you want me?*
*You know I don't believe it when you say that you don't need me*

*It's much too late to find*
*You think you've changed your mind*
*You'd better change it back or we will both be sorry*

And was I singing that to Justin? Or … *to Mum?*

I sat there on the sofa for an hour or so until a gay glass artist came and asked me to dance. I knew he was a glass artist because he had shouted it out when he had been sitting on the sofa earlier, and in a lame attempt to be sociable I had asked him what he did during the week.

'I'm a *glass artist!* I work a lot with sculptures.'

'Me too,' I had said, but he hadn't heard.

To be truthful I didn't know he was gay but he'd had his tongue shoved deep into some other guy's mouth a little earlier in the evening. I had no other proof.

I was hesitant at first about dancing, afraid to leave my secure, bribed place on the sofa, but he was so convincing in his enthusiasm that I gave in and we danced to a techno beat with a Hammond organ. And it was good, that track, but somehow I didn't manage to absorb it into my body, feeling all the time awkwardly self-conscious even though I had thrown the dregs of a few lime cocktails down my throat. I noticed someone else had taken over my role at the laptop. That stung a little because I really wanted to believe I was indispensable, but it's a heart-rending fact that people seldom are.

Debbie walked up to me and threw herself round my neck. I tried to duck, tried to protect my naked feet from her stilettos, and I almost toppled backwards with the weight of her alcohol-fuelled body. She felt my head, ran her hand over the back of my head and whispered that it felt like velvet. I liked it a lot, having her voice like that in my ear. Then suddenly she let go of me and carried on dancing. Her breasts moved unhindered beneath the fabric of her dress.

I remained standing there, looking at her, looking at the others and the liberated way they moved around the floor. Then all of a sudden I realised something: during the past few hours I had experienced a sprinkling of pure happiness, absurdly enough, despite the fact that Mum was missing. I decided to go along with that feeling and not let myself be held back.

The bass was so heavy that the air vibrated. I danced wildly. I danced even more wildly. More than anything I so wanted to feel like I was good at it, dancing. Perhaps it was the alcohol kicking in that made me go in for it a hundred percent, dancing with my arms above my head, my bandaged pulsing hand and all, so I shut my eyes and sang along. I felt as if I was floating in very salty water. I was *happy!*

Then I heard someone laugh. I ignored it at first but it didn't go away, that annoying high laugh. I opened my eyes. It was the glass artist.

'Ha! Is that how people dance these days?'

And then he imitated me, wiggling his backside exaggeratedly and moving his arms upwards as if shadow boxing. And sniggering. Not unkindly. Well, not *that* unkindly.

It was hard to dance after that.

I smiled at him even though that was the last thing I felt like doing. Like a puppy I lay down in front of the big German Shepherd.

I left the sitting room and walked upstairs. There was a couple sitting on the landing sofa, snogging with their eyes closed. I caught a glimpse of their wet, pink tongues. I stared at them indifferently. It made me think of a bizarre mating game between two squirrels that I'd seen on TV once. The programme was all about animals in Costa Rica and the squirrels were massive. During foreplay the male peed on the female, which appeared to send her into unbelievable ecstasy and made her dance wildly. After a while the male peed on her a second time and she danced just as wildly again. After repeated peeing and dancing the actual mating finally began.

You would never have thought squirrels could be so kinky.

Suddenly the guy opened one eye, as if he had felt he was being watched. Hurriedly I disappeared into the bathroom and shut the door. The music sounded muffled and distant. I stared at my face in the mirror. I looked stupid. Pale and stupid. My mouth half open, my eyes watery and glistening with self-pity.

'May every glass artist prick be eaten alive by Satan!' I whispered, and then raised my voice: 'Who cares about effing *art?* Who cares about making art out of effing *glass?* Who cares about effing *sculptures? I hate you! I hate everyone!'*

I screamed that last sentence out loud. Then I fell silent and looked around me. I cleared my throat. Above the hand basin was a large hand-written note but my eyes wouldn't focus; I couldn't read what it said. The paper had gone wavy, like paper does when it's damp. I imagined Justin's pale body in the bath, imagined him showering in hot water.

I strained my eyes to read, squinting, and made out:

*The most effective way for an organism to adapt to its surroundings is to die.*
*Sigmund Freud.*

Feeling slightly nauseous I unlocked the door and crept past the snogging pair on the sofa and down the stairs. I searched for the pale yellow down jacket that was lying in a pile of footwear and outer clothing, thinking how practical it was that I didn't have to look for any shoes. I looked around me, at the sitting room, at the kitchen. Everyone was busy with what they were doing: talking, dancing, flirting, drinking.

As I went out through the front door I thought about that note, thought about Freud. I wondered whether death really was adapting. Whether dying wasn't the most anarchic thing you could do in a society where everyone was so scarily glass-artistically alive.

## Saturday, 14 April

*A Malignant Tumour*

When I woke up on Saturday morning fully dressed in my bed in my sparsely furnished room there was only one thought echoing in my head. It was so insistent that I wondered if that was what had woken me.

*She may have sent an email.*

Of course. I had to check. Now.

It was strange I hadn't thought of it earlier. That was usually how we kept in touch in between the Norrköping weekends. I had been so busy checking Dad's emails that I had forgotten to check my own.

I got out of bed quickly, too quickly, and a heavy, leaden ache spread from one side of my head to the other, forcing me to sit down again. My mouth was dry. I touched my tongue with my finger. It felt as if it didn't belong to me. It felt like a foreign object, like a little animal that had curled up in there and died. I felt like doing the same. But I didn't; I made myself get up and walk the couple of metres to the office where I switched on Mum's laptop. I drummed patiently on the keys as it started up. I felt a sudden pressure on my bladder that I tried to ignore. I went into Hotmail and quickly scanned the lines. Spam. Spam. Spam.

Then: would you believe it.

There. An email from Mum. It had been sent yesterday morning and it was addressed to both me and Dad.

On the subject line it said: Can't see Maja this weekend!

Maja.
Jonas.

I am very sorry that this is such short notice but I have to let you know that Maja can't stay here this weekend. Unfortunately it is not possble for me to phone, the way things are at the moment, but I assume Jonas that you will read this in time to cancel the visit. I promise to make this up to you Maja and will phone as soon as I can. I hope you can get the money back for the train tickets, Jonas, otherwise naturally I will reimburse you.

Best wishes,

Jana

At first I only stood there in silence, staring at the screen. I didn't know whether to feel relieved or, well, what? She was alive, at least. Had I ever thought anything else? I didn't know.

Then I felt it come. The rage. Slowly at first but then more and more intense, like those burning pins and needles when your foot has gone to sleep. Hot and corrosive like caustic soda it raced around my blood stream.

I spent two days with her every other week. Was that too sodding much? Was that so sodding difficult? *Was that so sodding unimportant?* I seriously felt as if I wanted to damage something, kill something.

I tried to convince myself: this is good news; she hadn't simply disappeared. Wasn't that right? Then why was I in such a terrible rage?

There was something in the objective tone that was unbearably painful, that fed the flames. As if she didn't care at all about what she was writing, about what it would do to me. Actually the formal tone was not unexpected. Irritating and sad, yes, but at least it was like her. In fact that was the only thing that wasn't strange, even if clearly it ought to have been.

*What is more important than me, Mum?*

The thought detached itself suddenly and hung there, exposed. I didn't want to think it, didn't want to touch it. It was too ugly. I tried to force it away, suppress it, remove it like you remove a malignant tumour. Because I didn't want to care. But I did.

A less emotionally damaging question: why hadn't Dad said anything? He checked his emails at least fifty times a day. His job flipping well depended on it, or so it seemed. I quickly checked his inbox but couldn't see an email from Mum, only one from that pathetic Denise wanting to give him her door code just in case he turned up that evening, making her "such a very lucky girl". *Girl.* Pathetic. I felt exhausted.

Had he deleted Mum's email? There was nothing in the recycle bin but it could have been emptied, of course. I clicked on *Sent* but there was no answer to Mum. Odd. I double checked that she really had sent the email to him but yes, she had his email address was there after mine.

The whole thing was completely baffling! The questions attacked me, shooting through my head like projectiles: *why was she doing this where was she why hadn't she phoned why hadn't Dad said anything what was she doing when was she going to come back why was she doing this why was she doing this why was she doing this???*

All of a sudden my body took over and I had to run to the toilet. I just about got my trousers and knickers down before my bladder emptied itself. I let it run. I put my hands on my face and shut my eyes. It hurt. Everything hurt. My thumb, my heart, my brain. I washed my hands carefully to avoid getting the bandage wet and looked in the mirror which was covered in glittery lilac dinosaur stickers I had put there ages and ages ago. In my calmest voice I said to the reflection in the mirror:

'You are overreacting, Maja. Everything is all right now, don't you get it? She has been in touch.'

It could have been because I was looking at myself in her mirror but for the first time in my life I thought that I looked like her, as Dad kept telling me. It was something about the eyes. The look had become so sharp, almost hard. Had the anger done that? The disappointment? Wasn't it weird that I only resembled her when I was in such a state? And wasn't it sad that was the only time?

I went back to the laptop and sat down, feeling as if I wanted to be sick.

One weird thing was the spelling mistake. *Possble.* Mum never made spelling mistakes. She was far too obsessive for that. The incomprehensibility of the whole thing somehow increased my rage. I didn't understand! I stood up, feeling annoyed, and went down the stairs and into the kitchen.

The police. I should have phoned them a long time ago. Why did I feel so paralysed? I grabbed the phone that was lying on the window sill, recharging.

How strange. Now that I knew she was ... alive, I wanted to call them. Why was that?

*Does that mean I had thought she was … dead? Is that what I had been afraid of?*

I keyed in the emergency number *one one two*. Because this was an emergency situation, wasn't it? I put the phone to my ear, opened the freezer door, and allowed the cold to wash over me, seep into me. Why not? I let it make my head cold: I broke off a handful of snow-white frost and wiped it across my forehead. It made the skin go numb and that helped the headache slightly. I heard the ringing tone and I stood as close as I possibly could to the freezer, pulling the door towards me until I was enfolded by the cold. The hairs on my body stood on end, my nipples hardened. I scraped off some more icy-cold frost and crammed it into my mouth. There was a woman's voice in my ear:

'*SOS alarm. How can I help you?*'

And then.

'*Hello?*'

Suddenly.

'*Hello, is anyone there?*'

Suddenly I realised something wasn't right.

I cut off the call and stepped slowly away from the freezer. Purposefully I walked the fourteen stairs of the staircase. The screen saver had kicked in and a colourful ball was bouncing off the edges as if it was trapped inside a two-dimensional aquarium. I moved the mouse and the email reappeared.

Precisely as I thought.

Dad's email address. It was wrong. It said: filantropen@homail.com.

Homail.

The 't' was missing.

## A Kind of 'Right, That's It!'

The sun had been hiding behind a hazy covering all morning but then the sky cleared and everything became so blue and dazzling that I opened the terrace door, deciding to drink my juice outside on the steps.

It was chilly and I wasn't wearing enough clothes. It all felt pretty miserable and I thought about Mum and tried to understand how she was feeling. I wasn't good at it but then I don't think anybody is, really.

Mum wasn't like other people. That's the kind of thing you say about people, sort of in passing and dismissively when you can't be bothered trying to understand them, but in Mum's case it was true. It might sound cruel but she genuinely was socially inept. I'm not sure but I think she didn't really understand what made other people tick, what they were thinking, how they felt. Perhaps that's why she didn't know how to behave in social situations? Either that or — and this is what I sometimes suspected — she simply couldn't be bothered.

I almost laughed when I thought about how she actually spent her working life trying to understand others. But only almost, because how could such a thought be even the slightest bit funny?

A cold wind swept over my arms and gave me goose-bumps. I so wondered why she wasn't here, why she wasn't with me now. I felt empty, totally drained, and it was so desolate around me, so colourless and ugly, that the surroundings seemed to have been drained as well. I wondered if I really knew her at all, my own beautiful Mum. A teardrop fell into my juice but I was tired of crying, crying for Mum. I couldn't do it any more. Instead my body started itching with something like rage but not exactly that, and I got hot and the goosebumps disappeared. The lump of crying I had in my throat, that I refused to let out, became hard and it was absolutely impossible either to swallow it or to ignore it. I flung the glass down on the stone slabs beyond the terrace and it shattered into hundreds of small pieces and I saw the sun glittering on the juice, the glass, and the foolish lonely tear.

When I went back into the house I was overcome by a powerful anger. A kind of *Right, that's it!*

I moved about like a search and destroy robot, looking at anything that could possibly reveal something about her. Where she could be. Who she was.

I read all the journals that were lying about, especially the articles that were stained, wrinkled or torn, the ones she had read. I studied the dirty dishes in the sink, coming to the conclusion that she had been drinking tea, coffee and instant soup and eating sandwiches during the last few days, just like she usually did. I went through her wardrobe to try to work out which clothes were missing, but despite the fact that Mum's wardrobe is not what you might call impressively large it was of course impossible to remember all the items. Possibly a greyish-blue short-sleeved silk blouse was missing, but I wasn't at all certain. I searched a good half hour for the suitcase before I found it crammed into the hall cupboard and could dismiss the idea that she had gone away, at least with that particular suitcase. I switched on the radio to check which channel she had been listening to and not surprisingly it was P1, and I checked the DVD player to see which film she had watched last, but it was only the vampire series *True Blood* that I had loaded myself fourteen days ago when everything was still normal.

I flicked through the books that lay on her bedside table, concentrating on the dog-eared ones containing her notes and underlinings, question marks and one or two exclamation marks. The English was complicated and I hardly understood a thing, either the contents or the words. Even the Swedish books were fascinatingly incomprehensible. Small fragments broke free from the page and shone like sparklers against a black night sky:

> *Living is considered an art. As with all art the artist improves only through practice. Insight into the secret of the art can be achieved by making mistakes.*

Mum had underlined these sentences twice with a pencil so sharp it had almost perforated the paper. In the margin she had written: "Living is an art!" followed by one of those rare exclamation marks. That must be what she really thinks. That living is an art.

My headache intensified. My temples thumped so hard that I was forced to go to the mirror to check if it was visible from the outside.

I rummaged through the drawer of her bedside table and apart from the mouth guard, a packet of tissues, two yellow ear plugs and the DVD player manual, I also found a photograph.

A photograph in the bedside table drawer. To take out and look at before going to sleep.It must be significant, I thought. It *must* be a clue.

It was taken a year ago. The date was there in red digital letters in the bottom right-hand corner. It was a picture of Mum and a man with dark curly hair who I had never seen before. Even though the photo was out of focus you could see how beautiful she was: shoulder-length, shiny dark brown hair, conspicuous eyebrows and large grey-green eyes. High cheekbones. There was something special about her mouth, a strikingly full lower lip with a considerably thinner upper lip. You could make out the beginnings of a smile on her mouth, while the man was laughing as if he was on the point of insanity. I think you could see every flipping tooth in his mouth. She was wearing a dark-green long-sleeved silk blouse that I had just seen in her wardrobe. She liked silk, said it was like being caressed, that all other clothes felt heavy and shapeless in comparison. He was wearing a jacket and underneath that a white T-shirt. He was touching her, brushing her lower arm with his fingers. Her cheeks were red and since she would never do anything as irrational and meaningless as wear make-up, they must be roses in her cheeks caused by the heat or the cold.

On the back of the photograph in capital letters in blue ink was written THOMAS. Not THOMAS AND ME but just THOMAS. As if she herself was unimportant.

I looked for more photos, on shelves, in boxes and in drawers, but all I found was the photo album I had looked at so many times before that the corners of the hard cardboard covers were now worn smooth and rounded. This was the photo album I had looked in so many times that I could describe every single picture in the smallest detail, from Dad's patterned shirts to Mum's functional metal hair slides, and the concentrated look I had when I was eating my porridge. The photo album I had looked at so many times that I knew each unnecessary caption by heart: "Maja playing with a train", "Jonas, Jana and Maja at Kolmården wildlife park", "Jana and Maja in the kitchen". The photo album that showed me as a tiny newborn baby with thin hair, lying in Dad's arms, Mum standing close by looking serious, all the way through crawling, standing and the first staggering steps, to the chubby stubborn three year-old cycling on a bright-red tricycle.

Then suddenly the photos stopped. The rest of the album was empty. Fifteen blank white pages without a single picture. As if life stopped there, at the divorce. And perhaps it did, in a way.

But Thomas? I picked up the photo and examined it. I examined Thomas, his creased laughing eyes, his dark curly hair. Who was he, this man I had never met or even heard about? Did my mum have secrets from me? Did she? That had never occurred to me. Suddenly I realised that I didn't know very much about her, about her life on the days I wasn't here. I had assumed they were more or less the same as the days I was here, but perhaps I was mistaken.

I had a sudden impulse. I looked around the room for her phone bedside table, window sill, bed. It wasn't there. I whipped off the duvet and heard a thud. Her mobile. I picked it up from the floor and scrolled through her contact list again.

There it was.

Thomas.

No surname, just Thomas.

I hesitated for a split second and then I pressed call.

As taut as a wire and with the phone pressed hard to my ear, I stood there listening to the monotonous tones at the other end. I had no idea what I would do, no idea what I would say, if he answered. *Thomas.* I prodded my thumb and the pain immediately radiated through my hand and up my arm.

I needn't have worried. After what seemed like an eternity I reached his voicemail.

"Hi. You've reached Thomas. Leave your name and number and I'll call you back later. Ciao!"

There was a beep. I stood there in silence. Paralysed. "Ciao." Who says "Ciao", for God's sake? I ought to say something but I said nothing and the seconds ticked by. There was another beep and the call was disconnected. I had waited too long. After a few moments of indecision I decided not to give up so easily. I phoned again. The ringing tones, the recorded message.

'Hello. My name's Maja. Um … I'm Jana's daughter. You might know her? Jana Müller?'

I asked him to call me back, reeling off my number so fast that I muddled it up and had to start again. Then I rang off and went into the kitchen.

◆

I drank a cup of her herb tea that smelt of hay, ate some cheese-flavoured rice cakes and even smoked one of the evil-smelling cigarillos I found in the cupboard above the cooker.

This is what Mum likes, I thought a moment later, as I

uncontrollably threw up the tobacco-smelling, herb tea-soaked pieces of rice cake into the toilet, my head thrust deep between the white porcelain sides.

These foreign flavours were very familiar in her mouth. Or perhaps she had only bought the rice cakes on an impulse because they were cheap, or because she was distracted and picked up the wrong kind. *Here I am, jumping to the wrong conclusions,* I thought. *Like an incompetent archaeologist.*

What did I know?

What did I know about her?

What did I know about anything?

Nothing.

I wanted to stay there forever, there in the claustrophobic security of the toilet bowl, but I stood up. I very carefully stood up without any part of my head touching the inside of the toilet. Because I wasn't a mental case. I certainly wasn't that. I closed the lid and flushed the toilet, hanging over the lid like an alcoholic over a bar counter. I tore off some sheets of loo roll and wiped my mouth.

Oh well. Perhaps I had come to know her a bit better.

But I still didn't understand why she had abandoned me.

◆

After I had finished washing I heard my mobile upstairs. A text! Maybe from Mum!

I ran up the staircase in five leaps and threw myself onto the bed. It was from Enzo and that made me disappointed, but I was happy after I had read it. It reminded me of another life in another town, one where I had a parent close at hand and a friend. Where I wasn't so alone.

Ahoy! Wot u doing? How's yr thumb? How is Norrköping?
Have to tell u: finally bought control! My unsawn-off fingers really want 2 open the wrapper n watch the film but
course I'll wait till u get home. Film nite monday? Say u
can, pls! x E

I smiled, ran my fingers through my hair, noticed my
bangs were wet and realised it was water from the toilet.

Aloha compadre! 2 answer yr questions a) I'm throwing
up and b) my thumb hurts cos someone sawed the end
off and c) Norrköping is ... confusing. Luv 2 come Monday! So u can help me with my hair ... x M

*An Ice-cold Embrace. And a Warm One.*

I had to get some air. It wasn't easy, recovering from that cigarillo. The retching came in regular waves up from my stomach and into my throat. As I sat down on the outer steps and tried to push my feet into my trainers without using my left hand I saw a familiar head on the other side of the hedge.

Justin.

He waved. I stood up, walked down the steps and stopped on the bottom one, hesitating. I realised I hadn't changed my clothes since yesterday. Mint green jogging bottoms are hardly subtle but at least I had taken off the braces.

'Hello,' he said breathlessly. His cheeks were red with exertion and his eyes a shiny ice-blue. His eyelashes were so pale you could hardly see them.

'Hello … Justin,' I said, and walked the few steps over the drive. It struck me again how tall he was.

'I'm not called Justin,' he said, smiling, and my cheeks began to glow and turn as red as his. I waited for him to tell me what he was called but he didn't, and we were silent for a while. His breathing was the only thing that could be heard. Apart from everything else, such as the distant cars, the birds and my heart.

'How's it going?' he asked.

He was wearing the same trousers as yesterday, just like me. Now we had something in common. I liked having something in common. They suited him, those pink trousers.

'Yeah, good.'

'And your foot?'

And I thought: foot? What flipping foot? He took a drag on the cigarette he was holding between his thumb and his index finger like a gangster. Then suddenly I remembered his face close to the sole of my foot and I went hot when I thought how much I had liked it being there. Which was perhaps weird.

'Oh, my foot! Of course. Yeah, good, thanks,' I said, and idiotically lifted up my foot only to swiftly put it down again. He kept looking at me. I smiled.

'And how are you?' I asked.

'Good, good. I've tidied up. Couldn't sleep.'

He dragged on his cigarette again and blew the smoke out in quick puffs.

'I didn't see you leave yesterday.'

'No.'

He raised his eyebrows in surprise. 'I … I just went.'

'Oh?'

'Yeah.'

'Is that what they do in Stockholm, then?'

'No. Or … I don't think so. I, um …'

He disappeared behind the hedge again and my 'I …' and my 'um …' were left hanging in the air like annoying insects. Through a gap in the hedge where the branches were sparser and the leaves fewer, I could see him stubbing out his cigarette with his shoe. I would have liked to take a photo just at that moment: the glowing cigarette stub, his white shoes, his reddish-blond bangs, all filtered through that chlorophyll-green cover of leaves. When he popped up again above the bushes he was overtaken by a powerful fit of coughing and hid his face in the crook of his arm.

We stood there for a long time, each on our own side of the hedge, waiting for the coughing to die down. I wondered if it was a smoker's cough or if he had a cold. When he had finished coughing he said:

'I've got to go to the recycling.'

'Oh, right.'

He nodded towards the cherry-red Volvo I had seen the day before.

'My mum'll be back soon and she'll kill me if she sees all the bottles. Want to come with me?'

The question threw me.

'Now?'

'Yes.'

I looked at him, searching his face for a mocking smile and his eyes for a mysterious motive. It didn't work. I saw nothing. Then again I'm not so good at interpreting mysterious motives. I shrugged.

'Okay.'

◆

He drove like a car thief and that was good: anything that made me think of something else was good. A kitsch Virgin Mary figure dangling from the rear view mirror swung violently with every powerful acceleration and sudden braking. We didn't speak. The radio was playing de Blümchen's manic *Heit' ist mein tag* and I knew it would get lodged in my brain but I didn't care.

We worked well together, him and me. Efficiently, like a team. He did the plastic and I did the glass.

I deliberately chose the glass and threw the bottles hard into the black opening. I heard them smash against each other. I got beer on my bandage and I didn't want the noise to end, ever. I wanted to be surrounded by the deafening crashing, but the last bottle was approaching irrevocably and when that was also smashed the task was completed and everything went quiet.

'Your mum might want to spend some time with you while you're here?' he said.

'I don't think so,' I said bluntly.

He raised his eyebrows.

'I don't know why, but you are refreshingly straightforward somehow. And honest. Are you always like that?'

'No,' I said, in my refreshingly straightforward way, and he laughed.

'I don't feel like going home,' he said. 'It's such nice weather. Do you want to have a go in a kayak?' He happened to cough right in my face so that small warm spots of saliva sprayed my cheek. 'Oh, sorry.'

I lifted my hand to wipe them away but he said:

'Let me,' and he smiled and stroked his sleeve and wrist against my cheek. His jacket sleeve was rough but his wrist was warm and soft. A few strands of hair from my bangs got caught in a button on his cuff and were ripped out, but I didn't say anything. I just watched them trail after his hand like a long delicate veil.

Did he smile that nicely at everyone? Perhaps he did. I'm sure he did. But did it matter?

◆

We drove to Lake Ågelsjö, a short distance outside Norrköping. He smoked in the car, something I hadn't experienced since the last time I was in Germany five years ago, and. I had to breathe through my scarf or it would have been unbearable.

When he noticed what I was doing he wound down his window slightly and told me to do the same. That resulted in a fierce cross-draught which made it totally impossible to hear anything except the wind. We sat there in silence and froze, but at least I wasn't being asphyxiated.

The area around the lake was covered in forest and very hilly. On its northern bank the rock face dropped vertically into the water, or so Justin told me, but I couldn't see that from where we were standing.

The kayak was kept on a wooden frame beside a small hut covered in peeling blue-grey paint, and hidden under a huge military tarpaulin. Justin loosened a couple of rubber straps, stuffed them casually into his pockets and then pulled off the tarpaulin. It made a sound like thunder as it fell, creaking and heavy, to the ground. And there, underneath, was a dandelion-yellow one-man kayak. It was long, at least five or six metres. He lifted it up and began to carry it down to the water.

'It looks like a big banana,' I said, and he stopped, the kayak hanging heavily, his arms long and taut. I caught up with him and he smiled so beautifully at my stupid remark that I had to hug him. I hugged him tightly with my right arm, more carefully with the left, and then I ran my fingers through his red-blond bangs. I shut my eyes and his hair felt remarkably soft, and then I hugged him outside his jumper before my fingers made their way inside and I felt that tense, warm, kayak-carrying body.

*What the heck was I doing! He was too old for me! He was too old and he was too tall and most of all I didn't know him. And anyway he wasn't my type.*

*Who was I trying to kid? As if I had a type.*

Eventually he groaned loudly, not from desire but from exertion because of the weight of the kayak. And I said:

'Oh, the kayak. I'd forgotten.'

But of course I hadn't.

You don't forget that someone is standing there holding a flipping great bright yellow kayak.

I took my hands away but didn't exactly know what to do with them, so I let them hang uselessly at my sides. He gave me an odd look, kind of squinting, but he said nothing. My cheeks grew warm and I didn't know what was happening to me. Perhaps I was going insane and I didn't want to think this but I did think it: perhaps it's hereditary.

*Insane?*

*Or just a little bit in love?*

He carried his awkward yellow burden down the bumpy slope towards the water and I said something about not intending to paddle because it wouldn't work with my thumb anyway, but he just gave a loud sniff and grunted and I couldn't interpret that. I wasn't used to talking to people while they were carrying out physical work. I was hardly even used to physical contact, come to that. He gently lowered the kayak into the water and anchored it with the help of the rubber straps.

Then he climbed carefully into the kayak as it swayed.

'It's a sea kayak,' he said, and because I didn't know what to do with that information I kept my mouth shut.

He showed me how to sit with my back straight back and my legs slightly bent. He showed me how to paddle, how you use your whole body and your stomach muscles and even your legs. He explained all this as the sky clouded over above us. He showed me how to keep my balance too, and I resisted. I didn't want to. I couldn't. I didn't dare. And, to be honest, how would it work with a thumb that was exploding with pain?

Then he said:

'If a boat comes past, don't be scared if there are a lot of high waves. All you have to do is paddle straight towards them, towards the waves. Put all your effort into it and just paddle *right towards them.*'

And for some unfathomable reason, that appealed to me, that *one* particular thing. Quickly I pressed four painkillers from the blister pack and a moment later I found myself standing close to him in a neon-orange life jacket with a dangling whistle as he tied a transparent plastic bag around my left hand to protect the bandage. He helped me into the kayak with his arm around my waist and everything started spinning when he did that – either that or the fact that the kayak was "rank", as he called it.

At first the kayak did more or less as it wanted, and I found it hard to hold the paddle with my damaged thumb and with my hand in that slippery bag. It was hurting like mad but after a while I worked out how to steer and discovered the kayak was not going to tip over as easily as I had thought. Justin yelled loudly that I was a natural and his voice echoed between the rocks. I didn't believe him but I smiled when he wasn't watching and paddled determinedly into the waves.

◆

The water shone like a mirror, reflecting the mottled grey from the clouds overhead. It was as still as night time and all I heard was my own paddling and my breath. I saw the drops from the paddle form small rings that spread out across the water. I paddled past a jetty, a tree whose branches rested on the surface of the water, and a boathouse painted red. I stroked the green and cloudy water with my uninjured hand, and in return the wetness enveloped it in an ice-cold embrace. I didn't see or hear anyone else. There were no other boats, no people. The kayak glided slowly on past a small island with a rocky shoreline and scrawny pines. There were big yellow water lilies on long stalks that went all the way down to the lake bed. I tried to pull one up but it was attached so firmly the kayak started to rock so I let go.

I thought of nothing. Felt nothing. No pain. No longing.

I stopped paddling and closed my eyes. I breathed and glided, leaned back and looked up at the sky where the light grey clouds made a ceiling.

*Are You Okay?*

'Where *is* your mum?' asked Justin, as he drove up the driveway to his parents' house.

He turned the key and the car fell silent, but not the radio. A cover of Michael Jackson's Smooth Criminal was playing, but twice as fast and with rock-hard drums and bass.

*Annie are you ok*
*So Annie are you ok*
*Are you ok Annie*

I looked up at Mum's window. It was pitch black inside. The lack of curtains gave it an inhospitable impression, as if nobody really lived there. He followed my eyes.

'I don't know,' I said truthfully.

'You don't *know?*'

'No.'

'Do you know when she's coming home?'

'No.'

*Annie are you ok*
*So Annie are you ok*
*Are you ok Annie*

He turned to face me, letting his hand brush my arm. A tingling caress. I looked at it, that hand. The broad back, the long fingers, the black-edged nails. Why was he touching me? Why did he care? Was it brotherly? Was a sexual invitation? Then suddenly I remembered who had touched who down at the lake. Who had invited who.

'I … I'm sorry for that … down at the lake … touching … hugging you. When you were carrying the kayak.'

He gave a laugh and threw his head back. I presume he wanted to emphasise how little it meant to him, but it looked a bit exaggerated, as if he had just suffered a whiplash. His arm slid kind of unnoticed from my arm.

'It's cool,' he said. 'I'm used to it. Not.'

He cleared his throat and turned away, looking out of the window on his side of the car. I looked at him sideways. He blushed. I smiled to myself. There was something uplifting about it. There was something uplifting about the fact that *I* had managed to make *him* embarrassed.

He cleared his throat again, and then he coughed. At first it sounded theatrical but it led to a real attack of coughing with running eyes and a throat full of phlegm. Now it was my turn to look away. I might have enjoyed making him embarrassed but there was a limit. When the attack was over he blew his nose in a paper napkin that he pulled out of his jacket pocket. With his face hidden in the napkin he said:

'But, she's coming back soon? She'll be here tonight, won't she?'

His voice was strangely tense.

The light went off and we sat there in the darkness and I watched the silhouette of the Virgin Mary dangling from the mirror.

'I don't know. I really don't know.'

Then I opened the car door and stepped out, because I was ashamed. Now I was feeling ashamed for my mum, who wasn't there. For me, who had a mum who wasn't there. And because she had rejected me.

The person who was not called Justin stayed in the car with the paper napkin over his face as I slammed the door, walked across the crunching gravel and up the steps to the front door. He stayed there while I unlocked the door, while I went in, and while I softly shut the front door.

After that, I don't know what he did.

Carefully I lay down on the floor with my face against the hall mat, which said "Welcome". Its bristly surface dug into my cheek. It smelled of dust.

Welcome. What a crap joke.

I longed for someone to touch me, to comfort me.

I longed so much for something, for someone, that it hurt. But when has longing ever given any concrete results?

I lay there for a while. Maybe ten minutes, maybe an hour, I don't know. There was no one there to time me.

◆

Then the phone rang. It was like an electric shock through my body.

I rolled onto my back and worked my mobile out of my damp trouser pocket. It wasn't Mum. It was my admirable dad. My inspirational, responsible father. The disappointment was draining.

'Hello.'

'Hello! How's my little Maja then?' he said, just a bit too loudly, the way he did after he'd had a couple of pints.

*My perspiring, intoxicated dad.*

'Good, really good.' I said, my voice sounding husky, as if I had just woken up.

As I was lying there I realised everything was wet: my jacket, my trousers, my shoes. Water had dripped on them from the paddle.

'How's your thumb?'

'So-so.'

'Does it hurt?'

'You could say that.'

I knew he wanted me to tell him that it wasn't a problem, that it was fine, so that he could go back to doing whatever it was he wanted to do, but I couldn't. I wasn't that generous. Before he had time to say anything else I asked:

'Dad, what do you do?'

'What do you mean?'

'What do you do when I'm not there? I mean, what are you doing now?'

'Now? This very minute?'

'Yes.'

He coughed. I heard music in the background, a singer with a high, girlish voice. Could it possibly be Debbie Harry? I saw an image of the blonde, dangerous Timberlake fan, recalled the way she kissed me on the cheek as thanks, the way I got all sticky from lipstick and saliva.

'I'm sitting here with Ola, having a few drinks and chatting. Why?'

He sounded guarded, almost off-hand. He didn't want to talk about what he was doing. He wanted to keep the conversation short and simple, show some fatherly concern and then carry on with his life. I was disappointed because I wanted him to tell me the truth: that he was going to Denise's party. That he would drink like a fish, dance his arse off in some club he was too old for and, if he got lucky, shag Denise or some twenty-five year old culture victim with a bob. Someone who would be impressed that he was a semi-famous music journalist, as well as a single dad with an emotional, unstable teenager. Perhaps I should be happy that he talked about me but sometimes I got a feeling that he almost used me to show off, that he talked about me and my "problems" simply to score a few brownie points; that he used me to prove he was Mr Bloody Nice Guy, someone who could take responsibility, who didn't cop out. It wasn't just the stuff Denise had written – there had been others before her. Masses of others. All those relationships which went on completely outside my world, on his "free" weekends, at lunches, via text or email – he never said a word about them, never let on that they existed. But I had my own ways of getting information. And that's exactly the reason why.

'I was only wondering.'

This was the moment I ought to say something. To tell him Mum wasn't here, that she had never turned up, that I was *alone, alone, alone.* I opened my mouth but just when I was about to tell him I heard Ola laugh in the background and I wondered what he was laughing at. What could be so flipping hilarious?

'Well, Maja,' said Dad, in that summing-up voice he always used when he wanted to hang up. I interrupted him. Always be the one to leave first.

'Gotta go now,' I said. 'Jana's coming. We're going to … eat now.'

'That's great, Maja! Good! See you tomorrow then, yeah? Seven o'clock.'

He sounded relieved. Didn't he? And I hated it, that sense of relief I thought I heard in his voice.

I said goodbye, but I hung up halfway through the word because I wanted him to know that I was sad – no, upset. I wanted to make him phone me back, but he didn't. He never understood that kind of thing, so it was totally pointless.

*Jana's coming.*

That's what I had said.

*Jana's coming.*

I pretended it was true. I pretended that I heard her bare feet against the parquet floor, that sort of sticky sound of damp feet walking on polished wood. I pretended that I saw her coming round the corner, her hair swinging and dancing on her shoulders; pretended that she suddenly discovered me on the floor. With her eyes wide open in astonishment she bent down and gave me her hand, her voice gentle, sympathetic: *Oh, are you lying here?*

Yes. I'm lying here.

Little old me, lying here.

Laboriously I got to my feet, using my left elbow to lever myself up. I walked into the bathroom where I took off my clothes and ripped off the plastic bag covering my hand. The bandage felt spongy and wet. Naturally the bag had leaked. I stepped into the bath and sat on the pack of toilet rolls. I turned on the water and let it run, spraying down over me like cold April rain. My thumb pulsated aggressively. I was struck by the crystal clear image of its amputation, as if it was happening there and then. It was impossible to avoid it.

*The grating, piercing sound.*
*The metal teeth, hacking into me.*

*The flesh. Exposed.*
*The blood. Snaking, pulsating, spurting.*
*The explosions. The pain.*

I shook my head, wanting to shake off the memory, the images, the sound, the pain. I turned my head up to the shower head as if it were the sun, and sat there with my head rotating from side to side in one long denial. I allowed the water to run over my eyes, allowed my eyes to run. I allowed it all to run until the pack of toilet rolls began to soften and collapse.


Naked, I walked up to my room and dried the bandage with a hairdryer. It took ages and still it was wet on the inside, next to the skin.

I tipped my bag upside down on the bed. Clothes fell out over the duvet in heaps of black and white fabric. I pulled on a pair of black jodhpurs and a frilly white shirt that had very long sleeves. Dad called it my straitjacket. You were supposed to fold the cuffs back and fasten them with cufflinks, but I had left them behind in Stockholm. It was ridiculously hard to button the shirt without a functioning left thumb. I attached my smart black braces, the ones FAS-Lars had mocked, tied a silk scarf around my neck, carefully applied some make-up and put on a pair of big glittery earrings. Who was I getting dressed up for, I wondered?

I went downstairs again, opened the door and ate a few handfuls of muesli straight from the packet. It tasted like dry animal fodder. I looked around the kitchen as I chewed, at the crumbs under the table, the yellowing pile of newspapers, the overfull sink. I debated for a while whether to wash up but decided to leave it as it was. Shit, I certainly had good reason to.

I opened the fridge. Apart from a few bottles of carbonated water, an open packet of some thick, disgusting yogurt and some organic milk, it was empty. I took out a bottle of water and drank almost half a litre in a few ice-cold gulps. The bubbles tickled my throat. Then I took out the milk. It smelled okay but it was two days past its sell-by date. There was no butter, no juice, no cheese. No breakfast for me. She usually bought that, at least.

Were all these clues?

The emptiness of the fridge was depressing. The freezer, on the other hand, was stuffed full of colourful rectangular boxes piled one on top of the other. Ready meals: pizza, lasagne, pies. Junk food. Worthless, unwholesome junk food.

I slammed the door shut. I had completely lost my appetite.

It felt so ugly, so wretchedly impoverished. Mum would have preferred to inject food if at all possible, so pronounced was her lack of interest. As it was now, I would gladly have done the same.

I finished the water in the bottle and lay down on the sofa. I needed a plan. I had to deal with this. Perhaps I ought to phone the police after all? The hospital? That presenter of that missing persons programme on TV?

I dismissed my own options. No, I shouldn't. She had been in touch. She was alive. Not being here was her choice.

Quickly I got to my feet, leapt up the stairs a few at a time, and went into her office. I switched on the computer and looked at her email again. Perhaps I could read more into it.

*Some longing.*

I am very sorry that this is such short notice but I have to let you know that Maja can't stay here this weekend.

Then I noticed something else that wasn't right. Mum's email address. It was new. It was a Gmail address I had never seen before. Why wasn't she using her work email like she usually did?

*If It's Red the Blood Won't Show*

It started to get dark but the street lights hadn't come on yet. I walked outside and sat down on the steps for a while, feeling the cold through my trouser legs. I shut my eyes and tried to think. I was envious of smokers who could have a cigg in peace and quiet and give themselves time to think. How long could it take to smoke a cigarette? Five minutes? I sat for five minutes, puffing on an imaginary cigarette and letting the thoughts come and go. Perhaps it helped because afterwards I stood up decisively, cut across the driveway and picked up a handful of gravel. To avoid being seen I squeezed through the gap in the hedge with my aching left hand pressed to my chest. If I couldn't meet my own mother I was definitely unable to meet anyone else's. The gravel was sharp and cut into the palm of my hand.

There. There was his window. It was lit from the inside, a warm, yellow light. I hesitated. Then I thought: what the hell.

I took aim and threw, but the very moment I let go of the gravel I saw the window being opened wide. The stones hit the glass then ricocheted back at enormous speed, straight out at first and then down over me like a meteor shower. One hit me like a bullet in the forehead. As I fell over I thought dramatically: *I'm going to die now.* But of course I didn't. People seldom do.

'Whoa!' shouted Justin from somewhere up above me.

I managed to moan in reply.

It was a joke. It was a joke how I always managed to hit myself, be hit, saw pieces off myself, get splinters in my foot and stones in my head. I grabbed my forehead, looked at my fingers. Blood. Obviously it was blood.

'I'm coming down,' he yelled. 'Stay there.'

I had no other plans so I lay still and looked up at the darkening leaf cover of something that must have been an oak. I heard my own breathing, panting at first, then calmer. The ground beneath me was cold and damp. It smelled of wet grass. The blood ran; I could feel it running warmly beside my nose and cheeks and down to my mouth. I wiped my face with my shirt sleeve and watched the white cuff turn red.

*Yet again I was lying on the ground, in a white shirt, bleeding, unable to get up. It was getting so interminably boring.*

Justin came round the corner still wearing his pink jeans; his feet pushed into his unlaced grubby basketball boots.

'Hello,' I said, with a kind of forced neutrality.

As if I wasn't really lying bloody and knocked-out on the grass.

'Oh my God, Maja! How did that happen?'

I tried to shrug my shoulders but that's not so easy to do lying down.

'You sound like you've got a cold,' I said, because he did. His Ms became Bs.

He grabbed hold of my right hand and tried to pull me up, but never had gravity been so strong and never had my body felt so heavy. For a long time I hovered a few centimetres above the ground without either coming up or going back down. When I was finally on my feet I saw Justin smiling at me. A warm and – I hoped – tender smile. The corners of his mouth twitched as if he had been about to say something but stopped himself.

I wished he would say something. I wished he would say something lovely.

He continued to smile as he said:

'You look like a clown.'


From his sitting room, where I had been less than twenty-four hours earlier, came the sound of a TV, but no one was in there. I glimpsed a close-up of a drowned, swollen female corpse, the Danish pathologist offensively crunching on an apple.

'Where's your mum?'

'At our summer place in the country.'

'But didn't you say she was coming home?'

'No-o, what I said was that she would kill me if she saw the bottles.'

'What, so she hasn't been here?'

'Yes, but she went again.'

He noticed words. Like I did.

'She wanted to fetch a hedge trimmer or something. They go there almost every weekend, her and the old man.'

I groaned inside. All that blood for no reason.

We walked upstairs and into the bathroom with the Freud quotation. There was a strong smell of cleaning fluid. In the bathroom mirror I could see that unfortunately I really did look like a clown. In my attempt to wipe away the blood I had spread it all over my face and now my nose and cheeks were as red as my mouth, which was circled with blood. The braces emphasised the clown impression. I shrugged them off quickly, letting them hang down by my side.

'*Scheisse*. Now this shirt is ruined as well.'

'You ought to wear red clothes, seeing as you're so accident-prone,' said Justin. 'A red shirt. If it's red the blood won't show.'

I washed the blood from my face and dabbed the cut on my forehead with a piece of cotton wool, but miniscule fibres fastened in the sore. Justin sacrificed one of the guest hand towels, wetting it and pressing it repeatedly against my forehead. The towel was stained light red. Exactly the same shade as his trousers.

I looked a whole lot better once the blood was wiped off but there was an ugly cut with jagged edges.

'I don't think it needs stitching, but perhaps we ought to go to A&E and let them have a look at it,' said Justin, and blew his nose loudly. 'I can give you a lift if you like.'

'No, there's no need,' I said hastily.

He raised his eyebrows, then shrugged his shoulders and took a box of plasters from the bathroom cabinet.

'Well, it's your head.'

'Yes, unfortunately.'

He laughed, but I didn't even smile.

I met his look in the mirror and I noticed his eyes were bloodshot. The cold, or a hangover? Or a combination of both? He took out a large plaster decorated with skulls and stuck it over the cut on my forehead. I said:

'My mum's missing.'

He pressed the sticky ends of the plaster with both thumbs and said:

'I guessed as much.'

◆

'There has to be a logical explanation,' said Justin, after I had told him everything. His voice was so convincing and calm that I thought I must be overreacting to the whole situation. We were in his bedroom and I was sitting on the bed and he was in a swivelly turquoise armchair, which he restlessly rotated a half turn to the right and then a half turn to the left, all the time not taking his eyes off me. I hoped he didn't still think I looked like a clown.

'Does there?' I said hopefully.

'Yes of course. Where does she work?'

The cut on my forehead hurt and I cautiously touched the plaster with my index finger.

'Linköping University. The Institute of Psychology.'

He stopped rotating and leaned towards me where I sat on the bed, his bed. His reddish-blond bangs fell over his face.

'What does she do there?'

'Research, mostly. Gives lectures to the students from time to time.'

'Does she travel with her work?'

'Yes … sometimes.'

'You see! A sudden business trip. There you are, then.'

He flung out his hands and leant back in chair, looking pleased with himself. I was going to add: But not often and *never* spontaneously, but there was something in his tone that prevented me. It was so certain, so final.

And I so wanted to believe him.

'The only reason it feels so mysterious … so … calamitous is that you are in her empty house, where she would otherwise be.'

Calamitous? I smiled. I had never heard anyone use that word before, only read it in books, and with Justin's dialect, his distinct vowels, it sounded ridiculously old fashioned. *Calamitous.* Surely that had something to do with calamity? I resisted the impulse to ask what it really meant.

I ran my hand over the throw on Justin's bed. It was yellow and smooth. I said:

'The odd thing is, her laptop is at home, and her mobile, and she's had several missed calls, the first one last Wednesday.'

'If she's going to lectures or meetings then she doesn't need her laptop, does she? And she probably forgot her mobile. That can happen to anyone. Remember, she has actually sent an email.'

'From some odd new address, yes.'

'There could have been a pro memoria from work to only use the work email address for work-related things. Perhaps she was forced to set up a new private address.'

I looked at him doubtfully. He ran his hand through his bangs so that they lay flat against his head again. I stared at his hair and discovered to my horror that we had the same haircut! My hair was black and his was reddish-blond, but the actual styles were the same. We could never be together, I thought, childishly disappointed. Shit, you can't be together with someone has the same haircut as you.

'What does pro memoria mean?' I asked, after a moment's silence.

My curiosity won over my pride. Verbally he was my superior. That was both uplifting and depressing at the same time: uplifting to meet someone who also had words and could use them, like me, and depressing because words are my ace in the pack. *My* ace. Now I didn't even have that. He had stolen it from me.

'Hmm, pro memoria. It means a suggestion, but fairly strongly worded, if I have understood it correctly.'

I nodded thoughtfully and then blurted out:

'The milk is two days past its sell-by date. Mum never has old milk in the fridge.'

Justin laughed a dry, dismissive 'Please'.

But I didn't. I didn't laugh. He didn't know how important milk was for her. Or rather, he didn't know how important coffee was. He hadn't seen her whisk the milk for her cappuccino in that precise and frenzied way that was so typical of her. That's what it was like. She always did the simplest jobs, like brushing her teeth, cutting her nails, washing up a glass, with a bewildering intensity. They weren't things she did in passing, while talking, laughing, or watching TV. They were well thought-out, precise movements that demanded her full concentration.

'You don't know her,' I snapped, because I wanted to get rid of the lump that had just formed in my throat.

'No, of course I don't,' he said honestly.

'You don't know what she's like.'

'No, I don't. What is she like?'

*"What is she like?"* Did he really want to know? Did he? And if so, how would I be able to explain? How could you explain Mum to someone who didn't know her, who didn't know what she was like?

How did you explain her inability to be … normal? How did you explain the long sessions in the shower, the excessive planning and her intense look, her eyes that rarely blinked, like a bird? How did you explain that she was totally obsessed with relationships and social interaction on a theoretical level but could just about manage to answer a simple harmless question about how she was, or say thank you when she was given something? And at the same time: her fantastically dry sense of humour and her ability to remember everything I said, which made me feel really important. If I ever mentioned something I was interested in – a band, a film, a book – then you could bet that the CD, DVD or book would arrive in the post a week or so later. But no little note floated out, however long you shook the jiffy bag. No "Lots of love from Mum" or even "Jana." Never any comments.

How did you explain Mum to someone who didn't know?

'She's … she's special.'

'Okay,' said Justin gently, sniffing back the snot with a grunt.

'She is my mum,' I said, and stared at him defiantly, as if he had said something different.

He met my gaze and we sat like that for a long time, our eyes locked together. Finally he looked away and through the window where the dusk was a deep lilac blue, and that was lucky because a second later a tear ran down my chin. I wiped it away in irritation. I can't do this any more, I thought. I can't be here. I've had enough of myself and my pathetic excuse of a life. And as if he had read my thoughts he said: 'Come on. Let's go for a drive.'

*This is What Happens When You Go Out of Town*

We climbed into the old cherry-red Volvo PV and headed towards town. We randomly drove around the shopping centre and down the avenues lined with linden trees. The street lamps had begun to come on, casting circles of yellowish-white light. The radio was playing quietly. It was so nice sitting like that, next to each other, in silence. Justin was wearing a green woollen hat that was far too big and kept slipping down over his forehead. He had to keep pushing it back up.

Finally he parked on a small street called Västgötagatan, on quite a steep slope. It went noticeably quiet when he switched off the engine. He nodded in the direction of a run-down building with a dirty yellow façade. In front was an outdoor café surrounded by dark green screens. Judging from the sign it was called The World Bar.

'Shall we go in?' he asked.

'Okay,' I said.


Justin went first and I followed. There were only a few people inside the place and I guessed we were out early for a Saturday. On the tables stood onion-shaped oil lamps, their long, white wicks suspended in light green oil. Further in was a smaller room with framed film posters from the fifties and sixties on the walls, and a jukebox in the corner. Arranged around the walls were fold-down cinema seats in red velvet. The room was empty.

Justin raised his eyebrows at me and I nodded back. He sat down in one of the cinema seats and lit the oil lamp. I sat down opposite him, surreptitiously eased a painkiller out of my pocket and looked around, wide-eyed. I had actually *never* been to a bar on my own. Occasionally Dad and I had watched a football match in a dingy pub called Diset in Örnsberg, and another time in some shabby restaurant on Ringvägen, but that was it. When my eyes met Justin's he smiled and I became aware how very far from worldly wise I seemed. I corrected my facial expression immediately: I raised my eyebrows and lowered my eyelids to look bored.

Justin blew his nose in a metre-long strip of toilet paper that he pulled out from his pocket like a magician, and actually it wasn't very pleasant, that snotty piece of paper, but I made allowances. Oh, how I made allowances. I asked if he was getting a cold or getting rid of one. He insisted he was getting rid of it but his glittering, feverish eyes told a different story.

Then suddenly he fixed those glittering eyes on me and said:

'How old are you really?'

'What?' I answered, annoyed. 'How old are you?'

'I asked first.'

I didn't dare answer. I just stared defiantly back at him. He tossed his bangs back.

'Okay, okay. I'll be twenty this summer, in July.'

'Oh, well, you're a little bit older than me, then,' I said, pretending to look for something in my pocket to win time. He was younger than I thought and that made me inexplicably glad.

'And that is …?'

He blew his nose again and stared at me steadily from behind the edge of the snotty paper. I sighed to show how exceptionally uninteresting and idiotic the question was.

'Stop rolling your eyes. Can't you just tell me how old you are? How hard can that be?'

'God, the nagging! I'm eighteen, okay?'

'Okay. Eighteen. Why are you so pissed off?'

I made my voice a little less hard as I said:

'People always think I'm bloody sixteen. It's *so* irritating.'

'Okay, so now I know.'

With the over-exaggerated patience of a teacher he said:

'With that information I can actually ask my next question: Would you like some wine?'

I felt my cheeks go red.

'Yeah! Good idea! I can go,' I said eagerly, to convince him I had reached drinking age, but I regretted it the minute I stood up. Because what would I do if they asked for ID?

I walked slowly towards the bar. A girl with a slight sun tan and light red curly hair, and who didn't look any older than me, was busy looking through some receipts behind the counter. I waited patiently until she had finished. A beam of light was pointing to the very spot where she was standing and made her sun-kissed skin shine like bronze, and I thought she was so beautiful that she ought to stand there all evening. She looked up at me and smiled and then she stared at the blood on my sleeve, and my dirty bandage, and the skull-patterned plaster on my forehead and, all credit to her, she said nothing. I ordered my very first bottle of wine and by some kind of miracle she didn't ask for ID. That made me want to whisper 'thank you' into those light red curls, and I must have stared for too long because she looked away.

She looked at the wine bottle and then the price list, but the wine was new and she had to go into the kitchen to ask the price. No one knew so she guessed at a hundred kronor and even I, with my extremely limited knowledge of wine, spirits, bars – well, the whole world, while I'm at it – knew that was ridiculously too little. But I said nothing. Well, I've never been known for my high moral standing. I simply smiled at her until it suddenly struck me that I had no money, not a single krona, because my bag lay completely unsafe in Mum's unlocked house. I managed to stutter an inarticulate 'excuse me' and ran back to Justin, who came to my rescue with a crumpled hundred kronor note. When I handed it to the red-haired girl and her suntanned skin turned pink, the triumph whirled around inside me, because the wine was a find and Justin was a find – if only I could manage to grab a little piece of him for me.

I poured the wine, acting as if it was something I did on a regular basis. My earrings dangled hypnotically, or so it seemed to me anyway, judging from the reflection of my face in the colourful, framed poster on the wall, and we drank wine and talked about music and old school synth, and I pretended I knew what I was talking about. I was good at faking it, always have been. Justin didn't like that type of music, he said it felt fascist. I insisted that I liked it because I think a few differences of opinion can be small glowing embers which can turn into sparks and become a bloody great forest fire, and actually I like black shiny boots and Front 242. At least Tragedy for You.While he talked animatedly and splashed wine on his own top I noticed a birth mark on his cheek. It made him look particularly vulnerable and I didn't understand why, but when he smiled and the corners of his mouth turned up, I saw that the mark brought out something female in him, if not to say girlish, and I wondered if it was always female characteristics that gave the impression of vulnerability. How sad, in that case. I took a few gulps to drown any possible sadness, and Justin drank with me.

Well, we drank and drank and drank the dark red wine with its aroma of earth and iron, and we ate absolutely nothing at all apart from a few handfuls of greasy peanuts, even though the hunger was drilling a massive hole in my stomach. I asked him if he was cold because he had kept his hat on and he said he was, even though the place was as warm as Italy.

'Back soon,' he said, standing up suddenly and heading off to the toilets. He walked slowly, with one hand clutching the piece of disgusting paper. I shut my eyes and thought of him, and how naked he was under his clothes. Small shocks rippled through my body, right the way down between my legs.

I opened my eyes and stared at the table, and noticed something I hadn't seen earlier. Under the glass table top were masses of little pieces of paper: flyers, receipts, concert tickets, shopping lists, poems – even photos. It was totally amazing! I found an entry from a lonely hearts column that I memorised:

*Hi, I'm a guy of 22 who comes from Skärblacka. My hobbies are partying and doing stuff. Looking for a girl who likes parties as well as doing stuff.*

I giggled. It was good to be specific. Perhaps he had met far too many girls who liked partying but not doing stuff. And perhaps some who liked doing stuff but not partying? I wrote a note of my own that I pushed under the glass top.

*If you wanna make an apple pie from scratch you have to start by making the universe.*

Outside it was getting dark unnaturally fast, as if God had turned a dimmer switch, and when I looked up again two of the tables were full of people in their twenties. One of them must have put some money in the jukebox because it was playing something mellow by the Beatles. The noise coming from the main room was all at once significantly louder and it was so odd because a couple of hours seemed to have passed and I hadn't noticed.

They were lovely; it was moving to see how lovely they looked. They were wearing make-up, they had put a lot of thought into what they were wearing, and they smelled good. That made me wonder what I was doing there, because I was bloody and weird and far too young and *I really didn't fit in*, but on the other hand I never had.

I don't know if it was the wine – I tried to convince myself it was – but when Justin came back I had an overwhelming need to have his tongue in my mouth. Maybe it was me wanting to belong, to fit in, to be a part of it all. He sat down beside me on a wobbly seat, so close that his thigh was touching mine. We sat like that for a moment and I was painfully aware of his body. Every millimetre of my skin was super-sensitive.

Suddenly he took hold of my hand and said:

'Listen, this is the world's best song. We've got to dance to it.'

I instantly heard what it was, so I stood up, even though there was no dance floor, and he pulled me close to him.

*Slowly fading blue*
*the eastern hollows catch*
*the dying sun*
*Night time follows*

*Silent and black*
*Mirror pool mirrors*
*the lonely place*
*where I meet you*

*See your head*
*in the fading light*
*and through the dark*
*your eyes shine bright*

His hand crept under my scarf, which made it almost impossible to breathe, and perhaps he had read my thoughts because in the middle of all the dancing he bent his head and kissed me.

It wasn't fantastic, not at first. His tongue darted about too fast, too hard, but it calmed down after a while. His hand found its way under my blouse and it was madness because the tables were crowded and no one except us was dancing. I sincerely hoped he had washed his snotty hands and I took that lovely hand away, but it was as if it had left an imprint on my waist. Not of snot, I don't mean that. No, more like I could still feel the soft touch of his fingertips for a long time afterwards.

We kissed and kissed and kissed and I was amazed that my body could feel the way it did. There was something whirling and pulsating: tiny, tiny bubbles struggling upwards. Again and again. But then he wrenched his mouth away from mine and took a deep breath as if he had just surfaced from the bottom of a lake.

'Help,' he said. 'I've got to breathe.'

His nose was so blocked that it was hard for him to breathe in and it spoiled the feeling a bit, but we carried on dancing and he leaned his forehead against mine and it was beautiful because he felt so close. That was until he bumped against my plaster with the skulls on and I shrieked because it burned like fire.

*And burn like fire*
*Burn like fire in Cairo*

The track came to an end and everything seemed greyer but he took my hand in his – the left one first but I directed him to the right one – and his hand was warmer than mine. He must have had a temperature. We sat down and finished what was left in the bottle and he wiped his nose with the back of his hand. I turned towards him and kissed him on his cheek, right on the birthmark. I put my nose in his ear and breathed in. I felt a kind of indescribable thrill at the very centre of my fuzzy brain and I thought it must be love, and I hoped so very much that he felt the same.

◆

He wasn't well, I knew that, but even so it was unbearably painful when he said we ought to go home. I felt warm after the dancing and the kisses, and my shirt was damp from sweat. The sweat cooled in an instant. Humiliation ran in cold, salty tracks down my backbone to my knickers.

'I've got to get up early,' he said, without a trace of regret in his voice.

*Hadn't he felt it?*

'I understand,' I said, as neutrally as I could, but that was a lie because I understood absolutely nothing. I would *never* have chosen to go.

Then a track by Blondie came on – Blondie once again– and Justin nodded in appreciation towards the jukebox as if the machine had thought of it by itself, and drained his glass. I recalled Debbie's killer heels and how my feet had moved out of their way in his sitting room almost exactly twenty-four hours ago.

Justin pulled down his hat and put on his jacket and I stood helplessly looking on and then we went out into the April air that was sharp and the light that was blue-white and cold. Limp from the wine I hung un-independently round his neck. Like a heavy pendant I dangled there, my hands tightly clasped around his neck, my thumb sticking straight up in the air like a misleadingly positive sign. It hurt like hell. Something started falling from a tree close by, something fluffy and white, like small tufts of cotton wool. It couldn't be snow, surely?

I turned my face up to his and kissed him and he kissed me with a tongue warm from wine and maybe from fever and he pushed his groin against mine, worked his hands under my shirt, under my bra, and felt my breasts. I liked his hands and I loved the way he seemed to find it so difficult to stop touching me. I loved that I had that effect.

He looked a bit stupid in that hat because you couldn't see any hair, but it didn't matter. He said:

'Can't you sleep with me? I'd only want to hold you.'

And the remark was so ridiculously classic that I laughed. Didn't he understand that? Not that anyone had ever said that to me before but hadn't he heard the song, seen the film, read the book?

'Do you even believe that yourself?' I said, and I thought that perhaps now was the time to lower my eyes and appear to be attractively flirtatious. But I've never been one for that kind of thing.

A green car drove past, pumping techno through the open windows.

He kissed me again and I got goosebumps all over my arms and my nipples stiffened and he felt that because that's where he had his hands, there and everywhere else.

'I only want to hold you,' he said again and I considered the idea for a while, I really did, but then he wriggled his hand inside my jodhpurs and that in itself was an achievement because they were so extraordinarily tight, and then into my knickers.

It was extreme.

It was shocking.

It was like making five chess moves one after the other without waiting for your partner to move. It was too much.

I stiffened and loosened the cramp-like hold I had on his neck.

Was this what they did in the country?

Was this the way it was?

I came to think of my English hairdresser, Rob, back home in Stockholm, and the warnings he had given me the previous autumn. I had been in Norrköping over the summer and in a sudden panic about my hair had gone to a hairdresser's in some back street. I should have known better because the salon was dusty and the posters on the wall were from the eighties and there were adverts for some hair gel I had never even heard of.

I walked out of there with a crew cut. A frigging crew cut!

Not that anyone has ever looked good in that haircut, but me, I looked *terrible*. Rob had to make an emergency intervention as soon as I was back in Stockholm and I have never forgotten his words:

"This is what happens when you go out of town."

That's what he had said, and he had wagged a finger at me.

That's what I thought of as I stood there with Justin's hand inside my knickers.

*This is what happens when you go out of town.*

His fingers were cold and I felt that he felt that I was warm and moist, but I hoped he understood that was from his earlier efforts, and he groaned in a restrained way in my ear, which also became warm and moist, and then everything became just *all too much* and I was forced to drag his hand out of my trousers and pull myself away.

Quickly I backed off a few metres and shook myself like a dog shaking off water. He stared at me blearily, as if he had hardly seen me before.

But I have to admit it. Had it not been for cold hands and had it not been for restrained groaning or the fact that Mum could easily be dead there and then, well, I might have shagged him that night.

But as it happened, I didn't.


We took a taxi home. Just like that. "We took a taxi". That

was something I could tell someone I wanted to impress. Except I couldn't think who that might be. Enzo saw right through me; he would immediately notice the poorly disguised satisfaction behind the mock indifferent expression.

We sat a long way apart from each other on the back seat, each leaning against an ice-cold window while that unlikely white fluffy stuff fell from the trees or perhaps the sky. I didn't want to believe it was snow.

'Listen,' said Justin, staring dreamily out of the window. 'Why don't you just email her? Using the new address?'

He turned to face me, his mouth hanging open slightly, and at the same moment the car stopped outside his house.

Yes, why didn't I do that? I hadn't even thought of it.

I got out. Before I shut the door I heard Justin sniff and pay the one hundred and sixty-two kronor that I absolutely did not have.

The birds were twittering. I don't know why but to me they sounded desperate. Do birds really twitter at night like that or was it a sign that the world was off balance and about to go under?

Justin climbed out. We both watched as the taxi drove off and then we didn't know where to look. He stared up at the sky and ran his hand through his hair and I gazed at the asphalt and kind of like fell against him.

It was a last pointless hug with heavy arms that wouldn't reach all the way round.

◆

I sat at the computer for a long time that night, the wine pulsating through my bloodstream. My fingers were placed in the correct positions on the keyboard, precisely as my journalist dad had taught me – forced me – to do. Apart from my thumb, of course, which I held rigidly upright. My thumb in its filthy bandage.

I waited for inspiration but none came. Compulsively I ate one rice cake after the other and they tasted of salt and dusty air. I put my fingers back in the correct position again, trying to concentrate. The white screen flickered. The kitchen clock ticked and at regular intervals the tap dripped a fat drop of water that shattered as it hit the stainless steel of the sink. For a moment the sounds became synchronised but then the clock overtook and they were out of step again. After a short while they found their matching rhythm. It was somehow hypnotic. It wasn't possible for the sounds to get louder but it felt as if they did. I stared unseeing at the screen.

I wanted to be honest in my email but didn't know if I could. It was exhausting. My hands lay heavily on the keyboard and my head felt heavy. Finally I was so tired that I simply let a flow of words run from my fingers. The email filled just over a page and then I spent half an hour sifting out everything that was irrelevant or untrue. Eventually only the core remained:

Hello Jana

I wonder where you are. Why you can't see me at the weekend.
    Why you can't see me now.
    Please phone me.

Maja x

I read the email several times, reading the words one by

one. I held the cursor over the Send button ready to click, held it there a long time.

The clock ticked.

The tap dripped.

But I did nothing. I didn't click. I didn't send.

I couldn't.

Instead I saved the email in Drafts and went into Dad's inbox and then his Facebook page. I read a new pathetic message from lovesick Denise and regretted it the minute I did so. Not because I had a guilty conscience but because it was so revolting. She had sent it yesterday, before the party. It was insanely expectant and cluttered with jaunty, endless exclamation marks.

Great that you can come! You really know how to make a girl happy! *Sooo* cool!!!

I considered deleting it but took a deep breath, summoned up my common sense, and marked it as unread.

I went back to Dad's emails and sent the following fairly abrupt email:

Hello Jana

I received your email about not being able to have Maja at the weekend. I assume you have your reasons even though I really think you could have explained why. Contact me as soon as possible so that we can discuss your future contact with Maja, preferably by email because it will be very hard to reach me by phone during the coming week.

Regards, Jonas

I sent the email without any hesitation. Then I deleted it from the Sent file and emptied the recycle bin. Totally exhausted, I fell into bed.

*A Good and Honourable Initiative*

Suffering from the worst hangover I had ever had, I opened the top drawer in the kitchen – where I always thought the cutlery belonged, because Dad and every other normal person keeps their cutlery in the top drawer – only to find Mum's dark pink diary among the hundreds of pens that were rolling around in there. It wasn't meant to be in there. That drawer was exclusively for pens.

The diary was absolutely her most important possession, more important than her purse, her mobile, and her keys. She always carried it with her. I couldn't understand how she had left the house without it.

Something was wrong. *Terribly wrong.*

This was the first time since realising she had gone that I felt more concerned about her than about myself. A prickly wave of guilt washed over me. It was about her now, not me. Something must have happened to her. But what? *What?*

I hardly dared look at it, even less pick it up.

I gently closed the drawer, taking instead a spoon from the full cutlery rack on the draining board, and sat down to eat my cereal. My eyes wandered repeatedly towards the drawer and I ate so slowly that the cereal went soggy in the milk, the milk that was now three days past its sell-by date.

Mum wrote in her diary every evening and looked in it countless times during the day. I had given it to her as a Christmas present. It had become something of a tradition, me giving her a diary every year. It was the best present she could possibly have, she used to say, and she was always effusive in her thanks. I was painfully aware that it was also the only present she got apart from the box filled with salami, bars of marzipan, and hand-knitted socks that her parents sent from Germany each Christmas. Between ourselves, Mum always called it "the diary you gave me", never just "the diary." She would say: "Now I'm going to sit down and write in the diary you gave me", as if there was a shedload of other diaries to choose from. Once I asked her what she wrote in it. All she said was:

"Everything."

"Everything?" I had asked.

"Everything that is important."

I got up quickly, walked the few steps over to the draining board, and touched the handle of the top drawer. My fingers ran over the cool, smooth metal.

Looking in that diary would really be overstepping the mark. I felt nervous even at the thought of it. It was so incredibly private, so forbidden, so *wrong*. I walked back to the table and sat down heavily.

Yet there was, of course, something particularly tempting about it, about finding out what was written in that book. Perhaps it contained what she had been thinking about. What she had been feeling. *Where she was.*

It was strange, really, that without any pangs of conscience I could read Dad's emails, almost feeling like I had a right to do it, but I had such respect for Mum's private notes. It was as if her integrity had infected the diary and made it inaccessible.

◆

There was an unexpected ring on the door, an intrusive, grating sound. I don't remember ever hearing it before. We didn't get too many visitors. It made me drop the spoon into the bowl and the milk sprayed onto my night-dress. I was paralysed. I looked at the drops that hadn't been absorbed by the silk fabric, but lay like a string of pearls across my chest.

Perhaps it was the police? Perhaps it was the police who had something to tell me.

It rang again.

I stopped breathing and went freezing cold and then burning hot within the space of a few seconds. There is only one thing the police inform people on the doorstep. In my mind I saw images, silent images: raising my hand to my mouth, staring into their sympathetic eyes, collapsing in a helpless heap on the floor, being lifted up by strong police arms.

I regained my ability to move, stood up, and ran through the kitchen and into the hall to open up, but stopped myself and stood motionless in front of the door for a few seconds.

*Mum, let it be you.*

*Let it not be the police.*

I opened.

It wasn't the police. And it wasn't Mum.

It was stupid of me to think it would be the police because I wasn't living in an American TV series. And it was stupid of me to think it was Mum, because she would never have rung her own front door. But that's what I'm like. Stupid.

It was Justin. It was him standing there with his shiny copper-coloured stubble and his eyes full of self-reproach.

'Hello' he said.

He sounded worn out.

'Hello,' I said, unconsciously putting my bandaged left arm over my heart.

'Well, here I am,' he said, and he grinned and flung out his hands in the best sing-along style.

'Yes, so you are ...' I replied hesitantly.

'I thought of something,' he said, looking down at his shoes.

I stood in silence.

'Well ...'

A cold wind took hold of my hair and blew it to one side, revealing to him my entire unmade-up face, and that made me feel more naked than my naked body underneath my nightdress.

'Well,' he tried again.

I let go of the handle. It sprung back with a metallic sound.

'I was thinking, perhaps I ... perhaps I didn't take it too seriously, you know, what you told me yesterday. About your mum. I don't know, maybe I was ... She hasn't come home?'

'No.'

'Oh. Well, I thought ... I thought perhaps you ought to phone the police after all.'

'Yes.'

'I got a bit of a ... guilty conscience.'

I wondered if that was really true. Or was it because of his cold hand between my legs?

He stepped into the hall and because I didn't move he walked right into me and he opened his mouth and I opened my mouth and we kissed, standing there, and he kissed me and he kissed me and he was so tall I had to stand on tiptoe, and he fumbled about behind him and pushed the door closed with a slam and then he walked forwards, kind of driving me back, and I stumbled backwards through the hall, diagonally through the sitting room, and towards the stairs with him glued to me. Well, I might have steered a little.

I felt his body, which was soft and hard at the same time, and we went all the way up staircase with me first, walking backwards, which was good because it made him the right height, and he kissed me and he kissed me and he kissed me. His tongue was warm and he tasted of cigarettes and coffee and salt. I must have tasted sweet from the milk and that went well together, didn't it, sweet and salt, in some kind of contradictory way?

He was wearing his shoes and his pale blue jacket with the checked lining and when we reached the landing he laid me down on the floor, or was it me who pulled him over me? It wasn't entirely clear. Then he lay on top of me and my shoulder blades were pressed against the wooden flooring by his weight. I held my left hand with the thumb above my head to protect it. His hands glided over the grey silk, glided under it, glided. They were rough and his fingertips had blisters and I wondered whether he played the guitar. I felt him through his clothes. He was hard, and I undid the buttons in his jeans, those washed-out, faded pink ones, because they seemed so tight. I undid the buttons with one hand, I did, as if I had never done anything else, and he pulled down his underpants and I helped him, and I felt him in my hand and wasn't he smoother than silk? I touched him even though I didn't know what you were supposed to do, stroked him like you stroke a fragile little animal, and I wanted him even though I didn't know what you did because although I wasn't exactly a virgin I wasn't that bloody far from it. He pulled up my nightdress to my breasts and he worked off my knickers and I helped and he kicked off his shoes and they bumped down a couple of stairs. Then he yanked a condom out of his pocket and that surprised me because did he always go around with a condom in his pocket or had he planned all of this? Was he turned on by abandoned young women or was he turned on by *me me me* or what was this all about? And he asked:

'Do you want to?' And I nodded silently because I couldn't think what else to do.

He knelt up and rolled that pale, pale yellow condom onto his penis and as for the condom, well, it really was a good and honourable initiative *really really really* but it certainly was a little bit weird that he walked around with it in his pocket and, as I said, I'd had sex before, maybe once or twice, well sure, a few times, but not with such good and honourable people.

His cock was hard and stood straight up and I forgot what I was doing and pulled my hand through my hair, trying to get a good view, but it was my left hand and the bandage clip fastened in a strand of hair and it was so excruciatingly painful that I couldn't get a good view. No, there was no such view to be had because he was on top of me with his warm weight and his heavy warm body and I thought:

*help*
*what's happening?*

146

He moved and he moved, hard and purposefully, and I wanted him to be inside me – I did want that didn't I? So I said it:

'I want you inside me, I want you inside me, I want you *inside me.*'

And he did, he wanted to, there was no discussion about whether *he* wanted to, and it went a bit fast and it was as if someone had stuck a knife between my legs. Nothing but a warm, sharp knife and I screwed up my eyes as if that would make it hurt less.

Even so, I wanted him to continue. Why did I want that?

Somewhere I was probably thinking that it was taking away everything else: all the gnawing anxiety, all the embarrassing loneliness, all the pointless questions without answers. So he continued and I lay there with my hand above my head and it was a knife and it was a knife and it was a knife.

And then suddenly it wasn't a knife any more.

The sharpness disappeared and it was as if a warm wave drifted through my body. I opened my eyes with the surprise of it.

It got a bit nicer.

The only thing I could feel was his body inside mine, in me.

And it got a bit nicer.

The only thing I saw were his closed eyes, his thin, pale eyelids hiding that ice-blue gaze.

And it got a bit nicer.

The only thing I could hear was his heavy breathing and then mine.

It got a bit nicer and then it got even nicer and finally it felt so amazingly incredibly nice that I forgot *everything* to do with mums and dads, mysterious disappearances and sawn-off body parts, and I shut my eyes tight and then I looked up in astonishment and then he pulled himself out, backed away and met my eyes. And asked if I had a bed. Of course I did, and that's where we ended up.

*How* I don't remember; I don't recall the move itself, but I could have beamed us there, I could have teleported us, I could have developed every possibly supernatural ability to get us there, because everything else was so superbly amazing right there and right then that being able to do *that* wouldn't have surprised me in the slightest.

◆

Afterwards, when we were lying with our heads close, close together, I plaited his bangs with mine. Both of us with the same haircut. And surely that didn't matter? Because it looked so beautiful together, his copper-red and my black, that we simply had to belong to each other somehow.

He smiled and lit a cigarette, and blew out the smoke between the black bars of my bed, and I released the strands of hair and they unravelled and were free again. I looked at the glowing end of the cigarette and the ash it had created, and I looked at his fair eyelashes and freckly nose and I couldn't remember when I had last been so close to anyone, and it was like a film except that he was quite red in the face and they hardly ever are, in films.

'I feel almost better now,' he said and sniffed, contradicting himself. I looked at his black-rimmed fingernails and thought pathetically that even life had a black edge like that, so it suited really well.

'Weren't you going to get up early this morning?'

I tried to make my voice sound jokey but I have to admit it sounded more like a reproach.

'You might say it all went wrong from the kick-off,' he said, and either he snorted or chuckled, I couldn't decide which.

'What kick-off?' I asked.

He pointed at me and said:

'This kick-off.'

He kissed me with smoke in his mouth and amazingly enough it came out through my nose, and we laughed at that and I asked him if he played guitar and he looked at me, puzzled, and said:

'How could you know that?'

I smiled as if I knew it all, but I said nothing about the blisters I had felt. Like all guys who play guitar he loved to talk about his music so he talked and talked and talked about it and I listened good-naturedly as generations of women have done before me, and I thought about the things my body had just experienced. And what I had just experienced.

Because this – this was something else. It made my previous insignificant sexual experiences fade to nothing. Made that skinny, sweaty internet boy who I wasted my virginity on – as well as a few naked fumbling winter weeks – dissolve and disappear.

This was like a punch in the stomach!

A smack on the chin!

A saw in your thumb!

So powerful that I lost my breath, lost track of time and space. Not because it was perfect, because it wasn't, but so incredibly unsettling. At one point I didn't know which way was up and which was down.

With him, the internet guy, I had no such problems

orientating myself in space and time. I would easily have been able to point out the direction south-southwest if anyone had come past during the act itself and asked.

For over two hours we lay there, Justin and me, with our bodies pressed tight together, each with a headphone in one ear. We listened to Kate Bush and discussed American wrestling. Don't ask why.

What we did not talk about was missing mothers.

When the battery went dead and the music fell silent, we fell silent too. Justin pulled me close and hugged me from behind. I felt his ribcage against my back, felt it moving up and down. His thighs against the back of mine. His long body sort of cupped around my body. He was warm. His breath gradually became slower. He fell asleep.

For a long time all I did was lie there, staring straight ahead of me. I saw the yellow morning light filter through the lace curtains, saw it turn white and become daylight. I sensed a profound and overwhelming feeling of happiness, the happiness of being close to another person, another person's body. I think a little salty tear actually trickled from my eye. And with that on my cheek I fell asleep.

When I woke up it was cold and he was gone.

## The Horizon Starts to Tilt

It was almost three thirty and my train was leaving in just over an hour. I circled Justin's house like a restless spirit. It looked dead inside, as if no one was home, and the cherry-red Volvo was still not back on the drive. Ideally I would have phoned, of course, but I didn't have his number. I didn't even know his name, for goodness' sake.

At last I rang the bell, stamping nervously up and down on the top step, but no one opened and I was both relieved and disappointed. I wrote my name and mobile number on an old receipt and pushed it onto a nail that was sticking out of the door. Then I went, without turning round.

I had waited as long as possible before leaving Mum's house because it felt wrong, somehow. We always left together, me and Mum. We left at three forty-five even though it hardly took more than five or ten minutes to get to the station. Mum was definitely a pessimist when it came to time.

She drove well, my mum, calmly and confidently, and always to the uninterrupted flow of talk on Radio P1. But she went mental if anyone broke the traffic regulations.

If anyone overtook illegally she could get so worked up that she would sit there shouting behind the wheel. Those were the only times I heard her swear. At best she wrote down the registration number and phoned the police; at worst she followed the car until it stopped and asked the guilty driver for an explanation. It was awful. It not only made me feel excruciatingly embarrassed but also really uncomfortable.

If other road users did not commit traffic offences we usually had time to listen to the news on Ekot – even the shipping news, if there were queues – before we reached the station.

But not now. Not today.

I ran to the bus stop. If I missed the bus I would miss the train and I didn't have the money for another ticket, but after about twenty metres a thought struck me like a flash of lightning and I swung round and ran back.

Quickly I turned the key in the lock and rushed through the hall and into the kitchen. Then I came to an abrupt halt. I hesitated, hearing my own breathing amplified in my ears. I plucked up my courage and opened the drawer in slow motion. The pens rolled around and on top of each other. My hands were trembling as I picked up the cerise diary and put it in my bag.

◆

The train rushed towards something that looked like dusk but was in actual fact a huge black thundercloud. I stared out at the countryside, at the horizon that tilted as we rounded the curves on sloping rails.

I had bought a coffee even though I was as pumped up on adrenaline as if I had been swimming in a hole in the ice. I swallowed a few deeply desperate mouthfuls. It tasted burnt and bitter. I stared straight ahead, feeling tense.

I was about to do something extreme. Something shocking. Something forbidden. I released the elastic that held the pages closed and slowly opened the cover, having time to read her name, printed in the capital letters so characteristic of her, on the first page, JANA MÜLLER, before shutting it again. I felt hot and stood up restlessly, because I needed to go to the toilet. Didn't I?

The toilet was claustrophobically small and had a window of milk-white plastic. It looked as if you could open it about fifteen centimetres. I climbed up onto the hand basin and pushed down on the metal strip running along the top edge, hanging onto it with my fingertips. It was difficult with only one hand but even so the window opened about a couple of millimetres. Cold air whirled in along with a loud whining noise. I crouched down and almost lost my balance when one foot slipped into the hand basin, but I managed to regain it by pressing my hand against the paper towel holder. I hung there with all my weight on the window, which now opened a few more centimetres. The whining became a deafening scream and my hair whipped angrily about. I so wanted to stick my head out of the window but I couldn't, either because the window was too small or my head was too large, swollen from all the questions. I had to content myself with gazing longingly out. I saw the sky. The sky wasn't the only thing I saw: black clouds piled up against a dark grey backdrop.

*Help.*

Why was my heart beating so loudly?

*Help me.*

Why was it beating as fast as if it wanted to beat its way out?

Suddenly someone tugged on the door handle and that made me jump.

I hopped to the floor, unlocked the door, and walked out, defiantly meeting the eyes of those that sought mine.

◆

When I got back to my seat the diary was there, of course. Where else would it be? It gave off an almost unnatural cerise pink glow in the dim carriage. I looked at it for a long time, gathering courage. I took a painkiller and swallowed hard. Then I whispered:

'Sorry, Mum.'

With the pulse in my thumb beating like a hammer, I slipped off the pink elastic band again and opened the book. Then I changed my mind and shut it, and then immediately opened it again. I found myself in the middle of February. I scanned the pages, at first not daring to look at anything in particular. Considering how much time she spent with her diary there was surprisingly little written in it, on this page at least. Just a few brief notes about university:

UNI:

8 - 10 A.M. LECTURE DEV. PSYCH. (ATTACHMENT THEORY)

10 A.M. - 12.00 PREPARE LECTURE DEV. PSYCH

(PERCEPTION AND COGNITIVE DEV.)

12.00 - 1.00 P.M. LUNCH

1 - 5 P.M. WORK ON THESIS

I turned over a few pages. Day after day, page after page, were filled with similar entries: the things she planned to do at university. As I read I could make out a pattern.

Every Monday and Thursday it said "FOOD SHOPPING" and on alternative weeks it said "WASHING" on Saturday and "CLEANING" on Sunday. I flicked quickly through the pages and saw that these reminders were written all the way through to December. And every other weekend it said "COLLECT MAJA 17.33!" on the Friday, a simple "MAJA HERE" on the Saturday and "MAJA LEAVES 16.24!" on the Sunday. The times were ridiculously exact.

The matter-of-fact entries concerning me made me disappointed. I realised I had hoped for something more, something unreasonable. I banged my head against the seat in front of me because I had been so naïve. With the cut on my forehead stinging I realised that she would never have drawn a little heart around my name, if that was what I had been hoping for. It just wasn't her, and I knew it. I hadn't actually wanted her to draw a heart, especially. I only wanted her to reveal herself to me, reveal her feelings in a heart or anything at all, in a few words coloured by feelings, in some word that had broken away from that controlling pen.

I took a deep breath and opened the diary at the current week. It said as usual: "COLLECT MAJA 17.33!" on Friday, and the worry began to flap around in my stomach again like an anxious bird.

So, she had planned on doing it, but she hadn't done it. The notes in the diary were law. I knew that all right.

What had happened?

*What had happened?*

I looked up at the grey plastic mug holder and my cold coffee. I drank it down in one gulp as I stared out of the window at the dark forests and fields rushing past outside.

I looked down at the diary again. My thoughts were

interrupted by something unexpected, something that stood out from the strict weekly routine. On Wednesday the eleventh of April, two days before I was due to arrive, it said: "DR ROOS, VRINNEVI 14.00."

What was this?

Was she ill?

Was she seriously ill?

And in that case why hadn't she told me?

I felt as if all the blood was leaving my body.

Vrinnevi? Isn't that what the big hospital in Norrköping was called? I was almost certain it was.

I went back a few pages and my heart was beating so hard I was sure it could be heard from the outside. There was another entry about Dr Roos, on the eleventh of January, but of course I couldn't be sure she hadn't met Dr Roos the previous year as well. During my search a further two names appeared, Lundgren and Soltani. I counted five planned meetings with Lundgren in total: two in January, two in February and one in March. She had met Soltani three times: two in March and one in April. Was this connected to the hospital too? In the middle of February there was something strange: "CONTACT JONAS RE FAM. INT."

Contact Jonas?

"Jonas" as in Dad?

Contact Jonas re what?

*What?*

## An Unlamented Satellite

'I've made that fried cheese you like.'
Dad walked towards me holding a spatula in one hand
and dressed in a pretty awful lemon-yellow shirt.
   'Halloumi?'
   'No, you know, that cheese in breadcrumbs, with
Czech potato salad, the kind with peas and ... that sauce
... what's it called? We ate it at Bistro Bohème.'
   He looked at me, his brown eyes asking me to help him
out. He had a tendency to forget words the day after he
had been drinking. Mum told me it was called *aphasia*
but Dad got insanely irritated if I used that word. "Insult
me if you have to," he had told me, "but not with Jana's
words!"
   I stumbled on the mat and it occurred to me that for
the first time in our lives we had a hangover at the same
time. It felt tragic.
   'Oh, what's it *called?*'
   He looked intently at the hall floor as if he thought the
answer was written in the cracks between the floorboards.
   'Well, *I* don't know,' I said, and I really didn't. Even if I
had known I wouldn't have wanted to help him, wouldn't
have wanted to cover up for him and his shag hangover.

'That sauce, you know. Sauce ... what the hell is it called? It's got egg yolk in it.'

I shrugged. He helped me off with my jacket and was overly careful with my thumb. Then he gave me a quick, light hug, which I wanted to be longer and harder, and I detected a faint smell of alcohol, well-hidden by the more pleasant fragrances of soap and aftershave. Triumphantly he let go of me and burst out:

'Tartar sauce!'

'Ah.'

He took hold of my hand.

'God, what does your bandage look like! What have you done with it?'

I looked at the bandage. He was right. It looked disgusting. It was stained with dirt, grass and dried blood.

'And *what* have you done to your forehead?'

I touched my forehead, feeling for the plaster. I looked in the hall mirror and saw the skulls had come unstuck on one side, revealing the cut. Perfect. I wondered how long I had been wandering around with that hanging off my forehead. I pulled it off, crumpled it into a ball and stuffed it into my pocket.

What could I say? That I had been hit on the head by a stone? One that I had thrown myself? To give him yet another reason to believe I was self-harming? I recalled a T-shirt Enzo had that said: *I wish my lawn was emo so it would cut itself.*

Hilarious.

'It's not a problem. I fell. On some gravel.'

'Did you?' answered Dad.

His eyes were wide and questioning. He was waiting for me to go on. He would have to wait. He was not the only one who could withhold information.

*Contact Jonas.*

After a while he gave up and returned to the kitchen. I remained in the hall, unlacing my boots deliberately slowly with my right hand and then stepping out of them. I picked up a framed photo from the hall chest of drawers, one that had stood there forever. It showed me in the foreground at about five or six years old, swinging high up in the air. I'm fuzzy, out of focus. The wind has blown my dark brown hair off my face but a strand has fallen down over my nose and divided my face in two. On my feet are yellow Wellingtons. (I remember them very well. I loved them *so* much that I wore them long after I had grown out of them, with my toes slightly curled. I developed an odd way of walking, with short steps, waddling like a penguin. Eventually Dad worked out what was going on and bought a new pair that I refused to wear.) In the background is Dad, smiling, his arms outstretched and ready to push the swing, his contours sharp and clear. He looks so young. He looks about twenty.

I replaced the photo and thought: I'm hovering like a satellite. Disconnected. I have no brothers or sisters to lean on and dismayingly few friends. There is no generation before my parents, no paternal grandparents to offer stability and history, and even though my maternal grandparents do exist they are absent, in another country, the image of them blurred by distance and time. The roof constructed by my parents was precarious and full of holes. I thought:

Do we need a roof?

Do we need walls? Something to take the blows?

One more disappearance and I would be alone in the world. I would disappear into space like a forgotten and unlamented satellite.

I gave my reflection the evil eye and in a whisper forced myself to give up the self-pity. There won't be another disappearance. There will be a coming back!

I walked towards the kitchen, leaned against the doorframe, and stayed there. I studied Dad, who was standing at the cooker in the shirt that was either very old or very new, because I had never seen it before. He smiled at me and I smiled politely back. He turned the cheese and I saw the fat leap and splutter in the frying pan. I felt so dead tired that I didn't even make an attempt to help. He had made an effort by laying the table and lighting long white candles, but despite the nice touches I still felt that he was trying to hide something from me, though I didn't know what. Was it his alcohol-stinking yesterday with Denise, or something I really ought to know? About Mum? About himself? About me? About *Fam. Int?*

'You've made it look nice,' I said.

I wanted to add something but my words were forming thickly, like treacle. I wanted to say that he was all right. That he was an idiot. That Mum had never turned up. And that it was just as well. That I had been drunk and had sex with the first person to come along and who happened to be a neighbour. That I had spent the entire weekend alone in her big house. That I hated him. That I would always love him.

But I said nothing, because how do you talk about such things? Suddenly he said:

'So what did you and Jana do, then?'

He stood with his back to me, looking for something in a cupboard.

It made me jump. Now. Now was the time to tell him. Now.

No. Yes, now.

Now!

But I didn't. I tried instead to sound casual when I answered:

'Nothing special.'

'Well, you must have done something!'

He laughed, but it was forced. Then he turned around, expectantly, drying his hands on the tea towel that he'd tucked into his back pocket. I looked at him. I had to tell him now.

Now.

Now.

*Now!*

But I said nothing. Because suddenly I noticed I was angry. Furiously angry.

'Why do you always ask what we have *done* and never how it *was?* How *I* got *on?*'

I could have answered my own questions because I knew exactly why. He was worried that we hadn't done anything, worried that she had sat there reading constantly, that we had been indoors all weekend. And of course it had often been like that. But I liked it like that. Didn't I? Wasn't I allowed to like it?

'Well, but …'

'We did *nothing special.*'

He looked pleadingly at me.

'Maja, I only want …'

'Well stop wanting! Stop wanting her to do things, us to do things,' I said. 'You know nothing about her! I didn't see her read once.'

That was certainly true. I hadn't seen her. Read.

'Have I even mentioned that?' he said, hurt, and sat down.

We ate in silence. I tried cutting the cheese with a fork because I couldn't use a knife without my thumb resonating with pain. I felt the tears burning behind my eyelids. I stared stubbornly down at my plate and felt his anxious look. The cheese slid around and wouldn't stay in one place. Small green peas fell off the edge of the plate and onto the table.

Was she ill? Had she phoned and told him? Was this some bizarre attempt to protect me?

'Shall I help you?' asked Dad, when my plate was surrounded by green peas and a couple had fallen to the floor.

'No! I don't want you to!'

I threw the fork away from me and it bounced off the plate with a clatter and down to the floor. The tears came and my voice cracked.

'You think you're so nice ... so clever ... so frigging good! That you do everything so frigging right.'

Dad looked at me, bewildered. The yellow shirt clashed with his face and made him look a sickly green.

'Just because all those slags you ... you drag home are *so* impressed because you're looking after your poor loser of a kid who is *so* disturbed and weird that she doesn't even have any friends, it doesn't mean *I* am, get it? God, what do you want? Do you want me to be grateful or what? Don't use me as your bloody babe magnet. Have you got that?'

I shouted until my throat hurt, shouted until it became raw and fleshy. Like sushi.

'But ...'

'Shut your mouth, you *drunk!* I'm doing all right. *Don't interfere!*'

Then I ran, me who was doing all right, away from the

table and into my room, with tears streaming from my eyes and frustration boiling in my blood.

◆

I switched on the laptop and checked Dad's emails but there was no reply. On the other hand, ironically enough, there was a message on his Facebook page from pathetic Denise in which, to cut a long story short, she offered him her already well-used genitals.

I wrote back:

You perverted little slag! Get the bloody message and give up!

Jonas

PS. Definition of 'girl': as yet sexually immature CHILD of the female gender.

I lay on my bed staring at my mobile as if trying to magic up a telephone conversation with Justin or any sodding person at all, but I didn't succeed. That wasn't so strange. I wasn't exactly known for succeeding with anything.

# MONDAY, 16 APRIL

*Hole in the Head*

When I woke up next morning I felt heavy and feverish, as if my body was fighting an infection. I lay in bed for a while, trying to hang on to the small fragments of the dream that had moments ago seemed so real but was now fading and slipping out of reach. The only remnant was a feeling of sorrow and a prickling sense of frustration. I must have been lying on my thumb because it ached and felt swollen with blood. I blinked but found it hard to see: something sticky was clouding my vision. Perhaps it was the beginning of an eye infection. Perhaps it was yesterday's makeup dissolved by the tears I had cried in my sleep. I shut my eyes.

I heard Dad come into my room but I kept my eyes closed. He sat on the bed. The mattress was so soft that I unwillingly rolled a few centimetres towards him. He stroked my hair and then ran his fingers through it, and they fastened in a tangle of old hairspray. He pushed my hair to the side and behind my ear like he always did. When I was awake I hated him doing that, hated how proper it made me look. This time I let him.

'Maja, sweetheart.'

His voice was so soft. I mumbled something, pretending

I was more asleep than awake but I wondered if he had ever fallen for that.

'Time to get up now.'

I waited for him to say something about yesterday, some off-hand apology, even though it was me who ought to say sorry, or a gentle enquiry about what had happened. But he said nothing and only continued stroking my hair. Without opening my eyes I said:

'Dad, has Jana phoned?'

He was silent. For a long time. Too long?

'What?'

There it was. There was the "what?". Same as always, when he didn't like what I said.

'No. Should she have done?'

He stopped stroking my hair and rested his hand lightly on my forehead. Was he lying?

'No. I don't know, I just … just wondered.'

He sat like that for a long time while his hand got heavier and heavier on my head. We said nothing. I still had my eyes shut when a moment later he stood up and left the room.

I got up and checked Dad's emails and Facebook page. I was getting obsessive. Not a single message since yesterday. Even Denise had fallen silent.

I had a shower and the feverish feeling lifted slightly.

I realised I would probably be able to go to school after all. Unfortunately.

I felt fragmented and ugly and had to put on some of my reliable wardrobe favourites before I could even begin to tolerate myself. The black jeans, which were so tight that I had to lie on the floor to do them up, would have to stay undone for the moment. A black camisole and a black short-sleeved jacket that came to my waist, and

finally a pair of white silk gloves that came up to my elbows. I cut the thumb off the left glove to make room for
the bandage.

It took me forty minutes to do my hair that morning.
My first thought was to hide the cut on my forehead with
my bangs, which always covered half my face, to avoid all
the nosy questions from people who didn't care about me
anyway – Enzo excepted – and who I didn't care about
– Enzo excepted again. But if there was one thing I had
learned after going to school for more than ten years it
was that the more you try to hide something, the more
it shows. People tend to think you're ashamed of what
you're trying to hide and I wasn't going to give people like
Vendela and FAS-Lars the opportunity to get all excited
over my presumed shame. So I made my hair stand on
end using half an aerosol of ozone-depleting spray to keep
it in place.

Dad came and stood in the bathroom doorway, holding a cup of coffee and wearing that revolting yellow shirt
again. I met his look in the mirror. He didn't speak but
I felt the atmosphere had changed. I hoped he wasn't at
that very minute remembering what I was remembering.
My words: *"Shut your mouth, you drunk!"*

My cheeks blushed with the shame of it.

I didn't want to ask him for help but I had to.

'Can you do up my jeans?'

He rested his coffee mug on the hand basin. It was
hard to fasten the button. He had to stand behind me like
he used to do when I was little. Normally we would have
laughed. This wasn't normal. He said:

'Pull your stomach in.'

I pulled my stomach in and eventually he managed to
force the button through the buttonhole. He let go of me

immediately, as if I was contagious. I mumbled a thank you and looked in my make-up bag for eyeliner. I painted a thick black line on one eye but it was crooked. I didn't say anything but gave a low sigh and reached for a cotton wool bud. Dad took a gulp of his coffee. Then he asked me not to be offended but did I really have to make myself up to look like a prostitute?

He might just as well have slapped me across the face.

Not him as well.

Not whore in school and prostitute at home. I couldn't cope with it. I couldn't cope with any more.

'How could I *possibly* be offended by a remark like that?' I said. I was so shocked I couldn't even sound angry. When I had recovered I asked him not to be offended but did he really have to wear a shirt that made him look like a pimp?

'What?' said Dad, stupidly. 'Don't you like it?'

He looked down at his shirt and laughed:

'Does that mean I can keep it for myself?'

Had he not heard 'pimp' or was he pretending? I said nothing.

'What's wrong with it?'

'It's ... how can I put it so you'll understand? It has a kind of innate ugliness that passes all understanding.'

I was playing that we were joking, that it was banter, but there was no twinkle in my eye. And I couldn't see one in his, either. Inside I was cold.

'Maja, I ... perhaps it was ...'

Dad looked distressed, flung out his hand to say something, and spilled hot coffee over his shirt front.

'Ouch! *Hell!* Well, now I'll have to change it anyway.'

He went into his bedroom and everything went quiet. A few minutes later he waved goodbye from the hall, dressed in something grey and ordinary. His mouth was a straight line, his eyes sad. Before he went he said:

'Don't forget the hospital today. Your follow-up appointment.'

'I know,' I said quietly.

My stomach ached. I raised my hand to wave but couldn't bring myself to look at him. He shut the door softly as he left.

I stared at myself in the mirror. I spent too much time in front of mirrors. It was narcissistic and pointless. I was narcissistic and pointless. I prodded the sore on my forehead. It looked as if I had been shot in the head.

I groaned and rammed my fists into the shower curtain, right, left, right, left. It gave way gently but came back for more. Like a masochist. Was I one of those? Because I wasn't a sadist, surely?

Waves of pain pulsed through my hand and out into my thumb. I moaned and sat down on the toilet, my head in my hands.

*What was I doing? Why hadn't I said anything? What was I going to do?*

I stood up and studied the sore on my forehead in the mirror.

The memory of Justin.

*A flash image: the sharp stone in my hand, the window opening, the intense pain on my forehead, the fall onto the lawn, the smell of earth, warm blood on my face, the warm water, the tender hands, the damp towel, the stinging, the plaster over the cut, his face close to mine ...*

I had an idea. A bit sick, but that was what I was like, wasn't it? Psychotic? Sure. A whore? Sure.

I went into my bedroom, opened the turquoise cupboard, and spread the contents out over the floor until I found what I was looking for: flesh-coloured modelling clay. The clay was a little dry but I softened it with some olive oil. I kneaded it, pulled off a piece and formed a low ridge all around the cut, making a crater. Then I blended in the clay with foundation so that it would match my skin colour. I got out a bottle of blood-red nail varnish and painted some right in the centre of the clay crater, directly over the cut, which stung like mad. I finished by letting a drop trickle down my forehead, stopping a millimetre from my left eyebrow.

A hole in the head, *mothafucka*.

*The Walking Dead*

When I arrived at school Enzo was there, trying to stuff an oversized rucksack into his locker. We had gym that day and he always brought far too many clothes with him to cover all types of weather, all kinds of activities.

'Who's winning?'

'Yes, well, pardon my French but it's sodding well not *me*,' said Enzo, who spoke more fluently and less nervously when he was irritated. He gave up and dragged the rucksack out of the locker instead. He took a sideways look at me as he opened it and pulled out a pair of trainers.

'Wow! What have you … looks like you've …'

He took a step closer and examined my forehead closely.

'… been shot! Oh, it's fake. Shit, I was really scared there for a minute. Hair looks nice.'

'Thanks. Yours too. You have no idea how good it is to see you.'

Enzo looked confused, unused to signs of affection from me, or from anyone.

'Mutual. You look well,' he said, a little too quickly.

'Do I? That's strange. I feel like the walking dead.'

I wanted to hug him, but we didn't do that kind of

thing so I smiled and opened my locker and stared inside it, incapable of working out which book I needed.

'Was Norrköping such a pain? Not that your mum's a pain . . . I mean, I don't even know her but . . . I only thought that . . . the journey and . . . well, you know.'

I interrupted him.

'No, I know what you mean. Not a pain as such, but just – oh, you know.'

'Maths,' said Enzo helpfully, after I had been staring at my books for a while.

'Thanks,' I said, and at that precise moment I was close to saying something about Mum, and maybe something about young men with good and honourable intentions. I had a "You know what?" on the tip of my tongue, on the spot where you taste sweet things, and perhaps a bit on the sides too, where you taste salt, and I felt my heart beating hard against my ribcage. But as soon as I looked up at Enzo I changed my mind. I couldn't do it. It was something to do with his nice, kind look and the difference between his life and mine. I didn't want to lay myself bare and listen to his sympathetic, stammering, disguised expressions of tenderness because they would make me weak. I swallowed my "You know what?" and the "Y" cut my throat like a knife.

'It'll be cool this evening!' said Enzo.

'Yeah! Totally!' I said, trying to pitch my voice to sound happy, like a chipmunk in a Disney film. I had forgotten I was supposed to be going to his house, had forgotten *Control*.

'How's your thumb, by the way?' he went on, but before I had time to answer I saw Valter pass us in the corridor. I followed him with my eyes, taking in his well-ironed shirt, his curly hair, his expensive shoes. As if he felt my gaze he turned and noticed me standing paralysed, unable to act, my fingers still tightly clenched around my locker key.

'Maja!' he called. 'How are you? How's your thumb? Can I see?'

He walked quickly towards me and grabbed hold of my bandaged hand to get a closer look. He appeared not to see the bullet hole in my forehead. I caught Enzo's eyes briefly over the top of the locker door. His eyebrows were raised in astonishment. Valter was not usually this involved, this energetic.

'Yeah, good,' I said. 'It hurts a bit but …'

'You'll get over it, you're very strong.'

'Oh, am I?' I said insolently, but he seemed not to hear.

'I was thinking … you might like to finish your shelf this week?' Valter went on. 'I mean, if you can, with your thumb and everything. There isn't much left to do and we'll be spending the remaining few weeks on a photo project. It would be good if you'd finished the shelf by then.'

'Yes, that might be a good idea.'

Mum's forty-fifth birthday present. I wondered if she would ever have it, if I would ever see her again to hand it over.

'What did the principal say? Was she angry?'

'No, no, not angry. But we agreed it would be better if students devoted more time to sculpture during sculpture lessons.'

'A shelf is …'

'… a sculpture too? No, I don't think so. Still, I'll be here after school for a few more evenings, writing reports for the third years – oh God, I'm already having anxiety attacks about that. But it means I can help you, if you need any help.'

Enzo looked shocked and embarrassed at the same time. All this chummy interest. He muttered something about us having to go to our class. I indicated two minutes and he went on ahead. The corridor began to empty out and I thought that Valter ought to be going to his class too, but he stayed where he was with his Prince hair and with his hand cream-soft hands around my wrist.

When Enzo had disappeared I made an attempt.

I said 'Um … we really want to replace your T-shirt …'

'Your dad mentioned something about that, but don't worry about it.'

'No, I'd feel better if we did.'

'There's really no need. It wasn't as if you sawed off your thumb *deliberately*, was it?'

Always these insinuations. I felt like informing him, Dad, and the rest of the world that it was possible to wear black clothes without feeling the need to cut yourself. That you didn't have to be suicidal just because you refused to go around smiling all the time. That they ought to think about how they dealt with *their* anxiety before they started throwing massive great stones about in their glasshouses, because I certainly hadn't seen anything to convince me that they'd win any prizes at verbalising it, exactly. 'The school must have some form of insurance to cover things like that. I'll take it up with the principal.'

'Yeah, but I can take the T-shirt home and wash it, can't I? Just to say thanks for your help?'

Valter hesitated.

'Okay, okay,' he said finally. 'If it makes you feel better.'

I tried to wriggle my hand out of his grip but he didn't want to let go so I had to kind of twist it free. He was looking at me strangely. What was wrong with him? I closed my locker and walked away. It was only when I reached the classroom that I realised I had forgotten my books. I went back to the locker. In the distance I saw Vendela sauntering down the corridor, no doubt ready to attack the first person who deviated from what she decided was the norm.

◆

The school day continued in such slow motion that every minute felt like a quarter of an hour. Enzo had to help me button up my trousers twice, which was two times too many, and I think at least four teachers told me to go and wash my forehead. I did as they asked, removing a little bit of nail varnish each time, but insisted that it was impossible to get it off completely and that it was a real injury, which was at least partly true. And they said nothing more about it, or followed it up, fascinatingly enough, even though the maths teacher at least got all worked up and shouted, spraying us with saliva:

'Being shot in the head is nothing to joke about!'

I agreed. That seemed to make him worse, strangely enough. I don't think he likes me.

Our Swedish teacher Hanne took a plaster out of her massive Gucci bag and without asking stuck it right over the crater. Since I had her billowing chest in my face at the time it was only afterwards that I realised she must have seen it was fake. But she didn't say anything. It had its advantages, being able to write superlative haikus and heart-rending stories, to be able to verbalise things. Your anxiety, for example.

Although on this particular day I was not especially outstanding. I didn't write one single poem in free verse, which was our task, and only raised my hand once, but that was to go to the toilet, which I wasn't allowed to do.

It didn't matter. I didn't really need to go. I only wanted to check Dad's emails on my mobile and be left in peace for a while.

## A Shot of Adrenalin in the Heart

Just as I was walking across the square, past the little Italian café in Örnsberg, my phone rang. I stopped and looked at the display. It was a mobile number I didn't recognise. My heart did a double beat and I went hot.

*Mum. It could be Mum. Or ... Justin, maybe.*

I answered, but it wasn't Mum and it wasn't Justin. It was a hoarse male voice that said:

'Um, hello,' in a broad Östgöta dialect.

'Hello,' I said, and sat down on one of the café's bright orange plastic chairs. I couldn't hide the disappointment in my voice. I put down my carrier bag containing the clippers and the hair colour and felt the afternoon sun on my face. I looked around at the café tables: half of them were full.

'It's Thomas, Thomas Hansson.'

Thomas Hansson. That meant nothing to me. It sounded like a made-up name. A salesman, perhaps. I considered ringing off, just like that, without listening to what he wanted. I prodded the bandage on my left thumb. It had gone a beigy-brown and did in fact look pretty disgusting. I pulled away a thread that was hanging loose.

'Oh yeah,' I replied wearily.

'You phoned me,' he went on. 'Last Saturday.'

'What? I don't think … it must …'

Thomas?

Thomas on the photo, with the demented smile! It felt like I'd been given a shot of adrenalin straight in the heart. It was hard to sit still. The words poured out of me.

'Yes! Yes, of course I phoned you. You … you don't know me but … I'm Jana Müller's daughter and as far as I understand it you two know each other? You and Jana?'

'Yes. Yes, I suppose we do.'

He sounded unsure.

'Can I ask *how* you know each other?'

'Yes, but … why don't you ask her yourself?'

Did he sound annoyed? Or just curious? I couldn't decide.

'Well, it's just that…'

I scraped the paving stones with my foot and looked towards Hägerstensvägen where silver-coloured cars were moving past in a slow caravan. Shit, what was I going to say? I might as well get straight to the point.

'It's like this. She's disappeared and I can't get hold of her. I'm only wondering if … if you know where she is.'

It went silent at the other end. A little girl, about three or four years old, was running around the square in random circles. Her hair was white-blond and thin and she was wearing a dark blue jacket. The puller on the zip had been replaced with a keyring. She had a small yellow rucksack on her back with a cuddly dog sticking out of the top.

It just occurred to me that I had told Thomas Hansson something I hadn't even told my dad.

'What do you mean disappeared?'

He sounded sceptical.

'Disappeared. Gone. Not at home and not answering her phone. Disappeared.'

'Is that true?'

'Well of course it's true! Why would I make up something like that?'

He was silent for a moment, as if he was allowing the information to sink in.

'But, well, I still can't help you. We don't see each other any more. Not in that way.'

'Right. So you don't know where she is?'

'No. No, unfortunately not.'

The energy that had so recently made my body tingle drained out of me.

'How ... how do you know Jan ...?' I began, but he interrupted me.

'Have you contacted the police?'

The little girl came up to the table and stood right in front of me, looking at me with huge, remarkably blue irises surrounded by blinding white. So white it almost looked light blue.

'Yes.'

I said yes because it was easier. But of course, I should have done that straight away.

I heard him take a mouthful of something at the other end of the phone. I heard him swallow. But he said nothing. Neither did I. I looked at the little girl and she smiled at me. She was sweet, like candy floss, and I forced myself to smile back.

'All right. We met at the university. We are both doing a PhD in psychology, but in different fields. We ... well, we met a couple of times. Went out together, if you like.'

'You ... *dated?*'

I couldn't take it in. The fact that Mum was seeing

someone, that she was *dating* someone, seemed about as improbable as Dad becoming the pastor of a Pentecostal church and speaking in tongues.

'Yes, you could say that. But it didn't go anywhere, didn't get serious.'

'Why not?'

The girl ran off. Like a bee she flitted here and there among the tables.

'You're as straightforward as your mother, that's for sure. Listen, your name's Maja, right? This feels very strange. Why don't you ask your mother?'

'She's gone missing! I've already told you that! Missing!'

'Will the police be getting in touch with me, or what?'

'I can't imagine they would,' I said, truthfully. 'Would that be a problem, then?'

'What? No, no of course not,' he said quickly.

*Too quickly?*

He fell silent. I heard the twittering of the birds and his breathing in the phone.

'Okay. Just because it's you. Just because you're her daughter. I liked her. I still do. But, I don't know, I don't think she's so keen on me. At least, she doesn't show it.'

'That doesn't necessarily mean anything,' I murmured to myself.

'So I left it. We're friends. We have lunch together sometimes with a few other people and talk about our research. That's about it.'

'When did you last see her?'

'No idea. A week ago, maybe.'

'Isn't that a long time when you're working at the same place?'

If I had been in the police and this had been an interrogation he would have been the main suspect by now,

I thought. A rejected man punishing the person who has rejected him, who didn't give him what he wanted. Hadn't he looked a bit crazy in that photo? A bit ... disturbed?'

Thomas coughed.

'Yes, perhaps it is, but sometimes we have to go away for various things, or we're teaching or looking up information or material somewhere else, not at the university. Jana is quite secretive. She doesn't say ... well, she doesn't talk much about herself, what she has done, where she is going.'

'But think about it. When was the last time you saw her?'

'Good Lord, how would I be able to remember that? Erm, I know I saw her last Monday, that's a week ago, because there was some sort of information meeting ... but I wonder if perhaps I'm ...'

'How was she? How did she seem last Monday?'

'How did she seem? Well, she seemed fairly normal. I mean normal for Jana, if you'll excuse me saying so.'

'No.'

'What?'

I didn't excuse him. I looked at the sun and I didn't excuse him.

'Nothing. Was that the last time you saw her? Monday?'

'Look, I'm just checking my calendar here and I think I actually saw her last Wednesday. She left before lunch time. I thought I'd ask her to come with us, there are a few of us who usually eat together but ... she left a few minutes before.'

I sighed. The trail stopped there, then. Last Wednesday. Immediately before her appointment with Dr Roos. I got ready to say thank you but it was as if that thank you sat so deeply inside me I would have to cough it up like a gob of phlegm. A dirty grey bird of indeterminate species sat on the chair opposite mine and began picking at a few crumbs. I kicked out with my boot and it flew away, settling lazily a few metres further off on the paving stones. Birds in Stockholm are seriously damaged, I thought. They have no natural instincts left.

'She talks quite a bit about you, actually,' said Thomas, all of a sudden.

I sat up straight in my chair.

'Oh, what does she say?' I asked tensely, the sun shining directly into my eyes.

'What she says? That you go your own way, you don't care what other people think. That you are intelligent. You can tell she's proud of you.'

I said thanks and he said something about hoping she would come back. I shut my eyes. The sunlight burned orange through my eyelids. No, Thomas Hansson wasn't the reason for Mum's disappearance. He was too nice for that. It was more likely that Dr Roos had something to do with it.

I ought to phone the hospital. That would be the logical thing to do. I ought to phone.

*But I didn't dare. Did I?*

We rang off and I stood up. I phoned directory enquiries and was given the number for Vrinnevi Hospital in Norrköping and put through. But when they answered I hung up. I'll phone later, I thought. I'll phone … later.

My legs felt sort of springy. They did, in spite of everything. I waved at the little girl who had climbed into her buggy. She looked happily at me, but didn't wave back. Then I ran across the square, rounded the corner at Hägerstensvägen and passed the mysterious shop which sold watches and glasses and had dusty spectacle frames from the nineties in its window. The words were echoing in my head:

*She is proud of me, she is proud of me, she is proud of me!*

## A Bag Over the Head

I rang the doorbell and heard light footsteps that couldn't belong to anyone except Enzo's mother. When she opened the door she looked thinner than usual and when she hugged me I felt her ribs through the carefully ironed blouse. It seemed as if she went down a size each time I saw her.

'*Meu amorzinho!* Maja!' she exclaimed.

I smiled at her. I saw her looking at me, at my hair, my clothes, my cut, and my bandage. But she said nothing and I gave her credit for that. I had at least brushed the hairspray out of my bangs and removed the clay crater. Out of consideration for her. She did not appreciate macabre stunts. In fact, few people did. Fascinatingly few.

'How are you, my lovely girl?' she asked, and I replied 'Good' and she asked how Dad was and I replied 'Really good' and then she asked how Mum was and I replied 'Good, good' and then I got a pain in my stomach and I gave her a flower I had picked by a cable cabinet on the street. This small gesture thrilled her to bits and she said '*Muito obrigada!*' so many times that I felt ashamed, because it wasn't as if I had turned up with a bouquet of long-stemmed roses. After that she rabbled a long harangue in Portuguese that sounded lovely but was impossible for me to understand. Enzo appeared behind her in a T-shirt with an image of *The Godfather* on the front, smiled indulgently, and beckoned me in to his room.

I threw myself down on the bed and landed directly on top of a couple of CD cases. Enzo wasn't the sort to download. He wanted to own "the physical product", as he called it, and as a result his room was full of books, films and CDs. He waved the *Control* DVD under my nose while I did my best to remove the hard plastic case that was digging into my back. I whistled, impressed.

'You … you seem happier now,' said Enzo as I looked at the DVD case that showed a serious, glaring Ian Curtis with a cigarette hanging from the corner of his mouth.

'My manic depression is so unpredictable. Right now I'm in the middle of a manic phase.'

'Which lasts fifteen minutes, or what?'

'More or less,' I said, and grinned. 'Shall we start with the hair?'


I looked at Enzo in the bathroom mirror. He was being overly careful as he shaved the back of my head, and small tufts of dark brown hair were falling onto the bathroom floor. He had done it once before and, as with everything else, he was meticulous to the point of absurdity.

Having someone touch your hair can be surprisingly intimate. We didn't talk much. I held firmly onto my bangs; they were going to be saved or possibly trimmed a little, but I wanted to keep the length.

'Sometimes I miss my Leningrad Cowboys haircut. Perhaps I ought to let it grow out a bit at the back?'

'When did you have that, then?'

'Well, don't you remember? Last autumn, when we went back to school!'

'Oh, was that Leningrad Cowboys, then?'

'Yes. What did you think it was, for goodness' sake?'

'I don't know. I thought it had more of an Elvis during his fat-years look.'

'You swine!'

I turned round and stared at him, pretending to be offended.

'That was supposed to be a compliment, you know,' said Enzo, and I heard that he meant it.

'Oh, right,' I said, and he switched off the clippers and handed me a mirror so I could look at the back of my head.

'Looks good.'

I mixed the hair colour, some cheap stuff bought in the local supermarket, and Enzo pulled on the plastic gloves. The top of the index finger and the middle finger on one of them immediately split.

'What! I don't believe it!'

'We'll have to tape them,' I said, and ran into the kitchen to ask his mum for some freezer tape.

She showed me the flower that she had placed in a brandy glass and chatted for a while about how pretty it was and how happy my mum must be to have a daughter like me, and I wailed internally and made a mental note never to give her anything again. In the end I was given some normal tape but that worked just as well.

Enzo handed me an old towel to put over my shoulders. Then he massaged the colour into my roots, the back of my head and the sides and carried on until he reached my bangs, which dripped with the oily black liquid. To finish I put a clear plastic bag over my hair and fastened it by winding the tape around it a couple of times. I looked in the mirror and saw a black stain in the middle of my forehead, so I tore off a piece of paper that I wetted and pushed in under the bag. I managed to wipe off most of it so that only a grey shadow remained just below my hairline.

'There!'

Enzo stared in the mirror with exaggeratedly wide eyes and a horrified expression. He pretended his gloved hands were out of control, that they had a life of their own. His hands closed in on his throat as he simulated an agonising strangulation. He emitted a half-choking sound and then slowly sank to the floor, his tongue sticking out of his mouth. Then he jumped up and said:

'Now! *Control!*'

◆

The film put us in such an excruciatingly beautiful melancholic mood that we totally forgot my head was covered in black hair dye. As we watched the credits roll just over two hours later we were sitting as if paralysed in front of the screen. I thought about life and how fragile it was, and about Mum. The longing was like an echo in my heart. Enzo looked at me sadly but then he raised one eyebrow in amusement.

'Maja, you've got a plastic bag on your head.'

At that very moment I felt an intense itching spreading like wildfire over my scalp. I ran to the bathroom, tore off the plastic bag that was all warm and gooey, and bent my head over the bath. I turned on the shower without even thinking that the thumb bandage would get wet. The only thing that would help was ice-cold water. Immediately.

When the water running into the bath was no longer a dirty grey colour I turned off the shower. My head was numb with cold. Enzo came into the bathroom and surveyed my head for a long time.

'Nice,' he said. 'Except it isn't only your *hair* that's gone black. It looks like someone has painted your head with a roller. Your scalp is completely black. It's shining! You look like a boy doll with plastic hair! You look like Ken!'

And then he started to laugh, and he laughed so hard that he was forced to lean against the hand basin. I stared at myself in the mirror.

If only it was true. That I looked like Ken. But no.

I had the same flipping hairstyle as Hitler.

Well, obviously. If Justin had Hitler hair and my hairstyle was the same as his then it was logical.

A flipping Hitler haircut.

*Scheisse!*

# TUESDAY, 17 APRIL

*Sick in the Head?*

On Tuesday morning I was woken by bright yellow sunlight shining through my window and warming my face. I had forgotten to pull down the roller blind the previous evening. I stretched like a cat and without getting out of bed switched on my laptop which was on the chest of drawers beside my bed. Since coming home on Sunday I had checked my emails and Dad's thirty times easily. On Monday I had even gone online via my mobile during lessons to check them. To find out something. The truth, perhaps. But no email so far.

As all the icons slowly fell into place on the screen I ran my hand over my breast, trying to feel what Justin had felt. It was as white as an English virgin, and as soft and inviting as a fresh marshmallow. So why didn't he call?

*His body on top of mine, the weight of it, over my breasts, stomach, thighs. The red bangs, the ice-blue eyes, freckles like a golden spray over the bridge of his nose. His hands warm on my body, his tongue in my mouth, the sound of his shoes thumping down the stairs …*

My face turned warm at the memory and blood rushed to my cheeks. I hugged the duvet and fell back against the pillow with my eyes closed, trying to summon up the image of his face, but it didn't work. I saw the details – the long bangs, the blue eyes – but couldn't fit them together. Wasn't it odd that such an image could so suddenly disappear? It was only two days since I had seen him, after all.

I sat up, pulled the laptop towards me and went into Dad's emails. Nothing new from Mum. My thumb was hurting like mad so I pressed a painkiller out of the pack lying on the bedside table. I studied the bandage that in addition to beer, blood and earth now also bore traces of black hair dye. It really needed to be changed, I thought to myself. And then it hit me like a fist on the chin.

*The follow-up appointment!* I should have gone yesterday! Shit. I had *totally* forgotten. I groaned and hit myself on the forehead, which caused enormous waves of pain to radiate from the cut. God, I was a wreck. A leftover.

Still. No great damage had been done, I thought. All I had to do was phone and book a new appointment.

I went back to the laptop. Idly I clicked back to the inbox and furtively read a few uninteresting emails from journalists on some network that Dad belonged to, and an extra tragic message on Facebook with the heading "What happened??!!!???!!!" from pathetic Denise. She wrote that she didn't understand a thing and promised never to get in touch again just as long as he could admit to feeling *at least* some "primitive carnal desire" for her. What a fascinatingly dreadful woman. I deleted it.

I continued scrolling through the emails from April and backwards. March, February.

Then.

Suddenly one name stood out.

Jana Müller.

The air left my lungs and it became hard to breathe.

This one I had clearly missed. It was from her usual work email, sent on the twenty-sixth of February. I opened it apprehensively, as if I was afraid a bomb would explode.

Hello Jonas

I know you think I'm very direct but it's the only approach I know. So here goes.

For some time now I have been in contact with a psychiatrist regarding certain difficulties I have been experiencing, mainly in relation to other people. I'm sure you know what I mean.

We had our first meeting in October last year. After only a few conversations – too few, I think – my psychiatrist Dr Evald Roos suggested I undergo tests to establish whether my problems are severe enough for a diagnosis to be made. They suspect a particular diagnosis but I do not want to tell you what it is before everything is completed. Without going into detail I can say it concerns a social disability, in other words inadequacies regarding social interaction.

Over the last six months I have talked with Dr Roos and he has made a detailed background analysis. I have also met and been tested by a psychologist and also an occupational therapist. Now they want to carry out something they call a "family interview". I'm sure you understand that I can hardly expect my parents to leave Hanover, travel to Sweden and then be subjected to an interview, even if I wanted them to. And I do not want that. Naturally, Maja is also completely out of the question. I don't want to get her involved and I hope you will respect my wish not to tell her about any of this.

You can hardly be called a "relative" any longer but I still think of you as the person who knows me best, even though we have little regular contact these days. And I don't think – unfortunately, I might add, in this regard – that I have changed to any great extent during the past thirteen, fourteen years. What I want to say is that I feel you could provide a true picture of what I am like. And the difficulties and – I hope – the strengths that I have. My question is this: will you agree to a family interview?

Regards,

Jana.

I looked up from the screen. It felt as if someone had injected zero-degree water under my skin. A chilling feeling that instantly bored its way deep inside me. Fam. Int. Family Interview. Okay, now I understood. But:

*Diagnosis?*
*Psychiatrist?*
*Psychologist?*
Was Mum ill? Was she sick in the head?

*Are You Alone Too?*

When I arrived at school, a whole twenty minutes early for once, there was a carrier bag hanging from my locker. Inside were Valter's bloodstained T-shirt and a pale yellow post-it note that read:

> *Design studio open from 5. I'll come and lock up at 9. Ring if you need any help, I'll still be here. Machinery workshop open if you need sandpaper etc.*

Valter had drawn an arrow at the bottom so I turned the note over. It said:

> *BUT under no circumstances are you to use electrical tools e.g. electric drill, electric saw, etc! Not only because I'm afraid you'll cut off more body parts but also for the simple reason that I could get the sack. Valter*

I squashed the carrier into my own bag and there was a waft of Valter's sweet, heavy cologne as the air was pressed out. Why was he doing this for me?

I walked about like a zombie all day and in the school toilets the mirrors, cracked and smeared with dirty pink soap, told me I was pale and hollow-eyed. And despite the fact that the sun was shining as if it were the middle of summer, a November-grey, doomsday darkness hung like a sack over my head.

During the maths lesson I crept out and phoned Vrinnevi Hospital. I asked for Dr Roos and my voice was so shaky and weak that the receptionist had to ask me to repeat the name. But Dr Roos was busy and when she asked me if I wanted to leave a message I said 'No' and hung up.

At break time I went to the IT room and Googled diagnosis because even though I had a vague idea what it meant I could only associate it at that moment with school diagnostic tests. A quick search led me to:

A diagnosis is the process of attempting to determine a specific physical or psychological condition. The diagnosis is based on the patient's own description of the symptoms in combination with physiological and/or psychological examinations or tests. Additional descriptions of the condition, supplied by family members (especially if children are concerned) can complete the investigation. Diagnostics is a central part of medicine as the diagnosis forms the basis for treatment. Anamnesis (the history of the illness or disease) plays an important role in determining a diagnosis.

That might have made me a little wiser but it certainly didn't make me any flipping happier.

Enzo looked worried about my mental absence, which was decent of him but not especially attractive. Sympathy seldom suits the bearer. It's something to do with the altered position of the eyebrows in relation to the face.

He was to be admired for his persistent attempts to get me to react. He literally spat out nasty comments about our stupid fellow human beings, most of all FAS-Lars and Vendela, made politically incorrect remarks and from time to time gave me a friendly whack on the arm. That kind of thing would usually get me going, but I only groaned and went back to what I was doing.

After lunch, which consisted of a soup so thin it looked like snot-coloured water, soggy bread, and those rectangular, pale-yellow plastic squares they call cheese, I went outside. In actual fact I think it's ridiculous to routinely slag off school food. It's like kicking someone who's already lying on the ground and rolling about in the throes of death. It's not sportsmanlike. But on this particular day, I joined the crowd and despised it like they did.

It was crawling with students. Dressed for summer they ran about on the asphalt like frisky young animals, playfully tugging each other's pony tails, jumpers, dicks as well, for all I knew. I was the only one who was cold. I turned my coat collar up to my cheeks. An over-bleached blonde girl, her mouth dripping with lip gloss, shouted:

'Maja! Are you a vampire or what?'

And someone else added:

'No! Can't you see she's one of the undead?'

And I, who normally always had something to say, said nothing, but I knew what they were thinking because I had my gleaming black hair combed back, a hole in the head, and I was as pale as an English corpse. I was the walking dead.

With the sun in my eyes and Joy Division in my ears I slowly started walking. I walked past all the smiles because they weren't meant for me anyway, and I walked past all the warm, animated bodies because they weren't mine to touch. My feet walked forwards, onwards, away, home.

I left school and rounded the corner towards Fridhemsplan. I walked the length of Västerbro bridge and thought about all the people who had jumped off it into the beautiful, glittering water. But I thought even more about those who had managed to stay on the bridge despite their hearts which were heavy and their feet which were way too light. How admirable they were. How strong.

I passed Hornstull and walked over Liljeholm's bridge with its aggressive roar of traffic and cyclists whizzing past my ears like meat projectiles. I thought about the words that had been on a roof below the bridge for ages: ARE YOU ALONE TOO? Fat white capitals on a black background. But they were gone now, the roof sanitised and empty.

*Yes, I'm alone too,* I thought. *I am so very alone.*

And I was close, extremely close, to walking right into legendary tattoo artist Doc Forest's, slapping a few thousand-kronor notes down on the counter and shouting:

'Mixed dicks and swastikas, please!'

But naturally I didn't. And for the two hundred in my purse I would just about get the top of a knob.

In my ears I heard Joy Division singing:

*When routine bites hard*
*And ambitions are low*
*And resentment rides high*
*But emotions won't grow*
*And we're changing our ways,*
*Taking different roads*
*Love, love will tear us apart again.*

And wasn't love the root of all the suffering, all the evil in the world? Because if you didn't love, you wouldn't care.

◆

It was only towards evening that I started to come awake. As dusk fell and darkness began to fill the flat, I regained some energy, like the vampire I so clearly resembled. I pulled Valter's T-shirt out of the plastic bag. Without thinking what I was doing I picked up a marker pen and wrote right across the circular blood stain: I CAN VERBAL-ISE MY ANXIETY! Then I grabbed hold of my bangs and cut them off. Because I couldn't walk around looking like some old Nazi.

At twenty-past six, ten minutes before the time Dad had announced he would be home, I put on the T-shirt, threw my bangs into the bin, and set off for school.

◆

Dark shadows lay like thin, grey blankets in every corner of the design studio. Only one weak yellowish lamp was shining over by the whiteboard. Without looking I reached out to the right and on the three light switches lined up in a vertical row on the wall. The fluorescent tubes crackled and lit up one after the other. I discovered they hummed, quite loudly in fact, something I had never noticed in the daytime. One of the lights flickered nervously for a second or two before coming on fully.

I was back in the room where it had all happened.

There was a flash in my head.

*The grating, piercing sound.*
*The metal teeth, hacking into me.*
*The flesh. Exposed.*
*The blood. Snaking, pulsating, spurting.*
*The explosions. The pain.*

The horror of it made me shudder. It was the sound, the memory of the sound that was the worst. The sound when the metal teeth chopped into my flesh, cutting through the bone.

My thumb felt excruciatingly painful, as if someone had hammered rusty nails right into the bone. I lifted my left hand to my heart and cupped the right one over it protectively.

I walked past the rows of benches, stopping beside the one where I had last worked. Couldn't I make out a faint outline on the floor, next to one of the bench legs? I bent down but no, it wasn't my blood, just the silhouette of a lamp that had tricked me. The caretaker had obviously done a good job. For some reason I felt disappointed.

I carried on into the storeroom. My shelf was standing on the floor, half hidden behind a couple of oil portraits still in progress. I pulled it out and the underneath scraped against the rough stone floor. I turned it over. The blood had been carelessly removed: red streaks daubed the lower shelf as if someone had superficially dragged a piece of dry loo paper over the wood a couple of times. In one place you could see the blood clearly, a large, dried rust-red stain.

I took the shelf out into the main room, back to "my" bench, and stood it up. I studied it: the blood, the side supports with the flamingos, the pencil lines I had sawn along before the saw had suddenly lost its grip and sawn thin air, sawn me. Sawn *off* parts of me.

I walked to the machine workshop where the large dark-green saw, drill, and planing machines stood silent after a day's industrious work. I cut through the adjacent room, the bench workshop, where a remaining student was painstakingly oiling a beautifully-carved table. She looked up at me and I raised my hand in a hello. I asked her if she knew where the handsaws were kept and she looked uncertain but pointed towards a tall, narrow cupboard. I lifted out a handsaw. Obediently I was avoiding anything electrical. Then I heard her clear her throat behind me. I turned around.

'Excuse me, but aren't you the one who sawed off her thumb?'

She looked kind: brown, medium-length hair and a round face with no make-up.

'Um, yeah. How do you know?'

She gave a laugh.

'Who doesn't? That photo has circulated throughout the entire school by now.'

*What photo?* And the very moment I thought that thought, I understood. Simon's photo. Of course.

'Have you got it? Can I see?'

'Haven't you seen it yourself?'

'Nope.'

'Oh, I thought … sorry, I didn't mean to …'

'It's cool. Can I see the picture?'

She wiped her hands on her work trousers and took her mobile out of her pocket. It was a flashy new model with a large display. She scrolled down the screen with her index finger and then held the phone up to me.

It wasn't the photo I had been expecting. Not the one he had taken when I had turned to face him, or a close-up of my thumb. This must have been taken a few minutes afterwards. I looked at myself on the illuminated display as I lay unconscious in a sea of blood, my arms crossed over the splattered shirt front, my right hand protecting my left. It looked so peaceful. It looked like I was dead. As if I had finally – what was it Freud had said? – adapted myself to the world.

'So,' I said. 'That's me on the floor, bleeding.'

'Yes.'

She gave a nervous laugh.

I shoved the saw into a plastic bag I found on a bench and grabbed some sandpaper, one sheet of coarse and one of fine, from the sandpaper holder on the wall, as well as a tin of transparent wood varnish and a brush, and began to walk towards the door. For a second it looked as if she was going to stop me because she took a step forwards and opened her mouth. But when I ignored her she simply let me walk past.

◆

I sawed neatly along the pencilled lines, concentrating so intensely that everything else became hazy and unimportant and kind of disappeared out to the periphery. Slowly my flamingo materialised, its neck curved as if it had its head buried in a book. Pretty ugly, but a flamingo nonetheless.

I smoothed the edges carefully with the sandpaper, felt them with my fingers, and sanded again.

I took a piece of stiff paper and a pair of scissors from Valter's desk. Freehand I cut a heart-shaped hole in the middle. The edges were uneven but that's the way it was, I thought. That was how my heart was. Imperfect. Defective.

199

I lay the template over the bloodstained patch and fastened it with tape. Then I painted the varnish inside the heart-shaped paper hole. A shiny red heart. Tomorrow I would clean off the blood left outside the template, the part that hadn't been varnished. That way only the heart would be left, the heart made of my own blood. I tossed my head to get my bangs out of my eyes, an old habit, but simultaneously remembered that it was no longer necessary. I ran my fingers over my forehead, along my hairline. The hair was a few millimetres long on the left-hand side but got shorter and shorter the further right I went. I had cut it off exactly at the roots.

All of a sudden the door opened. I jumped. It was Valter. Already? I took a look at the clock and it was ten past nine. I had been there for over two hours.

'Hi,' he said. 'How's it going?'

'Good.'

He walked in. On his head he was wearing a beret. His soft curls stuck out from under the rim like clown hair.

'I thought I'd leave now, so you'd better start getting your things together. Do you need any help with anything?'

He went up to the front desk, pulled open the top drawer and took out a packet of cigarillos that he shoved into his jacket pocket.

'No, it's cool. I've nearly finished. I'll take it home and finish it there, if that's okay.'

I didn't want to say anything about the heart in case he thought I was being morbid, and maybe I was. But I didn't care about that. At least it was beautiful.

'Of course,' he said absently. 'As long as you bring it back so that I can give it a grade when it's completely finished.'

'Absolutely,' I nodded.

He walked around the shelf and inspected the flamingo.

'Nice. A bit more sandpapering to do just there. Who are you going to give it to? Or are you going to keep it yourself?'

He removed his beret and self-consciously straightened his hair.

'No, it's for Mum. It's her birthday soon.'

'Oh. Then that'll make her happy. It's a bookshelf, isn't it? Does she like books?'

'Yes, a lot.'

I returned the varnish to the storeroom, poured water into an empty glass jar with half a mustard label on the outside, and put in the brush. Before I put the lid back on the tin of varnish I breathed the smell deep into my nostrils, my eyes closed. I loved that smell.

It was unexpectedly silent in the design studio. Suddenly I realised I was wearing Valter's t-shirt under my jacket. Valter's T-shirt that I had now irrevocably destroyed. I stretched out the fabric, stared at the text and sighed.

I CAN VERBALISE MY ANXIETY!

Fuck. *What the hell had I done?*

I hung about, not wanting to leave the storeroom. Then he called:

'I assume you had to let on about the shelf when you damaged your thumb?'

It went quiet. I considered not answering but it was obvious I must have heard. I went back out into the room. Valter had sat down at the teacher's desk.

'No, I didn't, actually.'

'So she doesn't know about the shelf?'

'No, not that either.'

I looked at him confrontationally. He looked at me with curiosity.

'What? Do you mean she doesn't even know about the thumb?'

'No.'

He stared at me, mastering the art of looking both stupid and ugly at the same time.

'Why not?'

*Here we go,* I thought.

'She lives in Norrköping and … she's been away.'

'Oh I see. You don't live with her?'

'No.'

*Obviously not,* I thought. *Do you think I commute to Stockholm every day, or what? Moron.*

The irritation ate away at me as I lifted the shelf from the workbench.

'So you live with your dad?'

*Give it a rest!* I wanted to say. The words were just about to leave my mouth when I remembered how he had so readily, so unselfishly, offered me his time, his design studio and his T-shirt. Ah, his T-shirt. I crossed my arms over my chest to try and hide it.

'Yes. I mean, I go to Jana's – my mum's – at the weekends. Every other weekend.'

'I see.'

He forehead was creased and I could see how much he was longing to ask why. I saw it in his look, in the small wrinkles around the corners of his mouth. I had seen that look on adults before. I said nothing, allowing the wrinkles to slowly disappear. It seemed as if he wasn't going to ask and I thought good for him for making the more commendable choice. But just when I had relaxed a bit, it came. The question.

'Not that it's got anything to do with me, but how come you live here and your mother lives there?'

Why did everyone think it was such a massive problem that I lived with Dad? Or, let me rephrase that: why did everyone think it was such a bloody great problem that I *didn't* live with my mum? There seemed to be something really aggravating about a mother who didn't look after her child full time, but these days I couldn't even be bothered to go through the issue of different demands being placed on men and women, and how a child who goes to its dad every other weekend isn't put through the same invasive interrogation.

'She likes the dialect, the trams, the football team. How the hell do I know?'

He looked at me and I looked at him. I struggled to look indifferent and unmoved. I stared at him as if he was a dead object, a dead pointless object. I gave him that look. Mum's look.

I repeated to myself:

*He doesn't mean anything, he is nothing, he is a stone.*

Eventually he looked away. There was a concerned look in his eyes. I had won but it hadn't made me especially glad.

At last he seemed to notice the T-shirt and gave a start when he saw the blood stain. His eyes narrowed in suspicion and I saw him trying to make out the text. Then he looked at me again and I stared challengingly back. He averted his gaze, got up from the desk, and walked towards the door. He was halfway into the corridor when he asked me to switch off the lights. I put the shelf under my arm and walked towards the door, banging my fist on each switch. The humming stopped and it went black. I wished I had a switch connected to my brain.

So that it could finally be dark and silent.
No thoughts to think.
No longing to long.

## A Two-dimensional Aquarium for Tiny, Tiny People

I didn't go to school on Wednesday. I didn't even make a half-hearted attempt to get up when the alarm on my mobile went off. Dad had left early that morning so I didn't have to confront him. I was woken up anyway at nine o'clock by a dazzlingly beautiful sun that did not match my mood in any shape or form. Yet again I had forgotten to pull down the blind.

Out of habit I checked Dad's emails and his Facebook page but there was nothing there apart from yet another cry of desperation from a wounded Denise. I deleted her and that felt good. I was more than happy to delete a few losers here and there. Perhaps I had the potential to be someone who guns down her classmates? I had the clothes for it, anyway. I even owned one of those floppy sports bags and there was a full-length leather coat hanging in my wardrobe.

I lay down on my bed again and looked at the wallpaper. In its black and white psychedelic pattern I could make out virtuous little lambs as well as wicked devils. I phoned Vrinnevi a couple of times but Dr Roos was busy, so very busy, and did I want to leave a message? No, I'd phone back. It was both a bitter disappointment and a massive relief each time.

Enzo called during the mid-morning break and I stared at the display where his name was demandingly illuminated but I was incapable of answering.

At eleven-thirty, as I lay channel surfing and half asleep on the sofa, there was a ring at the door. I dragged myself up, tip-toed into the hall and peered through the peep-hole. There stood Enzo, just as I thought. It was now lunch break. He waved at the peephole and I realised that somehow he must have heard me. I opened up.

He stepped in and shut the door quietly. We looked at each other, embarrassed, and said nothing. He was wearing a green Adidas jacket with white stripes down the sides. It was nice – he looked nice in it. Several times he drew breath as if to say something, but he remained silent. I tied and untied the silk belt of my dressing gown, but it wouldn't go right, somehow. Eventually he managed to say:

'Have you … cut your hair?'

'Yes.'

I ran my fingers through my hair.

'It's, um, nice. Short, like. Aren't you well?'

'Yes and no. Depends how you look at it.'

He went on, falteringly. He was probably not too good at this sort of thing. But who is?

'How … how are you feeling, then?'

I shrugged.

'Okay,' I said in a low voice, and went back to the sofa, switching off the sound of the TV with the remote.

I heard him taking off his shoes. He followed me into the sitting room and sat on the sofa, on the saggy part, which made him lean awkwardly towards me.

'So … did something happen in Norrköping or … I mean, you've been a bit weird since you came home. Well, not weird but … up and down. Changeable. I mean, you don't seem to have been feeling very well.'

'No.' I laughed. 'I don't feel very well.'

'Do you want to … talk about it?'

I shrugged again. Did I want to talk about it? I didn't know. He looked at me unhappily and I looked unhappily back.

'What are you watching?'

'It's called a TV. It's like a two-dimensional aquarium for tiny, tiny people. Minus the water.'

He smiled as he said:

'Cool.'

We sat like that for a while, side-by-side, looking at the TV screen where the tiny, tiny people moved about and opened and closed their mouths like fish. After a while Enzo asked if he could turn up the sound and I laughed and said no, and he turned the sound up. I asked if I could rest my head in his lap and he looked surprised, but said yes. In the two-dimensional aquarium there was a film, an American comedy that wasn't funny. Enzo rested his hand on my shoulder. At first he was tense but then he relaxed; I felt his body become softer and his hand heavier and I don't think we had ever been as close as we were then.

And as I lay there staring at the screen with an unfocused gaze, something suddenly came back to me: a memory sharp as a knife and vividly illuminated in the magnesium white. Clear and cold.

◆

*I am about three years old. I'm standing beside Mum and she is reading in the armchair. I pull at her trouser leg, try-*

*ing to get her attention, to let her know I want to pee and need the potty. I know I'm not supposed to interrupt Mum when she's reading, not unless it's absolutely necessary, but I have waited so long and now I can't wait any more.*

*'You'll have to be patient,' she says distractedly, turning the page. 'I've nearly finished.'*

*I wait. I see particles of dust lit up in the afternoon sun and I hope Dad will be home soon, but I have a feeling he won't. Perhaps not for a very long time.*

*Some pee has leaked through my knickers – only a little, enough to make it feel cold between my legs. I clench as hard as I can, standing with my legs crossed, and I think one thing and one thing only: I mustn't wet myself.*

*'Jana,' I say again. There is desperation in my voice.*

*'You'll have to wait! Soon, I said.'*

*But I can't wait any longer, I can't wait another second, and the cold changes to warm. And for a couple of seconds it feels almost pleasurable as the pee comes, and I let go and let all of it out. It's a warm stream down my leg, to my foot and to the floor. I look at Mum. She is reading. She doesn't notice.*

*The pee turns cold immediately; it stings like the shame that swiftly and weasel-like replaces the pleasure.*

*Mum closes her book.*

*'So kleine. Done. Now.'*

*When she sees it is already too late she is furious. Her eyes – I am afraid of them. They are so harsh.*

*'I told you to wait, didn't I?' she says, and her voice is cold and angry and she holds my arm tight and drags me to the toilet where she briskly sits me down on the potty. I have to sit there for a long, long time, even though it is all fairly pointless.*

*There isn't a drop left to squeeze out.*

◆

Enzo got ready to stand up. I didn't let him. I made my head heavy.

'I have to go,' he said. 'Break's nearly over.'

Gently he lifted my head from his lap, stood up, and left me. I lay there with my cheek against the sofa cushion that was still warm from his body. I heard him carefully put on his shoes, open and then close the front door. And leave me.

I lay on the sofa all day in my silk dressing gown, like a glamour-girl in a detective novel. I saw the sun sink in the sky. At some stage, I don't remember when, I got up, fetched the phone and called Mum's mobile. It went straight to voicemail and I assumed her battery had run out. So I phoned Vrinnevi but by this time Dr Roos had gone home. Then I phoned the university. At first I heard Mum's recorded voice saying: Jana Müller, and then one of those automatic voices took over, saying: "Extension three four five six is not available. Please try again after the thirtieth of April. If you would like to leave a message …" I hung up.

I blinked, hard.

So she had been in touch with the university. I assumed that was good but I couldn't bring myself to feel happy about it. I only noted coldly that her plan clearly was to return. The thirtieth of April. In twelve days.

She had contacted the university. But not me.

I went out onto the balcony. The air was cold and clear, as it can be in spring. The sun was setting behind the trees and dusk was closing in on the horizon. Dead flowers were sticking up from the window boxes: brown snapped-off twigs with one small, light green stem that had survived the winter against all odds. I counted twelve cigarette butts in an old plant pot with a wilted stalk in a sodden lump of earth. Was that Dad's weekend ration? Or several weeks' worth? Or was it desperate Denise?

It hurt so much that no one had contacted me, that no one had phoned. Not Mum. Not ... Justin. I didn't know him but I missed him, missed his copper-red hair, his white body, his pale, pale blue eyes. Short fragments of memory flashed through my brain: his pink washed-out jeans and his hot breath on my neck. The tweezers and the whisky. Timberlake and lime cocktails. My hands under his top there in the forest, his muscles tense from the kayak. Dampness and pine needles and moss. His hands under my nightdress by the stairs, my shoulder blade pressed against the floor, his body heavy on top of mine. The smell of pale yellow rubber, of honourable intentions.

I didn't know him but I missed him. I didn't even know if I was in love, but I missed him.

*I missed him.*

I leaned my forehead on the balcony railing. It was icy cold and cooled my whole face as I pressed my cheek, mouth, chin against it.

The tower at Telefonplan changed colour again. It was now glowing a bright turquoise in the window. Stark and slender it rose like an exclamation mark over Hägersten. There was a number you could ring and choose which colour would light up each level by pressing different buttons on the keypad. It was some kind of art installation. I phoned directory enquiries and was given a number that I called. I was driven on by the hope of power. Power to make something change. Something big.

The voice at the other end said you could make every

colour by mixing red, blue, and green, but I didn't understand that. How could you make yellow? I became almost obsessed about making yellow. I phoned and phoned, mixed and mixed, and it went green and red, and cerise and lilac, but not yellow. Perhaps someone else was phoning at the same time because the colours in the mast were not always the ones I pressed. I phoned again and again, and pressed the numbers, heard the ringing at the other end, more green, three, three, three, less blue, four, four, four. But I couldn't get yellow. If only I could get green minus blue, I thought, but you couldn't press minus, only plus. In the end I made a pale pink colour and that was the closest, so I settled for that. I said to myself:

'I'm happy with that. After all, I'm not a complete head case.'

When I heard Dad's key in the lock I hung up and came in from the balcony. As silently as a cat I crept into my room and shut the door.

# THURSDAY, 19 APRIL

*Obsessed*

It was Mum's forty-fifth birthday and I had just stepped out of the shower.

Forty-five years. And she wasn't even giving me the opportunity to congratulate her.

I hadn't set the alarm for today either, but even so I had opened my eyes at one minute to seven, as wide awake as if someone had poured a bucket of ice-cold water over me. I still wasn't quite sure whether it was right to give into the enormous resistance I felt about going to school. I tended towards a "dunno". A resounding "dunno."

Dripping water I walked through the flat, looking for a towel which wasn't quite as wet as the one Dad had left on the bathroom floor. I went into my room and managed to bump my hip against the chest of drawers where the laptop was standing. I swore. The screensaver disappeared and Dad's inbox appeared.

A new email had turned up.

From Mum. It had been sent only thirteen minutes earlier.

My heart stopped.

I touched the screen gently as if it would bring me closer to her. Then I sat down on the bed and carefully lifted the laptop from the chest of drawers, balancing it on my wet thighs. I took a breath and held it, to steel myself. Then I clicked on the email and it opened out across the screen like a flower slowly opening its petals.

Jonas

Last week I found out I have Asperger's Syndrome.

Naturally the confirmation is completely overwhelming.

A total shock, to be honest.

I am familiar with the diagnosis. I read about it while I was studying and afterwards too, and I noticed certain similarities with my own behaviour, but I still thought the symptoms I read about were much worse than the ones I have.

In general you can say that the diagnosis concerns a dysfunction in the ability to socialise and communicate.

How ironic: me, who always thought I was so good at communicating. But over the last few years I have started to realise that I do not communicate in the conventional way. I know I'm direct — too direct, some say. Can you be too direct? For me that is incomprehensible.

When I talked to my parents they said that Swedes are difficult because they talk around the subject, they don't say what they really think. You have to work it out for yourself, interpret what it means when they look down or turn their head away. Germans are more straightforward. They are explicit, they tell you what they are thinking and what they expect from you. That's a simplification, of course, but it's the way I have been thinking. I thought it was a culture clash and I'm still not sure it isn't, even if I understand of course that it isn't *only* that.

A person with Asperger's finds it hard to read other people's body language, understand what others are thinking and as a rule is socially clumsy and therefore finds it hard to make friends.

It always worries me when I am with other people. There are few people I can feel completely relaxed with. You were one of them, before. Maja is one, of course.

So I want to ask you: is that why? Is that why I am so alone? And is it a relief, then, to understand why? Or is it a burden?

I had to gasp for air. It felt as if someone had forced me down to the bottom of the ocean and anchored me there in the dark, chained to a rock. I was desperate to come up to the surface, desperate to breathe, to get oxygen!

I looked around the room in confusion. There were my everyday things, my clothes, my books – meaningless objects that I once thought were worth something. I struggled to understand. The only way was to go back. So I dived down again, returning voluntarily to the dark water.

People with Asperger's frequently have special areas of interest that completely absorb them, that they become obsessed with. I do not want to believe that's true.

I do not want to believe it's that simple.

It feels as if the only things I am genuinely intensely interested in – literature, psychology – have been reduced to symptoms of my illness! Except it isn't an illness, they tell me, correcting me. Even if that's what I've been calling it all the time. No, not an illness, but a "syndrome", a "disability", "a collection of personal character traits", "a disposition".

Of course. You can recover from an illness, but not from this.

Many people with Asperger's are dependent on routine.

I blushed when the psychiatrist said that. He might just as well have given me a slap. It felt as if he had been reading my private notebooks.

My routines help me, I want to have them. They aren't a problem for me, they are the solution! He said he thought the upset in my routine explained why I had to be hospitalised after our divorce almost thirteen years ago. Yes, I said. And also because I felt sad, I thought, but I didn't say it. Perhaps I've become Swedish now, I thought, now that all of a sudden I'm not saying what I think. That was a joke, Jonas. You see, I am joking. It is a social skill to be able to joke. But of course you have to joke in the right way, at the right time. Was this the right way, Jonas? The right time? Oh, it's a hard balancing act. It's so hard that you keep falling into the ditch time and time again. Can you see how I am also using metaphors? People with Asperger's find metaphors and similes difficult, find it hard to joke and most of all to understand other people's jokes. The psychologist said it was something that could be learned and practised, but that in general it does not come naturally for someone with this diagnosis.

But I feel it comes naturally. Doesn't it?

I don't know anything any more. Nothing feels certain. I have to re-evaluate myself, my surroundings, my entire life.

They tell me I have a monotonous voice and that upsets me, it upsets me terribly. I have never thought about it but I assume it has to be seen as neutral information, that it is among the symptoms and that therefore I shouldn't feel upset. The intention of giving me information is not to hurt me, surely?

Is my voice monotonous, Jonas?

In which case, what should I do about it?

A social interaction impairment. I presume you could call it that, give it that description. And that's what it is. In which case why is it so painful?

As I wrote earlier, when it was confirmed I was shocked. Well, shocked is an understatement to describe the reaction that completely engulfed me. I was unable to speak. I could not communicate. I lay on the floor in my psychologist's office and stared at the ceiling and could not bring myself to get up. I didn't know what there was to get up for. What I thought was me was only a diagnosis. There was nothing of me left. They had to commit me, as they say. Now I have been committed. Committed to a psychiatric ward.

And I swore I would never come back here.

It is terrifyingly the same, as if thirteen years haven't passed but thirteen days. Thirteen hours or minutes.

I remember when Maja was here, how she came in wearing that white dress, the one I bought in Germany. The way she held your hand. Her hair was in plaits that hardly reached her shoulders. Her hair was thin, each plait no thicker than a little finger. I remember her coming here and how she stood in the doorway not wanting to cuddle me, not wanting to give me the hug I was asking for. I don't think I have been an especially competent mother.

I don't want you to tell Maja. I want to tell her myself. I don't know how to formulate it yet. I hope she can come to stay the weekend after next, just as usual, but perhaps I should be realistic and not make any decisions yet. On Thursday we will discuss my discharge from hospital. For your information I have taken sick leave from the university.

This is a long email, Jonas. I hope I have made myself understood, despite my documented difficulties in communicating. It is my birthday today, if you remember. Forty-five years old.

Jana.

◆

I was naked and cold and I stood up without knowing it. I held the laptop like a baby to my breast. I swallowed. I swallowed again, but I couldn't dislodge the hard lump in my throat.

I remembered that. Now I remembered it. I had only buried it deep, deep inside. That bare room with yellowish-white walls, the ruby cross on the gold chain that hung around her neck. Mum, with greasy hair, with her arms folded across her chest, inviolable – I remembered that. She was silent, and thin. I was afraid of her. Afraid of everything.

But behind the words in her letter was a warmth that

hadn't come out then, not that I could recall. It was hard to imagine she had even written that email, it was so . . . emotional.

Dad. I couldn't remember him there. He must have been, of course, but I couldn't place him there in my memory.

Couldn't see him.

Is that because he was so familiar to me?

Or ...

Because he hadn't been able to protect me?

*Phantom Pain*

I walked along Vinterviken's shoreline, moving like a robot. Like a super-efficient, unstoppable machine. I went past the boat club, the rocky outcrops, and the old, graffiti-covered blasting bunkers, and on past the abandoned sailing boat. Then round the bay and out along the promontory, where it was windswept and desolate. I heard my breathing amplified as if through small loudspeakers. I felt my heart about to burst in my chest and the tears running down my cheeks. When I had walked once around the promontory I did it again, and then a third time. The sweat soaked through my hat. I did another lap and I made up my mind never to leave that dreary spit of land. I would walk like this for all eternity, following the same track, like the arm of a turntable playing a scratched record. The same groove over and over again. That's how I would walk, until my footsteps wore a hole in the ground.

And I walked.

And walked.

And walked.

The sun travelled over the sky, shadows crept over the grass, and morning turned into afternoon. People came and went, their dogs sniffing in the gravel. They lifted their heads and looked at me. Then looked away. I imagined I looked normal. Yes, I think that's how I looked, because my body was hard and determined, and I walked and walked and walked.

And while my legs were moving mechanically, hitting the ground with the regularity of a machine, my thumb was hurting. The bit that had been sawn off hurt. A phantom pain. Wasn't that what it was called? I passed the fingers of my other hand through the air over the top of my thumb. I couldn't feel anything. When I touched the actual tip I felt a different pain that soon ebbed away. After a while only the phantom pain remained, quivering there in the air, just above my thumb. Was this my pain, even though it was outside my body? And if it wasn't mine, then whose was it?

I walked and I walked and I walked.

But when the body was created it wasn't designed to walk forever, however strong the will power. I fell. I let myself fall. I dropped straight onto the damp grass, the sweat running down my face, my back, my chest. I hit my shoulder but I didn't care. I lay there with my chest heaving up and down, up and down. Violent, uncontrollable gasps. And then I shouted.

'*Shit!*'

My shout was carried off by the wind. I sat up and sucked ice-cold air into my lungs.

'*SHIT SHIT SHIT!*' I yelled, and a bubbly string of saliva was snatched away by a gust of wind.

Then I stood up, walked to the shore, and tore off my clothes. A thousand needle-sharp spikes hit my skin. The wind was blowing so powerfully and incessantly that it hurt. It stung. It was like being lashed. My skin became hard and cold and impenetrable. At last.

I walked to the water's edge and sharp pieces of gravel dug into the soles of my feet. I looked out over the water. It was grey and the wind was whipping up small spume-topped waves.

My voice was harsh as I said:

'It's only phantom pain. It doesn't really exist.'

And then I fell headlong into the water.

*Asperger's Syndrome*

I sat wearing Valter's bloodstained T-shirt, searching the internet to get some sort of clarity. Everything was so confusingly blurred, so bewildering and difficult. My hair had dried but my teeth were still chattering and had been doing so for almost an hour. It was like they would never stop.

*Asperger's syndrome.*

I read about lack of eye contact and remembered Mum's large eyes following me, appearing not to blink. How nervous it could make me, how irritated I could get. How beautiful they were.

I was so cold that my skin shrunk. I went to the kitchen and poured a glass of whisky. My hand shook and the neck of the bottle knocked against the glass. Dad drank whisky when he was cold. But he drank it when he wasn't cold as well.

Then I went back to the computer.

*Asperger's syndrome.*

I read about the difficulties in understanding how others think and feel and recalled the numerous tragicomic situations she had landed herself in, recalled the amazingly literal replies to check-out staff and librarians. How confused they became, how dumbfounded they were. I contemplated her inability to understand why those thoughtless comments she sometimes aimed at me left me feeling hurt and speechless.

*I consider you to be moderately intelligent, Maja. Verbally gifted, very gifted in fact. I mean, what chance did you have with us as parents? But apart from that: mediocre. Don't get me wrong! Mediocrity is good, despite what people say. It makes life easier. The extremes are hard to live with. Being unintelligent naturally makes life, school work und so weiter difficult. You have fewer choices then. But to be gifted, overly-intelligent, is also a curse. I want things to be different for you than they were for me. That is why your mediocrity, your . . . your averageness, makes me so happy!*

And her voice certainly was monotonous, now I came to think of it. So maddeningly expressionless and monotonous.

How *could* she not understand?

*And would it ever stop hurting?*

It felt as if I had been chilled to the bone and that I would never get warm again. I drank the whisky which tasted so harsh and rough, which smelled of smoke and tar and petrol. A stream of warmth flooded my mouth and then my throat, but it didn't manage to spread further out into my limbs.

*Asperger's syndrome.*

I read about being obsessed by detail at the cost of the big picture and saw in my mind's eye Jana single-mindedly scrubbing the tiles above the hand basin for hours, only to totally ignore the rest of the bathroom.

I drank and I drank and I drank.

*Asperger's syndrome.*

I read about stubbornness, resistance to change and difficulties with social interaction. I read about the need for routine, a gift for language, and an obsession with particular interests.

It was as if everything was falling into place. I saw this "everything" fall literally, like three-cubic-metre blocks of concrete falling from the sky. Piece by piece they fell into matching-sized holes that opened up in the asphalt. It all made such amazing sense.

Such terrible sense.

And to think I thought it was just Mum being Mum. And it turns out it was only a syndrome. A diagnosis.

And I thought the same as she did: What was she without Asperger's? Was there a core inside or was it only a void? A shell? A body?

Somewhere inside me I wondered if it wasn't those thoughts that had kept her lying there on the floor.

I understood her. I would have stayed there too.

I looked out of the window. The sky was a whitish grey and the clouds hung so low they seemed to be resting on the rooftops. My thoughts were as thick as treacle.

I shut my eyes tightly. What now?

What the hell was I going to do now?

*So Afraid of Your Words. And Your Silence.*

I pushed my way through the crowd, forced myself past stiff, stressed bodies. I jumped over cases, ducked under outstretched arms, and dodged children who stepped unexpectedly out in front of me. My breath was straining and my pulse was beating hard at my temples. I held the shelf close to my hip and the wood dug into my upper arm. There was the bus. Through the tinted panes of glass in the first floor waiting room at City Terminal, I could see there was no one outside the bus. Everyone had already got on. There was one solitary man below a window, visibly moved, teary-eyed. The driver gesticulated with his hand to indicate departure.

I ran as I have never run before, with only one thought in my head: *'I've got to get on it, I've got to!'* I just made it inside the sliding doors of the airlock before they shut behind me. It took forever before the outer doors opened. Blue-grey clouds of exhaust fumes surrounded the bus. I dived in through the rear door, which was still open, while the driver was crushing a cigg to death with his well-polished shoe. I sank down on a seat and leaned back into it with the shelf on my lap and darkening spots of light behind my closed eyes.

◆

The bus was cold but the radiator at my feet was burning hot. I looked down at a bus shelter covered in graffiti, the scratched plastic cover of the timetable, and behind it a brown field. Suddenly heavy snowflakes started floating gently through the greyish half-daylight. Snow! Again! It had hardly snowed at all during January and February but now it was snowing for the second time in April. Weird.

The dirty ditches lining the road were slowly dotted with white. The engine sounded far-off. No one was standing at the bus stop and no one got off, but we stopped anyway. An icy blast of air swept in through the doors.

There was a girl sitting in the seat in front of me. I caught a glimpse of her between the seat backs. She was about ten or eleven, with tangled blond hair, a rustling red jacket. She turned round and looked at me with large wet eyes, and whispered so I could hardly hear:

'Have you got cancer?'

And perhaps it was the hair. Or perhaps it was me.

I shook my head many times, too many times, but I didn't say anything.

She turned to face the front again, not saying anything else. She just sat there, completely still.

*No. I haven't got cancer, but my mum's got Asperger's syndrome.*

The bus began to move slowly and then it swung away from the bus stop, picking up speed. It drove onto the motorway, skidded slightly on a sharp bend, and picked up even more speed.

I couldn't distinguish the trees. They had melted together into a black impenetrable wall. I leaned my forehead against the glass and felt a raw chill against my skin. We went into a tunnel. There was darkness and cold orange lights. I was breathing heavily. The mist from my breath lay like a skin over the window and I drew my finger through it. Thin brown water fastened in the fine lines of my fingerprints. I closed my eyes. The pulsating light forced its way through my eyelids, one pulse for every orange light we passed. I shut my eyes tighter.

It looked like fire, burning.

I thought:

*Mum*

*Mum*

*Mum*


*I'm so afraid of you, Mum, of your words and of your silence. I'm so afraid of sudden icy roads, of being crushed against the side of a mountain. Afraid of dying and not being able to think anymore. Except, of course, that would be sublime.*


But there were no mountainsides, only trees and fields where the clay-like earth had frozen in ploughed furrows. The only thing I saw in the window's reflection was myself, my eyes wide open and panic stricken. There it was again.

That look that wasn't mine.

That was my mother's.

It was 1 o'clock and we were travelling through an endless tunnel. It was as dark as night, or hell.

◆

When we swung into the bus station at Norrköping, like an hour later, the heavy snowflakes had changed into vile rain and the greyish-white light was back. I got off the bus, wet a tissue with rainwater, and gently rubbed away the blood around the varnished heart on the shelf. It didn't all disappear but it looked very nice anyway.

A heart with a floating, blurry halo.

*Was I Even There?*

Looking back it seems unreal.

Was I even there?

Was she?

The images are dreamlike. Indistinct and static, like grainy black and white photos taken by amateurs with artistic ambitions.

She was sitting there, wasn't she? On the bed with that pale yellow bedspread pulled tight across the sheet. Her hair a shiny brown, her eyes large and wide, like open windows. Her head bent over a book, her upper body unnaturally hunched, as if she had a slipped disc. Like a cat. Or … the curved neck of a flamingo. I didn't know if I ought to think it was a comfort or not, that she was sitting like she always did.

And me? I stood there, didn't I? In the doorway, with the blue-white fluorescent light in my eyes, the shelf pressed tight under my arm. So tight my arm trembled, that I trembled.

'Mum,' I said, but my voice was only a dry whisper, like when you pulverise crisp, dry leaves between your fingers.

*I said Mum. Not Jana. I don't know why but I said Mum.*

I tried again:

'Mum. Happy birthday.'

*Mum. It felt was so unaccustomed in my mouth. Like a pet name you are not used to using, unsure even if you are allowed to.*

She continued reading her book and didn't look up.

Her book.

*Happy birthday, Mum.*

Suddenly a thick, glutinous rage rose up inside me. Unpredictable, instantaneous.

*The books.*

As if I had eaten something that didn't agree with me and I needed to vomit.

*Mum. Happy birthday.*

I hated them.

*Those crappy books!*

My greatest rivals. Always.

But at the same time my shortcut to her, my way of getting close, of being included. Always.

*Congratulations.*

She licked a finger, turned the page.

I saw it as if through a strobe light, black pauses between illuminated still pictures. Pulsating blue-white light.

And then.

Precisely when I thought she would continue reading she looked up briefly.

Her eyes wide, her look unyielding.

That look.

*Dismissive and impenetrable? Or only dismissive? Not deliberately so? Would I ever know — was it the syndrome or her? Was it her or the syndrome?*

And all that rage simply fell away.

I put down the shelf.

Her look, however you described it, held me, nailed me fast. I stood there, my pulse like hammer blows in my thumb.

She went back to her book again, directing her eyes away from me.

Her eyes made of glass. And she carried on reading. As if I wasn't there. As if she had looked up because she had heard an unexpected sound and catching sight of the source judged it irrelevant.

I didn't know what to do, so I did nothing.

I just stood there, the heart showing between my hands, longing for her to say my name. But of course she was so very bad at that.

And then her voice, clear. Her gaze directed at her knees.

*Were her eyes moving over the lines, over the pages?*

'You shouldn't be here.'

*Was she continuing to read?*

I thought I couldn't be hearing right.

And then, louder:

'You have to go. You shouldn't be here.'

*Was she continuing to read while she was dismissing me?*

I took a step forward, approaching her slowly, the way you approach a timid animal.

*But it's me,* I wanted to say. *Me, Maja. You wrote that you could be completely relaxed with me. Only with me. Do you remember?*

But I said nothing.

Nothing.

She looked up at me, her eyes cold.

'You have to go. You shouldn't be here. It's wrong.'

I stayed where I was.

And then there was her voice, unexpectedly strong as

if it was coming from somewhere else, like out of a loud-speaker in the ceiling. Did her mouth even move?

'GO!'

I backed out of the room, my eyes glued to her, to her grey-green eyes that seemed not to see me but a point immediately beside me. Those eyes that could be looked out of but not into.

I backed out and tripped over the shelf, which fell to the floor with such a loud crash it echoed through the corridor. I staggered backwards but grabbed hold of the doorframe and hung on tight.

I hung on tight.

After a moment indefinitely frozen in time I regained my balance. I picked up the shelf. With infinite care I picked it up. I felt the sandpapered wood against my arm like a caress.

And then I ran.


Looking back it seems unreal,
    Was I even there?
    Was she?

## I Want to Be a Machine

The tears blotted out the reality, obliterated the sharp contours, and made the lights shine in the shape of six-pointed stars. Here I was, running again. I ran through the corridors with the shelf clamped under one arm. I wanted to run fast enough to fly, I never wanted to come down again, but my heavy boots brought me pitilessly back to the ground. I swerved to avoid some people in white coats who were all walking in the same direction but not together.

*Why weren't they walking together?*

I ran through the main doors and out, past the bus turning circle and on towards Gamla Övägen. The rain fell in hard drops and merged with my tears. I ran and ran and ran. I ran until I couldn't run any more and still I kept running. The air I breathed in was cold and raw and tore at my lungs. I ignored the stabbing knife pain in my side and put one foot in front of the other, over and over and over again.

I wanted to be a machine that never stopped running.

I wanted to be a machine that couldn't feel.

I wanted to be a machine, like her.

I ran past a car park, a cluster of trees, a roundabout.

I ran on asphalt wet with rain, through grass ten centimetres high, over lethally spinning gravel and back onto asphalt again.

Suddenly I lost my grip on the shelf and it fell to the ground with a noisy clatter. I ran on for a few steps before I was able to stop, like a runner who has just passed the finishing line. Slowly I walked back, my breathing laboured. I picked up the shelf and started to walk towards town again, but changed my mind. I shouted out loud, a high-pitched, unarticulated yell, took a firm grip on the shelf, and lifted it above my head before slamming it down onto the damp black asphalt. The impact was powerful and the wood creaked its objection, but the shelf stayed in one piece. It was solid workmanship: I had hammered as well as glued the joints together. I could feel my thumb throbbing but I didn't perceive any pain.

*If your heart should break in two, make it whole with Karlsson's glue.*

I picked up the shelf and smashed it down on the asphalt again.

*If your brain explodes, shrinks or erodes*

And once again.

*Do not fear, stand stiff or pale!*

And again.

*It can soon be mended with a five-inch nail!*

And then I stamped on the wood with my steel toe-capped boots; stamped on it, jumped on it, kicked it away from me in a shower of splinters.

The adrenaline was pumping through my body, making it feverishly hot. I didn't stop until all that was left of the wood was its original form, although more jagged at the edges. But the side pieces I had cut out with the saw were totally wrecked. You would never be able to tell they had once been in the shape of a flamingo.

I shut my eyes, reached out to grab a lamp post but missed and fell headlong into a ditch. A shelf edge dug into my side, between two ribs, but it didn't bother me.

The grass was wet and cold but it didn't bother me.

Mum was locked in a psychiatric ward but it didn't bother me.

Mum didn't want to know me but it didn't bother me didn't bother me *didn't bother me. Because I was a machine.*

## My Bloodstained Heart in a Ditch

I heard footsteps, heels against the asphalt. Regular, hard steps like the beat from a simple drum machine, one of those you get on a cheap synthesiser. I closed my eyes. It sounded like the introduction to New Order's True Faith. Probably the best track I have ever heard, perhaps the best in the world. The rain was falling in fat, heavy drops. I moved my lips but no words came out. It was only in my own head that I heard it:

*I feel so extraordinary*
*Something's got a hold on me*
*I get this feeling I'm in motion*
*A sudden sense of liberty*
*I don't care cos I'm not there*
*And I don't care if I'm here tomorrow*
*Again and again I've taken too much*
*Of the thing that costs you too much*

Suddenly the beats stopped. I opened my eyes but couldn't really focus. Directly in front of me someone was crouching, wearing black leather boots with killer heels. Someone I seemed to recognise but couldn't place at all.

'Darling! What are you doing here?' she exclaimed.

It was Debbie. I recognised her by that throaty, rasping, two-packs-of-ciggs-a-day-since-her-confirmation voice. She was wearing a leather jacket with chunky zips all over it. The jacket was so small it looked as if it belonged to a child. With it she was wearing jeans, which were so tight they seemed painted onto her body.

'Hello Debbie,' I said, and my voice was thick as if I had been crying, and of course I had been.

She laughed.

'I'm not called Debbie, love. My name's Sarah.'

And she pronounced it the English way and I wondered if she really was English or was only putting it on. But I couldn't detect an Östgöta accent, so maybe she was.

'Come on, I'll help you up.'

'Okay,' I said feebly.

She pulled my arm and while she was doing that I thought about the fact that Justin was not called Justin and Debbie was not called Debbie and Mum was not called Mum and it made me so indescribably tired that I was almost overcome by acute narcolepsy.

I got back up on my feet and she told me to turn around so she could brush off the grass and the gravel and the splinters, and she didn't ask me why I was lying in the ditch like a rough sleeper or a crack whore, and that was just as well because I didn't have the strength to answer. When she had finished she fished a packet of cigarettes out of her shiny red handbag, lit one, and inspected me critically. She picked a brittle leaf from what was left of my bangs with her cigarette hand, the orange glow only two centimetres from my eye. She stroked my hair softly, just like the first time we had met, and I swallowed a sob. She asked:

237

'Where are you going?'

It sounded as if she meant not only geographically but also existentially. But perhaps I was reading too much into it.

'I don't know,' I said, answering both questions.

She raised her eyebrows and started walking away, and I stood there, unable to decide what to do. For a brief moment I considered laying myself down in the ditch again, but I didn't do it. She had put so much effort into brushing off the leaves and grass and I wasn't the ungrateful type. Debbie whose name was Sarah pushed one hand into her jacket pocket – which sat so high up that it looked as if she was touching her own breast – and stamped her heels so hard in the asphalt that it sounded like pistol shots. She turned round, walked backwards for a couple of metres and nodded with her head on one side, indicating that she wanted me go with her. I obeyed like a homeless dog and caught up with her.

I left my bloodstained heart in the ditch. It would survive the rain, I thought. I had varnished over it, after all.

'Where are you going?' I asked.

'Only home. It feels as if I've been in Hades and been given one more chance to live.'

'What's … what's happened?

'Nothing's happened. Nothing that doesn't happen every day. I work on a geriatric ward, with old people, you know? It's a bit better than residential care but you still have to wipe their arses.'

I pictured her in a short, half-transparent white coat, unbuttoned lower than was respectable, bare legs, and red lips. If ever you were forced to have your backside wiped by anyone, you would choose her. She threw her cigarette butt into a puddle and immediately took out the packet again. This time she lit two cigarettes. She held the filters tight between her front teeth and as she searched for her lighter she curled her upper lip like a predatory animal ready to attack. Then she found it, drew on both cigarettes at the same time, and gave one of them to me. I didn't protest but even so she said:

'You need it, that's why.'

We walked in the direction of town, she in front, me half a metre behind, awkwardly smoking my cigarette. I didn't inhale deeply because I didn't want to cough. I would have liked to talk a bit to dispel some kind of cloud but I couldn't come up with a single thing to say. As we came to the southern part of town Sarah said:

'I live over there.'

She pointed to a row of low-rise yellow brick flats. A bright yellow and apparently empty tram approached and obscured the flats for a second. The ground shook. We stopped and allowed it to pass.

I felt the desperation return. Like carbon dioxide bubbles full of fizzing reluctance they filled my insides. I had kept it at bay while we were walking, as long as my legs were moving, as long as I heard the beat of *True Faith* over and over again, but now it was back, spreading from my stomach and out into my arms, my legs, my head. An aggressive, furious desperation.

I looked at her and suddenly flung out of me, vomited out of me:

'Sarah. Can I come home with you?'

My voice was steady but I was shaking inside. I hated asking people for things. I never wanted to risk being turned down, rejected.

It wasn't worth it. The split second before she answered

239

felt like an eternity and I squeezed my eyes shut and waited for the worst.

'Sure,' said Sarah, and spat out the chewing gum I hadn't seen her chewing. 'I've got to work an extra shift in a few hours, but no problem.'

◆

I lay on Sarah's unmade bed, on the duvet that smelled of musk and sweat. She was having a shower. I heard the water splashing against the tiles, splashing against her body. She was singing, something low-key, sensitive.

The bandage on my thumb was soaked through and indescribably filthy. I was reminded yet again of the follow-up appointment I had managed to suppress. The dressing should have been changed days ago. Without really thinking about it, I began to unwind the bandage slowly, unbelievably slowly. It was a long bandage, over a metre. The skin underneath was spongy and white. The tip of my thumb was dark pink but unexpectedly smooth under the stitches. Six stitches there were, in all: six small black stitches very close together. I compared my two thumbs. The left one was missing perhaps half a centimetre, precisely as Dr Levin had said, but strangely enough the end of the thumb that was now flat rather than rounded looked quite natural. On the other hand, the black thread against the red flesh did look macabre. I briefly pressed the sawn-off nail and felt the blood rush to it in orgasm-like pulses, minus the gratification. And here it was again, the phantom pain. In the sawn-off part, which wasn't there, which was thin air.

Sarah came out of the bathroom in a yellow robe without a belt, drying her hair on a threadbare towel. Before

I had the consideration to look away I glimpsed a pair of small breasts with pale pink nipples and, lower down, curly reddish-blond pubic hair. I felt a warm blush spread over my cheeks.

'Can I see?' she said, and pulled my hand towards her.

She held my hand in hers, studying it with her head tilted back a little, her eyes squinting as if she needed glasses.

'It actually looks okay . . . it's closed up well. Healed well. I can help you with the stitches if you like.'

'They're not supposed to be taken out until Monday.'

'Thursday, Monday, big difference. You do what you like.'

She let go of my hand and sat on a chair.

'Well,' she said. 'Are you going to tell me?'

'What?' I said, but that was stupid because she knew that I knew that she knew.

What was wrong.

She rolled her eyes and tried to blow the hair from her forehead. It didn't work because it was wet and stuck fast and was too short as well, although not quite as non-existent as mine. She looked so different without make-up, her face naked, almost childlike, despite the tiny fine lines around her mouth. Her eyes did not look quite so slanted and predatory.

'Sweetie, either you want to or you don't. Makes no odds to me. If you want to then I will listen whole-heartedly. If you don't want to then we'll chat about something else, about violence or the weather. Or wiping old people's backsides. That's not as monotonous as you'd expect. You can't imagine how many different types of backsides there are. The point is: you decide. But don't talk a lot of crap about nothing being wrong. No one bloody well hangs about in a ditch on bloody Thursdays at three o'clock in the afternoon. In a pile of broken planks. You're not some bloody park bench alkie.'


I told her.

I actually did.

There was something about her unsentimental attitude that made me. I knew she wouldn't humiliate me by throwing her hand to her mouth in wide-eyed horror. She wouldn't feel sorry for me or pity me with sickly-sweet words.

I lay on her bed with my eyes fixed on the ceiling, looking at the cracks where the emulsion was flaking off and hanging down like a child's outstretched hands, and I told her about Mum and Dad, and about me. And when I bent the truth, as I had learned to do, I told her that I was bending it, and the reason I did it was so Sarah wouldn't think my mother was too weird. So Sarah would understand her and sympathise with her.

Sometimes I turned towards Sarah and met her gaze, seeing those eyes narrowed in concentration. Sometimes she got up, fetched a cigarette, or some clothes to put on – a small pale pink camisole top with turquoise lace, a pair of dark blue ridiculously tight jeans – all items one or two sizes too small so that they squeezed her body and gave it bulges, even though she was as thin as a heroin addict. At those times she held up a finger and I stopped talking, paused, breathed, until she came back with her concentrated attention, a warm spotlight focused on me. If it hadn't been for the fact that I was telling her something painful I would have enjoyed it, enjoyed that undivided attention from someone I presumably admired.

It got to four p.m., then five and then six, and then

at seven my phone rang and I got up and looked at the display, and of course it was Dad, Dad who had realised I wasn't at home. I couldn't bring myself to answer, because what would I say? What would he say, and what would we say to each other? So I switched it to silent and put it back in my bag.

'That's it, I think,' I said, suddenly embarrassed that I had taken up so much time, that I had been given so much of that coveted attention. I felt hot, almost as if I had a high temperature, as I sat down on the bed again and the duvet was warm, too, where I had been lying.

'Was that it?' she asked. 'Was that all of it?'

'Yes … or no. I don't know. I think so,' I said and then I don't remember any more.

I must have fallen asleep from exhaustion.

# FRIDAY, 20 APRIL

*The Brain as an Accessory*

I slept and slept and slept. I slept for twelve hours and in that time Sarah left, worked her extra shift, and came home again. I woke up when the door slammed and she dropped her bag noisily onto the hall floor.

'Oh Lord,' she said. 'It's like having a little pet. A little lazy cat. Are you still sleeping?'

'Yes,' I said weakly, trying to prop myself up on my elbows. 'Or I mean no, of course,' I added quickly.

My head felt heavy and I thought that this is what it must feel like to be drugged. Sarah went into the kitchen without taking off her shoes, her heels tapping on the wooden floor. She filled a large glass with water that she drank in one go, standing up. I was overcome by a sudden need to pee and had to hurl myself out of bed and run to the toilet.

'You phone's buzzing again,' called Sarah. 'Do you want it?'

'Yes … okay,' I said, and heard her run into the hall and root around in my bag. After a while she stuck the mobile through the door I hadn't had time to close.

Dad.

I just missed the call and that was lucky because it

meant I didn't have to decide whether to answer or not. The display lit up. I had twenty missed calls. I went into the calls list: eighteen from Dad and two from an unknown number. *Oh God.*

There were seven messages on my voicemail, all from Dad, in which he sounded alternately angry or worried about where I was. His last message, which I had missed by only a few minutes, told me that he had reported me to the police as missing. I texted a guilty "dont worry home soon" and was immediately assaulted by a call from his mobile that I cut off.

Sarah's heels came closer and stopped right outside the door.

'Cat, have you got stuck in there?'

'No, I'm coming.'

I tore off a piece of loo paper and it got caught in the stitches at the tip of my thumb. I grimaced. The painkillers had worn off and the pain was immediate and intense.

When I came out she was sitting on the kitchen table, still wearing her outdoor clothes. She was about to say something when I interrupted her.

'Can you take out the stitches after all? They kind of like catch in everything I touch.'

'Sure, cat.'


She sterilised a small pair of pliars absolutely not meant for the purpose but for something else entirely – cables, maybe – and gesticulated that I was to sit at the table. She took a firm hold of my thumb and then she clipped off the stitches one by one, drawing out the thread with her nails, and using tweezers where they were too difficult and had grown into my skin. It hurt and I grunted primitively with every stitch. When she had finished she picked up the bits of black thread and put them in a flower pot. Lighting a cigarette she said:

'You know, I really don't know what I'm going to do with you. I can't have you here. Like, I've got to sleep and my sister's coming tonight from Bristol and well … it's not really convenient.'

She looked at me apologetically – but not *that* apologetically – and before the feeling of rejection seeped into my body and made me go cold I had time to think: 'Sister? Is there another one like her?' A small suspicion that she was lying rose up and stuck there, stubbornly refusing to leave. But what did that matter? The essence was: she didn't want me here. No one wanted me with them.

'But I've been thinking. It doesn't seem like you want to go home. I mean, I couldn't help noticing that your dad's phoned you a number of times. You'll have to excuse me looking in your bag but it buzzed once every fifteen minutes. Well, anyway. I could take you home to Jens, if that's okay?'

And I thought: 'Who the hell is that?' but I didn't know what else to do with myself so I looked her in the eye and nodded bravely. I felt the naked, soft tip of my thumb warily, over the skin where black threads had left their mark.

◆

Sarah and I took the 116 bus out to Smedby and it was only when we were getting off at Mum's bus stop by the shop that I realised it was Justin she meant. That Justin was Jens and Jens was Justin. I turned to her and said:

'No.'

And I began to walk back towards town and a cold wind made my body shudder.

'What do you mean, no?'

'What do you mean, "what do you mean no"? No as in no as in no.'

She ran the few metres I had walked to catch up with me and took hold of my arm, but I refused to look at her.

'Is it hard that your mum lives here?'

'No. Or, yes, perhaps, but that's not why.'

'Well what is it then?'

'It's nothing, it's just … *no*.'

'Come on!'

She held me resolutely under my arm and started to walk towards the houses. I resisted but she pulled me so hard my arm started to hurt and I stopped struggling. I didn't need any more pain.

'He's really nice. Kind. Funny.'

'I know,' I said. 'I was there, remember?'

She gave a laugh. I turned to her, questioningly. Her pale hair flapped in the wind.

'It's really weird, I can't believe we were together, him and me.'

'What?'

'But that was a hundred years ago,' she said swiftly, and added: 'At least.'

*He hasn't phoned me, he hasn't phoned me, he hasn't phoned me, and I'm so exposed now because we had sex and it to-tally knocked out my ability to navigate and I can't take any more, I can't fix it, and as if everything else wasn't enough, as if having a mum on a psychiatric ward wasn't enough, it turns out he's even shagged Sarah and why would he choose me after being with her? It is so embarrassingly pathetic to think like that but it actually does seem as if no one wants me. As if no one at all. Wants me. Me. I'll stand on the street with a For Sale sign round my neck – no, better still, I'll advertise myself in an online paper, or maybe even put myself up for auction online. That's more my style. Me, young me. Me who craps the internet.*

So Sarah rang his door and I stood like a victim in Valter's bloodstained T-shirt which smelled of sweat and stale cologne and was generally rank just like me, and Mum's house was dark, dark and silent, and that was to be expected because of course she wasn't there. I realised it was better before, when I didn't know where she was, when I could believe anything had happened, but not that, not the way it was now.

Sarah must have phoned him while I was asleep because he didn't look surprised to see me when he opened the door, with pale blue jeans and matching eyes, and he would have done otherwise, wouldn't he? He invited us in and we stood in his hall where I had stood before, barefoot that time with only splinters in my foot and possibly a thorn in my heart, but not like now with a sodding great wooden pole through my frontal lobe that had made my brain run out and lie there rather attractively on my shoulder like an accessory.

He asked if we wanted coffee and Sarah said:

'Hell yeah,' and I could clearly see them ripping each other's clothes off, taking it in turns to suck each other's nipples, their eyes closed in desire like in the movies, and I was a prop. My whole being was an accessory, an old, ugly, useless, pointless accessory.

But Sarah left before the coffee was even made, blowing a kiss at Justin and was it only me but did that kiss land on his dick? She gave me a kiss me on the cheek and said:

'Cat, it's all going to be okay. You don't think so now but it will all be okay, I promise you. I bet you a hundred kronor.'

A hundred kronor.

For some reason that didn't comfort me.

♦

After Sarah left it went quiet. I sat on a chair in the kitchen and Justin stood by the cooker. He cut off the top half of a coffee filter and said:

'It's too big for this machine.'

And I thought: I'm too big for this world or else the world is too small for both of us or else this kitchen is. Nervously I flicked through a newspaper. Idly I looked at the small ads. Found a perfect one that I tore out.

Am a well-built man, 58. Do you want to moor at my jetty? Obese need not reply.

Like a pensioner Justin counted out loud the number of coffee scoops he put in the machine and then pressed the red button. The machine began to gurgle and bubble. Then he switched on the extractor fan over the cooker and smoked under it, standing in what looked like a very uncomfortable position. I noticed his hands were dirty, oil stained, and there was a wound, fairly recent: a pink fleshy cut right across the back of his hand.

'Watch out your hair doesn't get caught,' I said, and I meant in the fan but didn't say that and it was a joke but neither of us laughed, and then it was quiet for quite a long time, an uncomfortable silence, and I became aware that we no longer had the same hair style. And I heard music playing quietly in the other room, something instrumental, jazz-like.

'I didn't think I'd be seeing any more of you,' he said then.

'Really? Why not? My mum lives next door, for God's sake.'

He looked at me from over by the cooker, he looked at me as if I'd said something unsuitable – inappropriate in fact – and then he poured coffee into two cups. When he replaced the glass jug he spilled coffee onto the warming plate and it sizzled. Then finally he sat down; sat down opposite me.

We sat there sourly drinking our scalding coffee, which was also pretty sour, and I would have liked milk in mine but I wasn't effing well going to ask him for anything, wasn't going ask anyone for anything ever again. So I looked out of the window directly across to Mum's house that seemed so inaccessible, so uninhabited, and I saw the flower pots, the garden tools and the lawn mower under the steps and realised that the hedge was shapeless and straggly and not, like everyone else's, well-trimmed. Hedges, lives. Then suddenly Justin took hold of my hand and placed it in his greasy one. He stroked the palm with the tips of his fingers, and then one finger at a time: little finger, ring finger ... my hand tingled and the tingle transplanted itself to my lower arm, through my upper arm, into my ribcage and my thudding heart. And I thought: don't you try comforting me.

'Shit, half your thumb's gone,' he said softly.

That was an obvious exaggeration but I said nothing and with his thumb he stroked the pinky-red flat part where the skin was so thin that you could feel the bone directly underneath. The bone. The chopped-off bone.

The filed-down bone.
There was a flash.

*The saw.*
*The flesh.*
*The blood.*
*The pain.*

He studied at close range the tiny holes where the stitches had been. Twelve tiny holes. He stroked and stroked and it felt as if he was stroking the piece that was missing, which was no longer there, and it hurt so much but it didn't matter because it was bittersweet and that's exactly how it was.

He smiled at me but I didn't return his smile and it slowly died.

I looked away. The kitchen clock ticked. The music in the other room had become wilder, more discordant.

'Why didn't you phone?' I asked.

He dropped my hand as if it had burned him. It lay there dead on the table, the thumb-top pink, like the nose of a stiff, lifeless mouse. Silently we sat there. His gaze on the table, mine fixed rigidly on his eyes. When he looked up I would capture it, his look.

'God knows. I thought of it but ... I didn't do it.'

He looked up and I tried, but failed, to capture it. Of course I couldn't.

I didn't want to ask because I already knew the answer, but still there was some wicked little masochistic part of me that could not leave it alone.

'You saw the note?'

I so hoped he hadn't seen it, that it had blown away as it had done in my imagination.

'Yeah.'

I was quiet. He went on:

'I've still got time to do that, to call you. It hasn't been that many days. More coffee?'

He stood up and went over to the coffee machine.

'So are you planning on doing that?'

'Do you want me to phone now?' he grinned and I said:

'Yes. I do.'

So he picked up his mobile, dug out my note from a traditionally decorated letter basket on the wall and keyed in my number. My phone started to ring in my jacket pocket and it vibrated against my breast. I made no attempt to answer.

'Are you playing hard to get?' he asked.

'No, it's just that I'm not home,' I replied. He smiled his lopsided smile but he was standing half turned away so I wasn't certain if that smile was cool or warm.

Suddenly I felt I'd had enough. Everything was enough. I stood up.

'Look, I really appreciate the ... um ... coffee and ... and I ...'

If I wasn't careful I'd start sounding like Enzo.

'... I really want to go home. To Stockholm. But I haven't got any money. I really *hate* to ask but can you lend me a couple of hundred kronor?'

He looked astonished. Caught with his trousers down. I thought about that expression. I didn't know if I wanted to catch him with his trousers down any more. I didn't know if I wanted to catch him anywhere. By his dick, possibly. But that hole I was feeling in my stomach, that sweaty void, surely that wasn't for him? It was only hunger and anxiety, not love, surely?

'Of course.'

He sat down again.

'But you know what,' he said, taking a gulp of his coffee. 'If you haven't got anything against it I can give you a lift instead. I've got to go to Stockholm anyway. I hadn't planned to go today but it's not a problem, I can do it. I've got to deliver the Volvo to Sundbyberg.'

He nodded in the direction of the cherry-red PV that was standing shining in the hazy sunshine.

'Have you? Why?'

'I've sold it.'

'What do you mean, sold? I thought it was yours?'

'It *was* mine but now it isn't. I buy cars cheap, wrecks really, recondition them and sell them on. For loads of money.'

He took a wallet out of his back pocket, a thin, well-used leather thing, and slid a business card across to me. In shining gold seventies-style lettering it said:

*Foxy Cars – we buy, sell, recondition.*

With a telephone number but no name. Suspect.

'Keep it,' he said. 'Then you can always phone me.'

'Fuck you,' I said, and stuck my tongue out at him. And he said: 'I'd love to', and did the same and his tongue was lovely and pink and I went over to him and he tried to get up but I pushed him down onto the chair again and straddled him, and then we kissed. I mean, we might as well, we were already halfway.

*'I'll Buy a Glock'*

It was six-fifteen by the time we arrived in Örnsberg. Justin pulled up outside the front entrance of my block of flats and as I opened the car door to climb out he grabbed my jacket sleeve and drew me towards him. With his fingers resting lightly in the spaces between my ribs, one finger for each space, he kissed me. It was a warm kiss with plenty of tongue and those pale eyelashes lay flat against his cheeks, but I didn't close my eyes. I didn't dare to because I was afraid he would disappear. When eventually I got out of the car I was accompanied by a slight feeling of giddiness. He closed the door from inside and raised his eyebrows in farewell before starting the engine and steering the cherry-red car round the corner of Torsten Alms Gata, down to Stenkilsgatan and away. The chrome trim looked like flowing quicksilver in the evening sun.

I stood outside the door for easily ten minutes. I really didn't want to go up. The sky was a whitish blue, a delicate spring sky, and you wouldn't believe for a second that it had snowed only the day before. *What is it with the weather,* I asked myself. It was as confused as I was.

Finally I made myself tap in the door code with my phantom-pain thumb and walk up the three floors to our flat. As I stepped in Dad immediately rushed up to me from some indeterminate point in the hall.

'Maja! Maja! Maja!' he shouted, hugging me hard, and I relaxed and sagged heavily in his arms and I thought he smelled of stale sweat and I wanted to stay there forever. But then he pushed me away so roughly that I almost fell over onto the hall floor, and he yelled:

'Where the hell have you been? Have you *any* idea how worried I've been, *any idea at all?*'

'Yes but …'

'Be quiet!'

'But …'

'Be quiet, I said! *BE QUIET!* I didn't get a minute's sleep last night, *not a single minute!* I phoned Enzo and Jana and anyone else I could bloody well think of who might know, who might just have a clue where you were!'

'I…'

'SHUT UP!' he roared, and he was so furious I actually backed away.

'I had something important to tell you yesterday, Maja. I spent all day wondering how *on earth* I was going to do it. And when I came home and you weren't here I thought at first, good, I've been given some extra time, but I was still anxious and believe me it only got worse. I ate alone but I was thinking of you all the time, how you would take it, how the make-up would run in black lines down your face. When it got to eleven o'clock and no one knew where you were I called the police. I reported you as missing. I thought if you've been raped I'll kill every bastard in the whole of bloody Stockholm. I'll buy a Glock on the street at Sergels Square and gun down every dealer and every pimp and … and … and if you're dead then I'll kill myself, I will! Can you understand what you've put me through? Can you?'

His voice was softer now, almost beseeching, and I realised where my mass-shooting tendencies came from.

'No,' I whispered, deeply repentant. The tears were brimming up in my eyes and about to run in those black streaks.

He stood silently, looking at me. For several minutes he stood like that. Time after time I saw the anger sweep across his face like a dark cloud, without him saying anything. Finally he closed his eyes and breathed out.

'Jana is … in hospital, Maja. She's been taken into a psychiatric clinic.'

He looked at me so gravely that time seemed to stand still. I heard every sound as if amplified: the cars on the street outside, his breathing, the humming of the computer. I saw every colour more intensely, radiating towards me as if from a TV: his blue T-shirt, the red hall mat, the yellow Wellington boots in the photo.

'I know,' I said.

His eyes opened wide. They were bloodshot and he looked old, my dad. He looked a hundred years old.

'You know?'

'Yes, I know. I know because I was there.'

# END OF APRIL, AND MAY

*Like Small Flames Licking My Ribs*

I didn't go to Mum's the following weekend. Even if she had been capable of having me it felt impossible to continue with those Norrköping weekends as if nothing had happened. As if she hadn't disappeared. As if she hadn't said: *You mustn't be here.* However hard I tried to see it from her perspective, the feeling was incredibly strong. I didn't want to. I really didn't want to.

I stayed at home in Stockholm instead. Met Enzo, went to an occupational therapist and was given exercises for my thumb, finished my project in art and design and did my best not to bring my grade down, at the very least. The theme of the art project was "contact", which was ironic now, in the aftermath of Mum's disappearance, because recently time has been marked by such a lack of contact. I made my own interpretation of the lonely hearts ads I had been collecting over the past months. I painted in oils, water colours, and inks, made collages and stuck on beads, razor blades, stones, and whatever I could find. Even a flamingo. They ended up completely over the top, those pictures, and that's what Valter said too, in a tone that sounded as if he couldn't decide whether they were good or awful, ugly or appealing. I couldn't either, even if

I leaned more towards good *and* ugly. The whole project had an air of more is more. Less has never been one of my strong points and anyway I've never been especially good at less or, for that matter, interested in it.

I managed to avoid telling Dad exactly how I had found out that Mum was in hospital. I mumbled something about finding her diary and phoning Dr Roos, "forgetting" to mention the fact that he had never answered my calls. What upset Dad most was that I had spent the weekend alone in Mum's house without telling him, and he droned on about how we shouldn't keep such big secrets from each other. But I replied that there were obviously a whole lot of things he hadn't told me either, and that shut him up.

Walpurgis Night came with its celebration of spring and Enzo asked if I wanted to cycle down to Vinterviken and look at the bonfire. I can't say I've ever understood the point of it but I went with him anyway. I hung like a heavy sack over the handlebars, forcing my legs to pedal. It was such hard work, as if I was ill or too much lactic acid had accumulated in my muscles. We parked the bikes beside a tall birch tree near the allotments, my front wheel embedded in a pile of cigarette butts. My thumb was throbbing with pain as it did all the time these days as soon as I overdid things.

The bonfire shocked me.

It totally silenced me: silenced my head and the words and thoughts inside it.

It was enormous. Gigantic yellow and orange flames licked the cornflower-blue sky. I approached it as if hypnotised, walking directly towards it and far too close, like a moth drawn to a flame. Enzo had to grab my arm otherwise I might have walked straight into it and allowed myself to be swallowed up.

It crackled. The noise was extreme. Deafening. I had never thought of that before, how fires crackle so much, how the wood makes them do that. But that's how it was.

People came and went. Some of our old classmates from secondary school called out 'hello' from a distance, and Enzo raised a hand and nodded at them. Not me. I couldn't bring myself to do it. All I could do was stand and stare straight at the flames, deep into them. The yellow part of the flame was so pale at the very centre that it was actually white. I felt warm, at last I felt warm, and I don't think I had felt that since the day I jumped into Vinterviken and barely came up to the surface again.

I thought to myself: *Burn like fire in Cairo.*

Enzo understood the need to keep quiet. It must have been an hour later when he stroked my arm and nodded in the direction of the bikes. I was startled to see anything apart from the fire, to see green budding trees and grey-green water. To see his kind eyes and soft cheeks.

We cycled slowly home. When we were about to go our separate ways I said 'thanks', but Enzo only gave me a perplexed look and shrugged his shoulders.


So, Walpurgis Night came and went. She phoned me a couple of times, Mum, but I didn't answer. Obviously I knew she had been having a really difficult time, but I couldn't do it. I simply couldn't do it.

Most of May passed and I hadn't been to Mum's once, and neither was I able to miss her, now that I knew she was alive and more or less safe. Dad kept me regularly updated: she's left hospital, just so you know. She's started working again, just so you know. She asks about you, just so you know.

They seemed to be in touch more often. Sometimes they phoned each other but mainly they kept in touch by email. I checked his inbox occasionally – quite often in fact – and saw her name there, but I never read the emails. I don't know why but I didn't want to.

Dad, who stayed at home every weekend even though I hadn't asked him to, started to look anxiously at the calendar after a while, clearly concerned about me, but also perhaps because his decadent weekends had abruptly gone up in smoke.

'Have you stopped going there?' he asked.

'I think so,' I said.

'I see,' he said, nodding slowly. 'Right.'

I don't suppose he had much else to say. And he could hardly blame me.

I might not have been able to miss Mum but I missed Justin all the more. I touched that ugly business card, stroked my finger over his name and over the shiny gold words:

*Foxy cars – we buy, sell, recondition.*

But I didn't phone. I was about to do it to several thousand times but I didn't call. I guess it had something to do with pride.

When he phoned me for the first time, on the twentieth of May, and said: 'Hello, it's Jens,' I didn't realise who it was at first. Who the hell was Jens? But then I remembered. That it was Justin. Who was Jens. And when he told me he was going to deliver a newly reconditioned Corvette to Skärholmen that afternoon and asked if it was okay if he came round for a while afterwards, it felt like small flames were erupting in my heart. Small flames were licking my ribs. Burning like a fire in Cairo. It was exactly one month since he had left me outside my front door.

I said to Dad, slyly:

'You don't have to be here all the time if you don't want to. I'll be okay. You can meet up with Ola or … Denise. That's perfectly okay by me.'

And he looked shocked, verging on horrified, when he said:

'De …Denise? What? Do you … How do *you* know who *she* is?'

And I shrugged my shoulders and grinned.

'No idea. I expect you mentioned her some time.'

He looked particularly suspicious, his eyes narrow, his forehead wrinkled, but he made the most of the opportunity and disappeared that evening, so I was alone in the flat when Justin came.

When he rang the bell I was so nervous I was shaking. But I looked in the mirror and adjusted my face – eyes open but not staring, a smile forming at the corners of my mouth – to signal "mild interest". I opened the door. We said hello. It didn't work. Forget mild interest. I was far too flipping interested. He sucked my gaze into his and then he bent down and kissed me and then he kicked off his shoes and staggering like that we snogged all the way to my room.

I think we kissed for three hours nonstop. The bedspread got more and more crumpled, the nervousness slowly evaporated. The only pause occurred after an hour when Justin noticed a diploma from a school athletics competition that was hanging on the wall. I had come second in the high jump when I was in year six, my one and only athletics prize. When he saw the date he quickly worked out that I couldn't be eighteen, as I had so stubbornly insisted, and he propped himself up on his elbows, opened his eyes wide and said:

'First year at college? Are you only in the first year at collage?'

I nodded and laughed nervously.

'I knew it! I ... that was why I asked, there ... that time! I thought you were in the third year, at least. That you were about to finish. Shit! I knew it! How old are you? *Sixteen?*'

'Seventeen, actually.'

'Seventeen?'

'Yes, seventeen. It was my birthday in March. That's not so bad, is it?'

And he stared at me and I said nothing. Instead I leaned against him, pressing him down against the mattress and kissing him again. At first he hesitated, his tongue was yielding and slow, and I saw him staring sceptically at the diploma, but after perhaps twenty seconds he shut his eyes and responded hungrily. I interpreted this as if he had recovered from the shock pretty quickly.

Just after nine he had to leave to catch the last Norrköping train. He and Dad met in the doorway and Justin greeted him politely, took his hand and said: 'I'm Jens.' That hand, with its grease lines on the palm, its nails edged in unidentifiable grime. Dad looked astonished but glad as well in some way, and he said: 'I'm Jonas' and something bizarre like 'Pleased to meet you.'

The following day, when I tried to check Dad's emails and Facebook page, I couldn't get access. The password had been changed.

*Perspective*

Late one Friday night when Dad and I were lounging on the sofa half-watching *True Romance*, he started talking about that family interview. He hadn't mentioned a word about it before, so I stared straight ahead like I was afraid to look directly at him, afraid he would stop talking. On the TV a bloody, trailer trash Patricia Arquette was stabbing James Galdofini in the foot with a corkscrew.

'At first they wanted me to go to Norrköping, but I couldn't … or rather, I didn't want to! Although I didn't say that. So we … we did it over the phone. It was so odd, being interviewed. It's usually me asking the questions. And she … the psychologist, Mia … Mia Lundgren or whatever her name was, she had a hundred questions about Jana. How she managed her job, her house, her relationships, even … even her hygiene, for crying out loud.'

He gave me a quick look. I concentrated hard on the TV, at Patricia Arquette in pink leopard-skin tights, off the shoulder blouse and turquoise bra. At the china figurine she smashed against Gandolfini's head.

'It was so hard to answer! I didn't exactly have up to date information. I've gathered some things – we've been in touch from time to time – and I've heard you mention one or two things, but otherwise I had to rely on what she was like thirteen, fourteen years ago.'

He took a sidelong glance at me and sat up straighter in the sofa. I grabbed the remote lying beside me. I needed something to hold, to hold on to.

'I don't know,' he said, hesitantly. 'Perhaps I should have told you about this? About the interview? About the … assessment?'

*Should he?* I shrugged and looked out of the window where the sky was a dull blue-black without a star to be seen. That is precisely what had made me so angry, the fact that he kept things secret from me, things that were important. But should he have shared them? I didn't know. I tried to see it from his perspective, but it was hard.

' …but Jana didn't want that, didn't want me to tell you. And in some way I felt I ought to respect that. I thought that if she doesn't get a … *diagnosis,* then it's unnecessary to even bring it up. More like … why worry you?'

The tower at Telefonplan lit up. A clear and practically neon yellow illuminated the windows on every floor.

Yellow! Someone had managed to get yellow!

Was that a sign?

I cleared my throat. To silence him. To gain time.

Because at closer examination I found I couldn't see it from his perspective. Not his and not Mum's. My own was too insistent and important; it lay in the way and blocked the view.

Because surely I was right about wanting to know about the speculation? About the assessment? Regardless of whether it had led to anything or not. I mean, I was her child! Wasn't I the one she was mother to? It was me she lived with, even if it was only every other weekend. Dad interrupted my thoughts.

'Then that psychologist asked a whole lot about Jana's competence as a ... as a mother.'

He fell silent. His forehead creased. He opened and closed his mouth repeatedly as if he couldn't make up his mind whether to say anything or not. There was a vacuum-like stillness between us, like when someone switches off a fan and it's only then you realise it has been on all day.

'That was the hardest thing. I knew so little! I know so little, I realised that then. I had no idea what it was like for you, and those questions filled me with anxiety, such huge anxiety. I sat there with the phone in my hand and that psychologist patiently waiting. But perhaps it wasn't anxiety for what it's like *now,* but more for how it *has* been. It brought up so many memories. She was so sensitive to stress, your mum. When you were difficult, you know, like all children . . . like if you didn't want to get dressed or whatever it was, she would just leave the room, leave you half dressed. She was completely inflexible. Or when you didn't want to eat the food she had prepared for you. She'd throw it in the sink, walk out of the kitchen and leave you sitting there, strapped in your chair. She kind of thought that ... that you ought to understand. You know: "I've *told* you to eat." As if saying it once was enough. She wouldn't try to talk you into it, coax you, or persuade you. Like you have to do with children. She didn't somehow . . . have that ability.'

Dad threw out his arms.

'Oh, I don't know! Perhaps you should have lived here all the time, but . . . you had the right to have her, to have your mother. And it gradually improved, I assumed. As you got older. And she's been so good about some things. She had enormous patience when you were in that phase, you know, when children are four or five and question absolutely everything. You were actually pretty unbelievable. Incredibly hard work.'

Dad smiled and looked affectionately at me. I felt the look against my cheek.

At that very moment Patricia Arquette made a firebomb out of a can of hairspray and a lighter and James Gandolfini's face was instantly covered in flames.

'You asked a thousand questions a day and it was driving me mad. We joked that you had inherited it from me, the probing journalist. But Jana was fantastic! When I left you there at the weekend and you started asking questions, she answered every one. Every single *one!* Every little question that came out of your mouth! And if she didn't know the answer, she would look it up, Google it or ring some department at the university. I remember one time, you had tormented me for a week with some question about space, or stars – I can't quite recall.'

He laughed.

'Anyway, I was taking you to Norrköping and we were sitting in the car and I think you asked me "why" every hundred metres, and I simply *couldn't* keep on answering! I just turned up the music. But as soon as we got to Jana's she phoned the astrological institute or maybe the meteorological service. And you sat there on her knee with your skinny little body and you were so happy!'

I smiled, because I could remember that. Not the question itself, even though it would almost certainly have been about space, but the feeling. The intensity of her attention. How important it made me feel. How valuable.

A little jolt of loss went through my body, because she was still like that.

We sat quietly for a few minutes, looking at the TV, watching them shoot each other. Christian Slater ducked in a red-splattered Hawaii shirt.

'But,' Dad went on. 'There was so much that didn't fall into place. Sometimes it felt as if nothing ever ran smoothly. Everything had to be planned, discussed, dissected. And her need for control! It almost drove me mad! That's why I had enough. That was why we separated. I couldn't cope with it any more.'

He stopped himself abruptly and looked sideways at me, guiltily.

'I probably shouldn't be talking to you about this,' he said.

'Probably not,' I replied.

On the TV Patricia said:

*Amid the chaos of that day, when all I could hear was the thunder of gunshots, and all I could smell was the violence in the air, I look back and am amazed that my thoughts were so clear and true, that three words went through my mind endlessly, repeating themselves like a broken record: you're so cool, you're so cool, you're so cool.*

And Patricia reminded me of Debbie who was called Sarah and her voice instilled in me some sort of courage and my heart began to beat hard with angry conviction.

'I … I think you should have told me.'

My grip on the remote hardened. As if it was crucial. As if I could control something with it.

'What? What about?'

Dad turned to face me. Our eyes met and I looked into

the golden-brown eyes that I hadn't inherited. I noticed how his hair curled and fell over his forehead.

'About the assessment. I had a right to know, regardless of what had happened. Regardless of whether she had been diagnosed or not. I mean, I'm her child! You're *both* my parents!'

He looked at me for a long time without blinking.

'Maybe you're right.'

'Don't you think I've understood that she's … *different?*'

'Yes…'

'I mean, what are you trying to protect me from? She's the way she is, anyhow! With or without the diagnosis.'

'Yes, yes, I expect you're right.

'Trust me, I *am* right.'

He sat in silence. After a while he said:

'Hmm. You are right.'

## Fucking Deadly

The last day of term was approaching. The last jittery days of my first year at college would soon be over. It was about as cataclysmic as picking your nose.

Dad had been insisting for ages that he wanted to be in church with us, but I thought that was unnecessary. It wasn't like I was graduating or anything. He allowed himself to be persuaded on the condition he could buy me some new clothes to wear. Not that I thought new clothes were essential – I mean, what was wrong with the old ones? – but I wasn't hard to convince. It's just that I hate it when people try to make clothes so absurdly important, as if they were some crucial statement of opinion. It's only material we cover ourselves with to protect our genitals and to stop us freezing. Okay, I won't kid myself, of course I cared. I didn't wear just any old thing. And clothes were a big concern of the New Romantics. But I refused to be a clothes *victim*, like the others of my fashion blog-damaged generation, and it would never cross my mind to wear ballerina pumps and cropped leggings or anything ridiculous like that just because they happened to be slightly fashionable.

I joked about wearing Valter's T-shirt. It was white and

genuinely made a statement, but Dad didn't think that was funny at *all*.

'With that T-shirt, all your inexplicable injuries and your concentration-camp hair style, I'd be reported to Social Services before the ceremony was over!'

I wasn't exactly delighted about that comparison of my hair, but rather that than looking like a Nazi. From one extreme to the other.

It ended up with both of us kind of having our own way: a mixture of new and old clothes. I bought a white dress with dramatically large red roses and a gathered waist at Judith's second hand shop on Hornsgatan. With it I thought I'd wear white gloves and my black steel-toed boots. I even sent a text to Sarah with a picture of myself and she swiftly texted back enthusiastically: 'Cat! You look fucking deadly!' and that made me happy because I'd rather look deadly than undead.

Anyway, the hole in my head had healed up well and I realised my fingers often made their way there to feel the place where the stone had hit me and where the skin was thin, smooth, and sort of shiny. Only a memory now.

As for my thumb, I had got used to it. I liked it. I'd relearned how to do up buttons with it, tie shoe laces and use a keyboard correctly. It was still painful and I still had nasty flashes of memory about the saw's metal teeth vibrating through my flesh, cutting off a piece of me. But I could put up with that. And that little part at the tip, the part that was no longer there, only hurt occasionally. Only occasionally did I feel that weird phantom pain.

# THURSDAY, 7 JUNE

*Mum*

At our end-of-term service in Kungsholm Church, the stillness and the atmosphere of weighty responsibility were striking. Even FAS-Lars kept his mouth shut and looked appropriately moved. Perhaps his parents had secretly crumbled a few sedatives into his breakfast cereal so he wouldn't embarrass them, what do I know?

While the principal gave a relatively cliché-free speech about that over-used word "future" that we evidently had "ahead of us" and how we still had two years left in which to "achieve great things", I stared at the other first years. There were a few straight-backed young men in well-fitting suits and well-combed hair, but the majority wore informal T-shirts and were apathetically lounging in the pews. A couple of girls on the drama course had pulled out all the stops, with blindingly white dresses and flowers in their hair, hands intertwined and massive great tears glistening on their cheeks, as if they were practising for their graduation.

I looked at them and tried to understand what they were feeling, because perhaps I was missing something here, a dimension of life or something. Perhaps I was detached, but if that was the case I had nothing against it.

Crying because I wouldn't be able to see my classmates for a couple of months? Crying because I wouldn't have to be bullied by Vendela and FAS-Lars? No, I don't think so. I simply couldn't imagine feeling like those girls in their white dresses even when I finished school for good. I would be hanging out with Enzo anyway. And the others? No. There wouldn't be even a fragment of sorrow to squeeze from it. Not for this. Not for them.

I was so wrapped up in my own thoughts that Enzo had to tug at my arm when it was time to stand up and sing Uti Vår Hage which we had apparently been practising for over a month without me really noticing. And as I stood there singing about lilies and columbines and roses and sage, wondering what sage had to do with it – as I stood there with my mouth on autopilot, who did I see right at the back of the church, closest to the wooden doors, in a light green coat? Who did I see there, with big eyes and shiny brown hair?

Mum.

My Mum.

And I think the whole church went quiet. Yes, that must have been what happened. Her eyes were looking straight at me, straight into mine, which were green and so painfully like hers.

And my heart stopped in my body and stayed like that. Utterly still.

*I'll Love You Always*

When the ceremony was over I watched my classmates rush shrieking towards the doors and out of the church.

But not me. I didn't rush. I didn't shriek.

I walked towards Mum, my Mum, who was standing immobile despite all the people who were pushing and shoving, forcing their way past, like cattle which had been indoors all winter and now longed to get outside to the first green pastures of spring.

When I was a few metres away from her my feet stopped suddenly. It was like I couldn't go any closer. I was unable to put one foot in front of the other, as if an invisible wall had been built and I couldn't get past it. I looked at her helplessly and then, then, she began to walk towards me. And she came up to me and hugged me, and it was a different sort of hug from the one she usually gave me. She said:

'I'm so sorry, I'm so sorry, I'm so sorry.'

Over and over she said it.

And I was also sad. I was so profoundly sad, and as proof my eyes filled up. And I breathed in the smell of her hair and I cautiously put my arms around her and we stood like that for an eternity.

Eventually a hunched church warden with skin as fine as paper gesticulated at us and said apologetically that we had to leave the church so that he could get it ready for some choir that was going to sing there that evening. So we walked out into the blindingly yellow-white sunlight and there was Enzo and his mum in a circle of other people, talking about how fantastic something was, although I couldn't hear what. And Mum, who had never met Enzo or his mum before, stretched out her hand to Enzo first, which I thought was lovely of her, if a little unorthodox, because it indicated that she understood how much he meant to me. Me: who before today was never even sure that she remembered his name. And Enzo smiled and looked spectacularly stylish in a black suit that wasn't the slightest bit overkill, and his mum was proud and happy and, as usual, as thin as a vanilla pod, but there was nothing I could do about that.

◆

We didn't talk about Asperger's but we did go to an Italian restaurant in Södermalm and eat dinner together like a real family. Dad must have known she was coming because he met us at the underground station. There were checked tablecloths on dark wooden tables and it was weird and unfamiliar, but it was okay.

I sat between Mum and Dad with a silvery dish of parmesan in front of me and felt like I was four years old. That wasn't surprising: we hadn't sat all together at the same table since I was that age.

They spoke to each other falteringly about the décor, staring at me continuously. Looking for help. I didn't offer any help. Not on principle: I simply had no words to say because my fragile heart was in my throat. I had to stare hard at my spaghetti to make them look at each other. When even that failed I made an excuse and went to the loo. I opened my report in there, sitting with my knickers around the top of my boots. The expected, far too frequent letter Ps for pass were sweetened with a couple of crucial Ds for distinction. The distinction in Swedish was to be expected, something I had coolly counted on.

The most amazing grade was the one for design: a massive D for distinction radiated up from the report, even though I was clearly lacking on every level and even though Valter hadn't even seen the shelf, as requested, to be able to give it a final grade.

*A shelf is not a sculpture, Maja.*

That grade stank of positive discrimination, but that's never a particular problem when it concerns you personally. And perhaps I was given a little clue when Valter had said in a lesson: "It's easier to trim a flourishing tree than it is to get a barren one to flourish," just happening to look at me. Ugly but good, then.

I thought about the shelf and how the debris from it lay in a ditch alongside Gamla Övägen, with its flamingo, heart and everything. Thought about how I had been lying there in the same ditch, like debris myself, my heart thudding in my thumb but with no varnish to protect it. Thought about how I had stayed there, unable to get up. And how lucky it was that I did finally get up and go on. With a bit of help from a chain-smoking Justin Timberlake fan.

I flushed the toilet, washed my hands meticulously and looked at myself in the mirror: the black hair, the stupidly short bangs, the green eyes. I looked at myself and whispered:

'I'm not average. I'm a flipping flourishing tree.'

Then I went back out. Mum and Dad looked gratefully at me, as if I had saved them from each other. Dad had loosened his tie and Mum had drunk up all her sparkling orange. I suppose I had been gone a long time. I sat down and we went back to that awkward conversation about the décor, talking about the checked tablecloths and the copper saucepans nailed to the walls.

But we didn't talk about Asperger's.

We absolutely did not.

The one indication that it was the only thing we *were* thinking about was that no one mentioned a word about it. The closest we got was when Mum mentioned in passing that I hadn't been to Norrköping for a while and perhaps I would like to come down for a couple of weeks to stay, immediately after Midsummer? Yes, I said, hiding my mouth behind my napkin, sure, I could do that, and in the middle of it all my phone vibrated with an incoming text. It was from Justin. From Justin who was called Jens. I read it in secret under the table as the dessert was being served by a gorgeous young man in a white shirt and a shiny green waistcoat.

Congratulations sweet Maja! One year over! Only two to go till you are respectable. Guess what? Can't sell any more wrecks in the Stockholm area. So … come here! J.

That made me so very happy! I was so very happy that it hurt. And I couldn't help smiling, one of those stupidly wide smiles that idiots in love smile, because perhaps we could be together now, now we no longer had the same haircut? And that text made it easier to agree to Mum's suggestion, so I repeated myself and said:

'Sure. Sure I'll come and stay, at the end of June.'
And she gave a wide smile and said:
'Good!'

Mum had made up her mind to pay and nothing could stop her; not Dad's proffered bank notes or barely audible reminders to add on a tip in that case. Mum paid and as usual it was precisely the amount on the bill. She picked up her coat and walked briskly out of the restaurant. I followed her. When I looked back I saw Dad quickly throw another hundred kronor note onto the silver tray. When he caught me looking he put his finger to his mouth, to silence me. But he needn't have done that. I was already silent.

We stood outside on Götgatan, looking at each other. No one said anything. After a while Dad asked Mum if she would like to stay the night on the sofa, but she said no in that liberatingly direct way that is so much a part of her, that really does mean no and absolutely nothing else. Nothing hidden, nothing concealed or disguised. And that's why he didn't insist but simply accepted it with a nod. I'm almost certain he felt relieved.

As we slowly walked along Folkungagatan, Dad said he would take the underground home and asked if I wanted to go with him. I hesitated. It felt like something else needed to be said. And as if she understood, as if for once she understood, Mum said:

'Maja, would you come with me to Central Station? We could walk there. It's not too far and the train doesn't leave until nine forty-five.'

It was gloriously light out even though it was approaching nine o'clock. The streets were buzzing with people: students dressed in white and wearing velvet caps, women in high clicking heels and men who had turned up their shirt sleeves and thrown their jackets nonchalantly over their shoulders. There was chatting and laughter and loud, pounding music coming from open windows. There was a smell of lilac and exhaust fumes and frying hamburgers. I imagine we had masses to say, that we should have talked nonstop all the way, but we didn't. We walked in complete silence. Sometimes I sneaked a look at her to see if she was about to say something, but it seemed she was wrapped up in her own thoughts and made no attempt to start a conversation. We walked all the way to Central Station from Götgatan without saying a word.

The train went from platform eleven and I walked with her onto the platform. My pulse was racing now. I couldn't decide whether I should really say something or whether I ought to think we had plenty of time ahead of us, like the principal said; that we had two weeks after Midsummer and the whole of the rest of our lives. Perhaps I ought to say something *now now now,* but she should be the one to say something, shouldn't she? Say sorry, explain herself, tell me what happened. It was up to her, surely?

Before she boarded the train she hugged me. It was a long, hard hug and she smelled good. Like something flowery, lady-like, and I thought it was touching, that she had put on perfume when I knew it was something she never did otherwise. She let go of me and I felt something, a sort of powerful, throbbing desperation, not just in my thumb but all over my body, and just as the doors were about to close she pushed an envelope into my hand. She stood in the window and she didn't take her eyes off me. I felt the desperation fade, felt my heart slow down and begin to beat normally again.

As the train pulled out of the station I stood on the same spot, watching her go. For a brief moment I saw her, saw her dark hair, her eyes. Then, clutching the envelope in my hand, I continued looking at the place on the train where I knew she was standing.

◆

## Maja

*My darling daughter. You are so grown up now and that's hard for me to understand. How did that happen? How did my little baby become such a beautiful and strong-willed girl? I'm writing to you because I know it will come out right, what I want to say. I'm writing to you because when words come out of my mouth they tend to go wrong. This mustn't go wrong.*

*I'm looking out over the fields. I'm on my way to see you and I dearly hope you will accept me. I know that what I did was unforgiveable. In history, in literature, in reality, a mother must never disappear, never collapse on the floor and be unable to get up again. Neither should a father, of course, but the judgment that falls on a mother who disappears, who collapses, is always harder. Most of all in the way she judges herself. I disappeared and I fell and I cannot make it undone. I could not deal with my surroundings, the outside world, of which you were a part. That is why.*

*But do you know what made me get up again? Do you know what made me get up from that cold floor?*

*It was you, Maja.*

*You are a part of me. You will always be a part of me. You are my daughter and I am your mother and that side of me does not belong to any syndrome. I'm totally, totally convinced of that. It was as if it started to turn around when I realised I am something else apart from the diagnosis, that there is something else within me, a core, which belongs only to me. The darkness became a little lighter, the struggle became a little easier. It was you who made me realise it, that I am something more.*

*I will always find it hard to understand how people function, how they think and feel. It is a great source of sorrow for me and I am beginning to understand that it is a sorrow for you, too.*

*I hope you will help me, help me to understand, because I cannot do it by myself.*

*I am your mum, Maja. I am your mum who also has a syndrome called Asperger's. I am a mother with hundreds of failings and thousands of faults.*

*But I am your mother and hopefully even I do some things right sometimes.*

*I will love you always,*
*Your mum.*

◆

I stuffed the letter back into the blue envelope and looked along the rails that curved into the distance, where Mum's train had long ago disappeared into the tunnel. I let my eyes drift up towards the blue horizon, where a pale and misty cloud thinned out and evaporated.

The quote on p. 79 is from the song "4 minutes", written by
Madonna, Tim Mosley, Justin Timberlake and Nate Hills

The quote on p. 81 is from The Smiths' song "Panic", written by
Steven Morrissey

The quote on p. 83-84 is from Human Leauge's song "Don't you want
me", written by Philip Oakey, John William Callis and
Adrian Wright.

The quote on p. 95 is from *The Existential Conversation* by
Emmy van Deurzen

The quote on p. 109 is from Alien Ant Farm's version of the song
"Smooth Criminal", written by Michael Jackson

The quote on p. 132 and p. 133 is from The Cure's song "Fire in
Cairo", written by Robert Smith

The quote on p. 195 is from Joy Division's song "Love will tear us
apart", written by Bernard Sumner, Peter Hook, Stephen Morris and
Ian Curtis

The quote on p. 236 is from New Order's song "True Faith", written
by Bernard Sumner, Peter Hook, Stephen Morris, Gillian Gilbert and
Stephen Hague